DANGEROUS SLEUTHING

Minutes passed and Teal's anxiety mounted. She fiddled with the radio until it came on. Opera. The soprano's big, Wagnerian voice drowned out all thought. She closed her eyes.

Teal then heard the car door open, and as her eyelids flew up, a hand clapped them shut. The opera stopped. She heard doors slam shut and the motor roar. She rocked as the engine turned over and the car pulled into the street.

"Sorry to inconvenience you, Miss Stewart, but, you see, you have inconvenienced me far more." The voice quavered, high and thin, the voice of an old man. "I will be very direct, very simple. Your dangerous game could involve me with inconsequential men. Men who posed no threat to me. That radical reporter. The overreaching politican. They were harmless. But the tragedy of their deaths—and how I hate wasted life—that tragedy could hurt me because of your persistence."

In one swift motion cloth replaced the hand. Teal's sight blackened beneath the press of a blindfold. She regretted the loss of pink filtered light.

"Do not try to turn, Miss Stewart. Do not allow your animal instinct to succeed. It would only jeopardize your chances of walking away from this car alive."

S0-BDQ-991

QUESTIONABLE
BEHAVIOR

J. DAYNE
LAMB

Northeastern University

ZEBRA BOOKS
KENSINGTON PUBLISHING CORP.

Chapter One

Teal Stewart dropped her blue eyes as a reflex to avoid the man's fixed stare. She shifted, acutely reminded of her stylish Italian dress and the long curve of leg it revealed. She looked up to watch him casually lean against the edge of a parting door. He still gazed at her as he pulled away from the elevator.

Men often gave her an uninvited second glance. Less often did they rock in slow motion from heel to toe and dive for her feet. Teal froze as his lips grazed her right knee. Embarrassment stiffened her face when the clutch of waiting businessmen turned to regard her with horror.

Then everyone fixed their eyes on the prone man. He gazed back. A twitch twisted his head to the floor. Red hair sprayed out from the band of his ponytail. Quivers shook his body. Teal looked away.

The initial shock that had held the stunned group dissolved. Words returned.

"Jesus Christ! I think he's dead!"

"Guard!"

"Hey, we need a doctor here!"

Teal stepped back.

Security trotted over, impatient with authority. "Now what's all this? What's going on?"

Sensing gridlock, Teal slipped away. She located the second guard at the far end of the lobby. She steadied her voice to cut the bluster short.

"Please. There's a man who needs an ambulance. He fell out of the elevator in the forty to forty-nine bank. And maybe you should call the police."

She returned to find the curious gawking and rife with rumors. Teal watched the first guard finish his inspection of the ill-fated car, now keyed open and immobile. The awful scene replayed in her mind again and again. The incongruity struck her with a thud. He had dropped from an empty elevator.

But that seemed impossible at this time of day when the elevators labored to disgorge the lunch crush. Ivy Club members and overworked certified public accountants like Teal Stewart were the sole upward-bound riders at noon. Ivy, situated on the forty-ninth and top floor, remained the only barrier, Teal once quipped in mimic of a Yankee saying, between her employer, Clayborne Whittier, and God.

The guard removed the key and released the car. No one from the still-growing crowd joined Teal and a lone construction supervisor as they entered. The supervisor pressed forty-one, a floor under renovation by Clayborne Whittier to accommodate the firm's recent growth. No wonder she felt like she was working like a dog, Teal thought, hitting forty-eight.

The near-empty elevator whooshed upward. Such silence contrasted with her typical noon commute when members of Ivy conversed, oblivious to Teal. Oh, the men slid surreptitious glances across her form, but these alumni of the Ivy League dismissed women as too un-important to temper their talk. More than once, Teal had ground her heel to the foyer tile as her unflattering opin-ion of an Ivy education grew. More than once, she had been trapped in the rear of a car listening to their silly exchanges.

". . . if they think they can ease George out, they are crazy. He's one bastard who won't be dumped."

"Say hello to Beth for me. . . . Oh, it's not Beth; new wife, eh? Well, say hello to her, then."

". . . yes, ha, we leveraged the taxes and didn't pay for a year, naturally, so it had a reverberating effect."

Today had seemed no different until the man sprawled prostrate at her feet. No leveraging that one.

She shook the irreverence from her head. Memory revived the staring face into the image of a man ani-mated with conversation. It did not spring from the lobby below. Teal concentrated. The image sprang from this place, the elevator interior, when the man stood not a foot from her. But when? Two days ago, she decided. Three at most.

The supervisor got off at forty-one. Forty-two through forty-seven flashed by. *I came in to pick up a document before lunch. The day I planned to eat with Hunt.* The muted bell rang her stop. *Three days ago, definitely,* she decided. She glanced down to step out, and a gold pen wedged between the carpet and elevator wall caught her eye. Teal stooped to retrieve it, then walked down the hall, pen in hand.

Kathy smiled. "Hi. No cancellation on tomorrow yet."

Hunt. That's who Kathy meant. The man who too

7

often couldn't make lunch. Teal nodded past her secretary before she backtracked.

"Kath, could you call the lobby for me? Tell the guard that the police can reach me here . . ." Teal faltered. The words sounded a little silly.

"Because?" Kathy prompted.

"I had them called. A man, I don't know, he fell out of the elevator downstairs. He touched me. Anyway, the police may want to question me about it."

Teal entered her office and leaned against the shut door. She absently rolled the gold cylinder between her palms as a question rolled through her mind. *I remember the man, but why?*

Monday. Three days ago. She had been rushing to join Hunt at the club for lunch. The men in the elevator were the same as usual except for one incongruous pair. They presented as odd a contrast as herself and Hunt, and stood out from the rest of the group as much.

Teal wore dresses of impeccable cut, sharp-heeled shoes and her chestnut hair pulled into a small knot. Hunt favored baggy trousers, worn corduroy jackets and skinny ties knit by his mother. His hair exploded in frenetic curls and usually caused Ivy's head waiter, Walter, to grimace as he greeted Mr. Huntington Erin Huston, but Teal knew Walter to be pleased that Hunt, the controversial architect, belonged to Ivy as a bond to his alma mater. Hunt should, of course, as he had received his first big commission from the university.

But—ah, yes. Teal fetched the random threads back into a pattern. The two men in the elevator had appeared no better matched. A patrician blond in Brooks Brothers with a touch of Louis Boston decadence in the European cut of his shirt had stood beside a man with fire red hair barely constrained in a ponytail who'd sported a tweed jacket with frayed edges and an unspeakable tie. He'd grunted his words and stood too close to his friend when he talked. One fierce gesture had smacked Teal's back with a freckled hand.

Teal had planned to point the pair out to Hunt over lunch. But Hunt had cancelled, the ''While You Were Away'' slip propped beside her telephone by Kathy. The message had forced Teal to eat at the crowded, overpriced deli across the street. She'd not been happy.

But that had been the man. The ponytailed, tweedy man now lying below. Teal pulled herself from the reverie. Her afternoon held more pressing problems.

The shrill of the intercom startled Teal out of her concentration on the financial statements spread before her.

''A police person is here to see you, Teal. Shall I send him in?'' Kath asked. She sounded the penultimate in blasé. Only irate clients made her pretend to be more relaxed.

Police. Teal considered the word, at once wary.

''Yes. And, Kath, I'll bend to your rules today. Ask him what he wants in his coffee. I'll take tea.''

She could hear Kathy's laugh across the wire and through the door. The request represented a victory for the two-year-curriculum Katie Gibbs career secretary who loved her job and relished the five o'clock finality of her work day. She insisted on getting Teal's tea. It had become a running battle, the race to beat her boss. Today's unexpected invitation would be heaven.

Teal looked up, alert and vigilant with executive authority, when her door opened. *Rubbish*, she admonished herself. She stood.

Kathy ushered in a young man who towered like a thin reed over the secretary.

"Detective Daniel Malley," she intoned without inflection.

"Dan Malley, ma'am, and I, uh, was s-s-sent to ask you a question or two."

Teal said, "Sit down," sweeping her hand to indicate the only other chair in the office while she sat back down.

Kathy paused in the doorway. "Cream and two sugars, right?"

Dan snapped up from the half crouch of easing into the chair. "Yes, oh, fine, yes, if it isn't a t-t-trouble to you."

Kathy flicked her eyes up before she smiled. Her expression said that Teal's compromise and her own Katie Gibbs training were wasted on this one.

Dan struggled to begin. He looked more naturally a chemistry teacher than a cop, more one to reflect than to act. With a name like Malley, Teal suspected Dan had entered the family business. Forget chemistry.

"How may I assist, Detective?" She chose her words to lend the formality necessary to buttress his position.

"Oh." Dan focused on her. "He's dead. That is, the body you reported is dead. I mean the man's a body."

A shudder rippled the fine hairs at the back of Teal's neck.

"Is this your first dead man, Detective? It's mine."

She hadn't meant to say that, but relief suffused Dan's face.

"Yes, ma'am. At least my first dead case." He swallowed. "Tell me what you saw, and why you didn't wait for the police to arrive."

The last held an accusing overtone. These questions turned Dan into police through the solid offensive play to establish his rightness and Teal's probable wrongness. Detective Malley had put his visceral fear of mortality behind. He could proceed.

Kathy tapped and opened the door. She set the tea on Teal's desk and handed the detective his coffee. His business like "Thank you" brought a smile to her eyes. Maybe Katie Gibbs was not lost on him after all.

Teal drew her mug closer only to knock the gold pen she'd found to the floor. She dropped it in her drawer, and she gave her full attention to the detective's questions. Dan asked what she had seen and interjected salient questions as he took notes.

"And why did you leave the, uh, scene?" he asked to avoid using the word corpse.

Teal shrugged. She'd thought the man rude, then ill. She'd never considered dead, or what dead could mean. "I wasn't needed. The police had been called, after all, and a guard was with the body. What good could I do joining the crowd?"

She didn't mention that she was busy today.

Teal considered what she'd seen earlier in the week. That elevator ride might give the detective a lead. She spoke, condensing memory and surmise. Dan listened.

"Do you believe this fellow was a regular at the Ivy Club?" he asked.

"I thought I did, but it's unlikely. He didn't look right. You could say my friend Hunt doesn't look right either, though, and he's often at Ivy with me since I insist. It gives me clout here"—in a flip of the hand Teal indi-

11

cated her professional world—"to frequent there." A finger thrust up. "His companion is the candidate for member. Ivy's head waiter will know. Walter remembers everyone."

Dan Malley gulped the last inch of his coffee and rose. Teal stood to join him, her hand extended.

"If I can help again, please call."

"I doubt I'll need to trouble you. H-h-however, if you remember anything more, contact me."

Teal had to ask. "Did he just die?"

"No knowing until the autopsy," Dan replied.

He gripped her hand again. Teal watched his shy nod to Kathy on the way out. How inexplicable were the impulses of life even in the face of death's finality. Teal didn't envy Detective Malley his profession, aggravating as Clayborne Whittier could be.

Teal realized that she didn't know the dead man's name. The anonymity chilled her. She decided to ask Walter tomorrow when she met Hunt at Ivy for lunch.

"Huh," she snorted aloud, "if he makes it at the right time on the right day!"

Clayborne Whittier's expansion had forced a new office and a new design. Once accepted, the partners' initial reluctance shifted to restrained enthusiasm as the firm moved to the most controversial of Boston's skyscrapers. In contrast to the building, they chose a decor intended to emanate discretion and prosperity.

Soft wool felt covered the wall. Elaborate moldings added dimension to the lobby and other large rooms. Some manager's offices, like Teal's, gave stunning views of the Boston waterfront. Others overlooked the

Boston Common, the Public Garden and the State House. Partners could boast of offices in the corner which paired the harbor or Common with the mundane expressway.

Teal like the environment of efficiency and hush. One never acted impetuous, loud, silly or scared at Clayborne Whittier. One never argued a raise, cried over a mistake or shouted down the hall to a colleague. One worked on behalf of the firm's clients.

As Teal knew she should be doing now. Her day was falling hopelessly behind schedule, but she could not forget the dead man kissing her knee. A man without a name, without an explanation for his death, without mourners. All of which would come, Teal understood. Still, for a moment, death reduced him to so much matter.

The image of his fall surfaced her own repressed anxieties.

I'm thirty-four, Teal mused. *Ambitious, overpaid, self-sufficient—the adjectives of success. Adjectives that make it easy to avoid the uncomfortable questions. I am afraid to risk and love, afraid to ask if this*—she surveyed the ordered office—*is what I want.*

She bit her top lip. *I'll think about it later, when I don't have my work uniform on, when I'm not surrounded by Clayborne Whittier. Later.* She stabbed the intercom.

"Kathy, do you have the Fruiers' report?"

"It came when the police person was with you," Kathy teased Teal with the carefully sex-neutral vocabulary. "I'll bring it in."

Fruiers Construction Company made Teal forget bodies, mortality and meaning. Fruiers, her favorite client, was growing with a major contract to build waste treatment plants. The company had asked Teal to review their cost accumulation system. On fixed-price contracts such as these, one large overrun could wipe out the expected profit. Everyone understood that bad data lead to bad decisions and worse results.

Teal scanned the computer printout after Kathy dropped it on her desk. The variance column displayed expenditures in excess of the budget in brackets. Easy to read. Easy to interpret. But Teal always questioned data so polished, so apparently remote from the disorder of mortal minds and hands.

That was the gist, she thought. Computer output looked untouched by an individual's imprint. In reality, programs and input were subject to human error, manipulation or fraud. Program the computer to represent over-budget variances as under-budget and the tidy report misled and misdirected.

Teal smiled at her discomfort over the dichotomy, order versus chaos. Where did she come down? She tried to manage her life to escape the anarchy so enduring in her childhood. How better than to become a CPA? Ironically, individual client motivations, actions and desires, not a mystical discipline of numbers, dominated her days. So much for tidy.

She brought her attention to the report. Mistrust always led to imagining the worst. Anyway, who at Fruiers stood to gain by playing with this program? It couldn't shift money to anyone, although it might mask failure for a little while.

What was it she had overheard in the elevator?

". . . new program is unbelievable. It matches the inventory purchase order against receipt and dates the

14

payable. We play it for the maximum float on our money!''

Inventory, Teal concluded, *there's the place for fraud.*

Chapter Two

If Hunt is going to be late, Teal decided, *I might as well wait at Ivy as here.* She tapped her desk for a second, willing him through the door. He did not make an appearance. She stood.

Old aggravations filled her mind. Why couldn't he just be on time? Instead, he was sure to be annoyed by her anger, and the whole damn thing would start again.

She slammed to a halt in front of the Clayborne Whittier receptionist.

"Tell Hunt I'm upstairs," she said to the man behind the mahogany desk. "Ask him to leave the paperwork here. I'll look at it when I have time."

Teal turned into the elevator corridor and punched the call button. If Hunt wanted her to review his cost proposal for his affordable housing bid, he would have to wait. This lunch, intended to blend business and pleasure, was materializing to no business and precious little likelihood of pleasure.

Seconds later, Teal stepped into the Ivy Club. The sparse foyer revealed two imposing, closed doors. Neither hinted at the entrance. Club policy endorsed the premise that one should know.

Teal pushed the far door and walked into the bar. A graduate degree from California's Stanford University did not qualify her for membership. Ivy's accessibility came by proxy of Hunt's account.

She settled into a low chair and gazed out at the water.

The vista transcended pretty. Boston's complex harbor mixed a working port and residential living. Restored granite warehouses now functioned as expensive condominiums, not as storage for items in trade. Commercial fuel depots, not marshes, rimmed the Mystic River. Logan Airport across the wider bay separated downtown from East Boston. Below, day sails, power boats, yachts, tugs and tankers maneuvered over the water's choppy skin.

Teal surprised herself. She ordered a Pinch, neat. Damn Hunt. Damn her whole careful life.

She leaned back and dropped her mind into the view. A plane lifted off a Logan runway. Teal imagined an exotic destination before it banked from the city and view. She concentrated on the two red tugs headed for a lone tanker stalled on the horizon.

"Ms. Stewart."

Teal turned. "Walter! You're seldom in the bar."

"Ms. Stewart, so good to see you. Should we expect Mr. Huntington to arrive soon?" Walter asked.

He spoke in a hushed, reverential tone. Ivy, in its exalted name and exclusivity, gave purpose to his life. Teal realized how little he wanted to make his request explicit, but he needed the table.

"You know Hunt—don't hold our table." Teal considered the maitre d'. "Walter, did the police stop up yesterday?"

"Humph. Yes. A busy time, I kept it brief." Walter bobbed his head in a stiff jerk to indicate displeasure at the involvement of the club with such elements as the police.

"I imagine you dismissed them with ease." Teal smiled. "Did you know him? The man who died?"

She appreciated the delicacy of her question. Walter identified with Ivy and was loathe to reveal information he considered privileged by position. Members trusted his discretion implicitly and probably assumed their every utterance to be classified. Walter surely did.

"Mark Konstat, editor of the *Alt Paper*. A Yale man, but he never joined us." Walter sniffed.

Walter believed that to be an alumni of such an institution and not to join Ivy indicated a serious flaw of character. Rather worse, it marked one conspicuously as an outsider. Teal knew that despite her tenuous school history, Walter viewed her quite favorably. The reflected glory of Mr. Huntington could be annoying. Right now it had its use.

"Then, which member did he know?" Teal asked.

Walter looked impatient to seat his patrons. The question might push to the limit his sense of propriety and hurry him from her side. But Walter surprised her.

"Averill Cunningham," he said. "Wonderful fellow. Good family. Classmates at Yale." His head of lustrous white hair bobbed. "Until this week they lunched together maybe once a year."

Infrequent contact gave an excuse to the unlikely relationship.

"And this week?" Teal pushed.

"Twice." He shook his head again, and he turned to leave. "Twice. When Mr. Huntington arrives, I will endeavor to fit you in straightaway."

Teal wondered if Walter held opinions about all the members and their friends. He certainly disapproved of Mark Konstat. But then the *Alt Paper,* short for alternative, stood in opposition to everything Walter cherished, and championed all he abhorred. Increased taxation to fund social welfare, a halt to defense spending, constitutional gay rights and the unionization of Harvard University's hourly workers—Walter felt deeply affronted by such threats to the status quo.

How interesting that Hunt managed to escape the brand of radical in Walter's view, Teal mused. Walter counted Hunt among the club's bevy of eccentrics, a category of individuals one was permitted to like, despite their extreme differences from oneself. That Konstat held no such status was evident. Yet Walter ardently defended, though he could not quite admire, Hunt's most infamous building, the one in which Clayborne Whittier and Ivy resided.

The First New England Bank design had been the talk, the scandal and, ultimately, the perverse pride of Boston. The forty-nine-story triangle of mirrored glass insulted the new wave of humanistic architecture. No critic admitted an enthusiasm for the structure. No paper had reported anything but the delays and lawsuits that dogged construction. Not until the building soared above the ground did these opponents voice reluctant admiration for the unwelcome landmark's purity of form.

The *Alt Paper* led in all but the admiration. The FNEB building was, according to the *Alt,* a monument to greed (boasting a silver skin), insensitivity (dwarfing

19

the gentle city), stupidity (resting on filled land) and inaccessibility (its austere facade). Hunt had shrugged.

Hunt. Teal looked at her watch. Damn it, over half an hour late. She clenched her drink, then relaxed. She knew when she was defeated. She could imagine his voice: *If I'm late, just enjoy. I don't get mad when you're delayed.*

The last line set her back to wanting to smash her glass. *I don't get mad when you're delayed,* she mimicked silently. Sure—because she was never late. Resignation made Teal laugh out loud at the too familiar complaint.

"I beg your pardon."

She focused. Black wingtip shoes and trouser cuffs in an expensive, muted navy crystallized in her consciousness. She looked up with raised brows.

"I do beg your pardon. I hope I'm not interrupting. I'm Averill Cunningham. Walter was kind enough to point you out. I understand you saw Mark when Mark—" He stopped, distress evident, and extended a hand.

"Yes," Teal said, completing the handshake. "I'm sorry."

"So am I. Another drink?" He motioned to her empty glass.

"Why, thank you. Yes. Certainly. Do sit." Teal smiled her confusion.

Averill Cunningham was a graceful man. And an athlete, Teal decided, watching him lower himself stiffly to the chair. She overdid her workouts when under emotional stress. He had a real reason—the death of a friend.

"I don't mean to intrude," he said. "If I am, I hope you can forgive me. I feel awful about Mark."

Teal switched to Evian when the waiter took the order; then she turned to Averill.

20

"There's nothing to forgive. And you're not intruding. In fact, I'm afraid I've been stood up by my lunch companion."

"Then, join me. Please," Averill offered. "The detective, Malley, said you work for Clayborne Whittier. I know Don Clarke, your senior partner."

"The police talked to you, too?"

Teal didn't care that this interesting man knew Don Clarke. Don made a practice of glad-handing everyone in Boston's business community.

"The police twisted my name from poor Walter. The questions made me feel they expected a confession. When did I last see Mark? Why wasn't I with him when he . . ." Averill sighed. "Still, if only I had stayed with him. That's why I wanted to meet you. You were."

"Not exactly—"

The bartender interrupted with a message on a pink slip of paper. Mr. Huntington apologized for an unexpected problem at his office. Perhaps she could stop by his place after work. The communication mollified Teal's ire at Hunt.

While she read, Averill dispatched the bartender to notify Walter that they required a table.

The maitre d' soon had Teal and Averill seated in the Carpet Room. The name honored the sumptuous garden pattern Bachtiari covering the floor. Teal considered the generations of crumbs and bearnaise sauce ingested by the sturdy Persian. Better fed than its makers, she imagined.

Averill returned the conversation to Mark.

"I feel so responsible. That detective didn't have to do much to get to me. You see, I had lunch with Mark yesterday. Did you know?"

21

"No. But I had seen you on the elevator with . . . him . . . earlier this week. I told the police. I guessed you, the blond, were the member here."

"That's quite a memory when all sorts of strangers use the elevator. You actually remembered us?"

Teal launched into the explanation she'd given Dan Malley—the similarity between the two men and herself with Hunt, why Averill appeared the likely club member.

"With Clayborne Whittier right below Ivy, anyone riding past my floor has to be heading here. It's not all that clever of me," Teal concluded.

"I've . . . I'd known Mark for years. We roomed together as Yale freshmen and got on well enough after I moved out. We saw each other now and then in Boston. Still enjoyed disagreeing on the issues." Averill looked amused before he looked chagrined. "Did Walter mention the intensity? He tactfully hid us away in a corner."

"No. He didn't." Teal laughed.

"The soul of discretion. Anyway, Mark and I could become pretty animated. If I'd thought it would kill him . . ."

They sat through a moment of silence.

"Kill him?" Teal said.

"Oh, figuratively. Mark suffered from asthma, allergies and a congenital heart condition. About everything you can name. A walk turned him blue. I think my participation in crew gave him a vicarious thrill. He probably enjoyed the damned sport more than I ever did. Anyway, he had that heart. I hate to think five minutes earlier and I would have been there to help."

"You couldn't have saved Mark," Teal whispered.

"No, but Christ, I should have thought. The excite-

22

ment of our discussion, the extra stress—this time he couldn't take it. And I left him when he ran into someone he knew because I was too impatient to wait, damn it.''

Just then their food arrived with the flourish of positioned plates and refilled water glasses. Teal shifted against the stiff seat. How could she exculpate Averill's private grief and guilt? She wanted to.

"If we hadn't argued. If I'd kept him calm." Averill stared out the window.

He withdrew, behind his fine face, tight and closed. Teal felt powerless. Her knife and fork clicked sharp rhythms on the china as she moved her veal piccata around her plate.

Finally she couldn't stand the silence. "I'm so sorry. There's nothing I can say which will make things better. Chance put me at that elevator yesterday. You aren't to blame for Mark, but saying it can't make you believe it, I know.''

Averill pulled out of himself. "It helps. Thanks. Talking with the police brought such guilt. I realize I couldn't have done anything, but I wish . . . well, at least it happened quickly. God, I hope for your sake he didn't cry out.''

Teal's heart lurched. The most urbane man she'd lunched with in months seemed to be pleading with her for a comfort no one could give.

"Think of it like this—his death was quick and as painless as quick can be.''

Teal didn't want to describe Konstat's glazed eyes or the slow twist he took from the doorway before he arced to the floor. She didn't want to remember the sound of him meeting the tile.

23

"He lay silently, Averill. Visualize your friend as at peace."

Teal wished she could take her own advice.

Chapter Three

"My guess? Dead before he hit the ground." The coroner shrugged. "Family insists on an autopsy at Mass General. Their boy couldn't have died from a heart condition: 'He was under the best care.' So fine, their experts can give him the best autopsy and I'll take notes. Seen enough?"

Dan nodded. "I've seen enough. Uh, what's your g-g-guess? The bruises mean anything?"

"Yeah, they mean Mom and Dad's best boy took a nasty fist or two. They mean the most expensive cardiac care, a restricted diet and asthma inhalators can't keep the vicissitudes of life or death at bay."

"Vicissitudes, hell, you going to make me look it up?"

"Danny-boy, life is hell. Here's a thought. This stiff lost a fight and, scared witless, his adrenaline shoots up, blood pressure races and lungs about burst. Normal, except with his heart who knows? Maybe it killed him or maybe he died of embarrassment. Point is, nothing's better than a guess until we dig through the corpse."

25

"You think the fight would have been a couple of days before he dropped?"

"Yeah, that's my opinion, but wait a few weeks and we'll all have the best autopsy report money can buy." The coroner laughed.

"And your opinion—his death was natural?"

"What's natural these days, Danny? He wasn't blown apart with a .38, if that's what you mean. Other than that we'll—"

"Have to wait," Dan finished. "Thanks for the time. Call me on the autopsy. Oh, one more thing—his mother keeps screaming about a hypo. Says he always carried a load of adrenaline for his food allergies 'just in case.' "

The coroner rolled his eyes. "He ever use it, did she say?"

"Once, in college. Other than that, she wasn't sure," Dan said.

"Well, my experience, which mind you is mainly with the dead, is people get sloppy about gizmos like loaded hypodermics. Without a scare, they lose the urgency. A diet like this guy apparently followed and he might forget the need. Or he lost it, I don't know. Professional guess? He didn't use it. Look harder."

"Well, thanks. And the report?"

"Will do, Danny. Say hello to your old man for me."

Dan masked his excitement. Konstat had been assigned to him as routine. Dan was too new to the department to expect to head more challenging investigations. Most of his time went to grueling, mind-numbing background work for senior detectives. They treated him well because they had admired his father and respected his intelligence, but it was the traditional apprenticeship and no exception.

He learned a lot as second and third man, but now Konstat belonged to him. In one day the case showed possibilities. Some. He didn't want to fool himself, make it more than it was, but he was not prepared to close it prematurely, either.

He had already talked with Konstat's boss at the *Alt Paper*. The man offered little to encourage further ambition.

"You do understand," the publisher had said with that look that meant no cop could, "despite Konstat's editor title, he was a first-class reporter. He'd started a story before he died. The *Alt* won't drop it."

The guy acted as if Dan cared about the paper's policy. Then he refused Dan a look at Konstat's files and gave the barest sketch of the project. The mob, an ambitious political hopeful, misdeeds at a bank—Dan wanted to groan. Couldn't an alternative paper come up with something a little newer? But if Konstat had been beaten up, he'd better pursue the story.

"The name of the bank?"

The publisher stared. He shook a no with a smirk. Maybe he thought he was clever.

"Look, make this easy. I need a name for my notes," Dan said.

"University Bank, but don't go around blowing our investigation." The publisher pouted.

Konstat's death wasn't murder, not yet. Most likely not ever, Dan realized. He fished, hoping for something useful from Konstat's employer.

"Uh, sounds like a tough assignment. The *Alt*'s lucky to have you to keep at it," he said.

"Not me," the publisher snapped. "I don't write here. Francesca Mettafora will be on it when she's back."

"From?" Dan asked.

"Vacation." The publisher had then waved Dan out.

Maybe Ms. Mettafora would be more cooperative, Dan now thought as he straightened his poor excuse for a desk. Teal Stewart had cooperated. And usefully, too, with the Ivy Club.

Maybe he should give her a call—warn her about Konstat hitting on a tough crowd and maybe getting beaten up—but the impulse seemed a little silly. The CPA had been at the elevator that particular day. She wasn't involved.

Admit it, Dan admonished himself. *I want someone to take this case as seriously as I wish it would turn out—there's no issue of trying to protect Teal Stewart.*

"Yet," he added aloud and smiled at the melodrama.

Teal was not aware of Dan Malley's thoughts as she walked through the financial district to Hunt's loft on South Street. It was an easy ten minutes from her office.

South Street once had been the center of Boston's leather and wholesale district. Display firms, wallpaper jobbers and leather goods manufacturers had occupied the square brick and granite buildings. Hunt had purchased one of the first warehouses to empty as businesses relocated to cheaper locations or closed, victims of a shifting economy.

He'd bought because the building was large and the street quiet at night. He'd bought because he did not want to live in a structure he designed. He'd gutted the

28

interior to a virtual shell, then sold the first four levels as raw space and kept the top himself.

Teal had lived with Hunt in Cambridge her first three years after receiving her MBA from Stanford. He had been trying to survive as an architect; she, to endure the first stultifying years at Clayborne Whittier. After they separated, when Hunt moved into the warehouse, he had had the decency to offer her a space, and she had had the decency to decline.

Teal couldn't help thinking about this as she turned her key in the elevator to send it to the fifth floor. Neither of them could explain why living together had not worked. But it hadn't.

Argyle nearly knocked her down as she stepped out. Excitement made him dance, nails clicking on the hardwood floor. Teal knelt to murmur her affection as she scratched his head. Silly murmurs to the big, beautiful Scottish deerhound.

"Poor old Argyle," she said into a misty, gray coat, "you've never understood I don't live with you anymore."

Teal shook off reflections and dog hairs as Hunt called out.

"Sorry about lunch, I—"

"Don't want to hear. Thanks for the message. You should try it more often." *Censorship*, Teal thought. *I'll never learn*.

Hunt laughed and leaned across the prone dog to hug her. A careful kiss on the cheek and they straightened.

"I know, I know. Edit the last remark. Anyway, I ate with Averill Cunningham, the guy I saw earlier with the dead man, who is Mark Konstat by the way. Memory served me well. Averill's not a bit like Konstat, but very proper. Even Walter thinks so."

"Averill Cunningham?" Hunt exaggerated the lift of his dark brows above deep brown eyes. "Don't know."

"That's not surprising since he's not your type." Teal heard her voice sharpen. What did she want from Hunt?

"Wine? The Ravenswood zinfandel is here somewhere." Hunt gestured toward the open kitchen.

"I'll find it."

"So, the guy was Mark Konstat?"

"Yup, editor of the *Alt Paper,* your favorite critic. Averill thinks it was his heart. Some congenital condition, I guess. Ah! Do you want a glass?" Teal straightened with the bottle.

Hunt waved his beer. "Nope. The histamine gives me a splitting headache. I bought it for you."

"Thanks. Anyway, Averill acted pretty upset. Lunch without the death of his friend between us on the table would have been much nicer."

"A heart attack? That makes sense, I guess." Hunt stayed with the subject of the dead man.

"I don't know. Probably. I think I'll ask Detective Dan Malley and consider it closed." Teal poured and lifted her glass. "I hope you remembered to bring your proposal home."

The evening lapsed into an old routine. Teal fed Argyle and made the salad. Hunt threw bay scallops into a mix of garlic, butter, white wine and brandy, then slipped the pan under the broiler. The big dog lay at Teal's feet as they ate.

Conversation picked up old threads—friends, work, *The New Yorker.* They both groaned. Hunt hated the stink of perfume strips, the altered layout and false chic.

Where was Elizabeth Drew? Still, he renewed. Not so Teal.

After dinner, she reviewed his proposal and the status of his bid on the mixed-income, suburban housing. Hunt's reputation as an architect had originated with his work for Harvard. Now fame brought him commissions for buildings meant to signal an institutional image. Modular-based condominiums represented quite a departure.

About ten-thirty they glanced at each other.

"Well, I should be going," Teal said.

It was the new-old dilemma characterizing the relationship since their separation.

"You're welcome to stay. I'd like your advice on getting the garden ready for winter. The roses have spots, but I waited to spray until you looked. And yes, you were right about the bittersweet with everything else going brown. The color is great."

Teal grinned. "Promise to replace the lock at my place tomorrow, and I'll stay."

Teal owned a three-unit town house on the flat of Beacon Hill. Brimmer Street. The purchase represented a final act of independence after she'd refused Hunt's loft space. But she still consulted on his plantings, and he still did her repairs.

Argyle whined to be let out to the roof garden stairs.

"Teal?" Hunt paused as she turned from the door. "I care, you know. I'm not sure how I'd feel if you have lunch with that guy again. Your voice changed describing him."

"Oh, Hunt." Teal sighed and pushed stray hairs from tickling her face. "We could be in the old lovers' ring of hell. Don't you miss thrilling at a certain voice on the telephone? Or your heart pounding when a certain make of car passes on the street? You don't feel like that about my old Mercedes anymore. So what are we doing?"

She kissed his cheek.

"Hey, that's no answer." He pulled her to him. "That's dirty pool."

When Argyle began to whine fifteen minutes later, they did not even look toward the garden door.

Saturday passed without event. The roses exhibited a mildew along with the last spectacular blooms of fall. Teal cut long stems for the house and sprayed with an organic sulphur solution. Together they dug up gladioli bulbs and buried snowdrops and early Kaufmania tulips under the friable earth. In the end, Hunt was too tired to change Teal's lock; Teal, too exhausted to walk home.

Sunday started bright and clear with only a faint yellow smog threaded through the Boston skyline. Hunt went out for the Sunday *Boston Globe* and orange juice. Teal made waffles, everything organized along familiar lines.

Hunt exited the elevator with the paper balanced on the carton of juice. He read as he walked, navigating from memory. He dropped everything on the pale gray counter and leaned around Teal to whisper in her ear.

"This should stimulate your life. You're in the thick of it!"

Teal hated being teased. She hated the interruption to preparing breakfast. Hunt interfered with protocol. He was in the way.

"What on earth do you mean?" she asked. She snatched the paper off the counter.

For a second she froze, her eyes on the headline: *"Alt Paper* Editor Konstat Dead. Is It Heart or Heat?"

She spun around to Hunt. "What's this about?"

"Konstat, doll, and you're in the thick of it. The *Alt* was investigating alleged underworld infiltration of our pristine banking system. The investigation may tie to Konstat's death. Malley is mentioned. And, I quote, 'A woman in the First New England Bank building stood close enough to catch Konstat when he fell. Witnesses say he clutched her knees and tried to speak.' You, in the *Globe.* "

Teal hardly registered the teasing. She tried to recall an *In Boston* article on organized crime and a Boston bank. The mob used unsecured personal and questionable real estate loans to penetrate the operation. She had only skimmed the magazine piece. The fraud was discovered after a loan officer died from bullet wounds. Seven bullets, actually. The bank folded.

The *Globe*'s story mourned a respected competitor. It alluded to Konstat's interest in a Cambridge bank, organized crime and William Carroll, whom the *Globe* described as "A prominent Cambridge businessman with political ambitions." The writer hypothesized that Mark had been near a breakthrough, prompting someone—the article became vague, libel in the writer's mind—to want Mark "out of the way." The police were "looking into the allegations."

"What do you think, Teal? Was Konstat a mob hit?" Hunt nudged her.

"In an FNEB elevator where no one can slip on or off without passing a zillion receptionists? Not to mention the hordes pushing on at every stop in a rush to lunch. Look, you are driving me nuts!'' Teal shoved Hunt away.

"You." She pointed to the table. "Sit and don't get in the way."

"Poison," Hunt said from his chair.

Teal put down the spatula. "What?"

"Poison. They poisoned him at Ivy."

"Sure, and Walter served it and Averill didn't notice. Hunt, mob murders are designed to keep the troops in line. A kind of dramatic instruction to those who value their lives. Guns that leave craters in the human body, cement shoes and shallow rivers are weapons of choice. If Konstat was killed, which he wasn't, the hit was not executed in the underworld style."

"No pun intended?" Hunt laughed, and Teal bared her teeth. "Okay, what about this businessman? They are efficient. Maybe he went for the discrete removal of an unfortunate obstacle to his lust for high office?"

"Hunt! I haven't eaten—"

"And you're a little testy. Just exploring the possibilities. But I bet you'll call Malley for sure now."

"Umm." Teal nodded to silence him.

She spooned buttermilk batter onto the waffle iron and poured boiling water into the French Melior pot. She adjusted the heat under the cast-iron frying pan.

"One or two sausage?" she asked.

"Two, and four waffles."

The morning returned to the lazy pattern of Sunday. Hunt read the comics and clips of the headlines aloud. Teal ate. Together they argued old positions and new ideas that the paper brought to mind.

Mark Konstat as mob and murder victim was not mentioned. Too implausible, Teal decided. Implausible and impossible. But chills dusted her skin at the memory of his staring face.

Chapter Four

"Detective Daniel Malley, please." Teal tilted the telephone away from her earring and responded to the tiny voice. "Yes, I'll wait, thank you."

Impatient in the abyss of hold, Teal glanced at her calendar. Crowded! Fruiers wanted her final critique on the cost control program. BiMedics, a biotech start-up three years ago, was considering an initial public offering of common stock. Teal had been asked to join the company's investment bankers at a working group meeting tomorrow. One sure topic for discussion would be the draft management letter Teal had written for Clayborne Whittier to issue.

Such letters evaluated the financial management and accounting practices reviewed by a CPA during a financial statement audit. Professional standards required inadequate controls be disclosed, making the letters a target of the investment bankers in their due diligence investigations. Serious inadequacies could jeopardize a deal. Fortunately, the BiMedics audit had revealed no significant problems.

The telephone came back to life, and Teal tugged off her earring.

"Detective Malley? This is Teal Stewart, the woman—"

"Who was kind enough to t-t-tell me about the Ivy Club. I remember."

"I read yesterday's *Globe*. Do the police really have questions about Mark Konstat's death?" Teal asked.

"The paper exaggerated. C-c-catchy headlines sell."

"So you won't tell, is that it?" Teal smiled at the silence, then broke it herself. "I met Averill Cunningham at Ivy last Friday. I guess you talked with him. He thinks his friend died from heart problems."

"We're looking into all possibilities, uh, although some evidence points to that," Dan said. "I'd planned to call you, actually. I'd like to stop by to talk again."

"You do have questions," Teal mused. "I expected you to laugh at the *Globe* article. When do you want to see me?"

"How about three?" Dan asked.

"Let me just take a second to check my appointments."

Teal left Malley to hold. She assessed the name in her appointment book and buzzed Kathy.

"Kath, try to move Roger to three forty-five, will you? And block in Detective Malley at three."

Teal brought him back on the line. "No problem, Detective. At my office?"

"Yes, ma'am. I appreciate your willingness to be bothered."

"No 'ma'am,' please, and it's no bother." Teal made an impish face imagining Roger's reaction to the switch.

37

"You'll be breaking the routine. For me, that is. I guess this is the routine for you."

The morning passed as Teal reevaluated the points BiMedics' investment bankers might question. No issue raised in the draft was more significant than a general recommendation for improvement.

Teal contemplated the letter, smug with self-approval, when Roger burst into her office.

"Teal," he barked. "What's this about pushing me off an hour?"

Teal looked up, still unsettled by Roger's new partner demeanor. Last winter while still a senior manager, he had acted like a peer. Summer brought Roger the invitation to join the partnership. He had earned it through years of sixty-hour weeks and firm bolstering, but the change in him made Teal think of Jekyll and Hyde.

Roger had transformed instantly into one of them. Staff joked that new partners took mind-altering drugs. Roger made Teal wonder. Or maybe new partners experienced a psychic explosion of dominance after the years of repressed self and sacrifice.

"Roger, it's a forty-five-minute delay, not an hour, and stop being pompous," Teal said. "I've been asked to see the police at three. I expected you to understand."

Police—that should bring him down to earth, Teal thought. *He's running the word through his mind right now. Possibly in a panic. He's debating whether it's because of a client or because of me. Good Lord, he's thinking, either way this could hurt Clayborne Whittier.*

Teal smiled graciously as she contemplated Roger's dilemma.

"Police? I'm sorry. Of course civic duty comes first!"

Roger's show of conviction didn't disguise his curiosity.

Teal tried to keep the mirth out of her blue eyes. *He's playing fish, clever him,* she thought and decided to be a pretty agile trout.

"Thanks, Rog, I knew you'd understand."

"But, Teal." His tone transformed. "What is this all about? Do you need help?"

Teal decided not to prolong his agony. She explained what she knew.

"Fraud in Cambridge? No kidding—that makes sense of something I heard from Joe Morgan the other day. Has to be the same; University Savings and Loan is his client. He was pounding down the gin and tonics." Roger chuckled.

Joe Morgan, Teal remembered, was a senior partner at a Clayborne Whittier competitor.

"So that's what Joe was in a funk about." Roger tapped a finger to his chin. "I'll dig up what I can on University Savings and buzz you before three. The delay of our meeting is no problem."

Roger did not come up with much. University Savings and Loan flirted with bankruptcy a few years back through sheer bad management. The bank offered high-rate loans and lagged the market move to networked machines. When it finally began to change, it was almost too late.

Special services to preferred clients brought back customers as well as rumors that members of the underworld did business with the bank. Teal wasn't surprised; University's precarious condition made it a perfect target for the unscrupulous. The fact was the bank survived.

She mulled over the information while waiting for Dan Malley. It wasn't a good position for a bank, not at all, but it had happened before in the city. Unlike Mark Konstat, the *In Boston* magazine writers who had covered that story were alive. Teal remembered no hint of a threat to the authors.

Earlier in the day Teal had asked Clayborne Whittier's librarian to search for information on William Carroll. The librarian found a recent issue of *New England Manufacturers' Monthly* with the text of a speech given by Carroll on "Massachusetts: The Benefits and Costs of Doing Business In An Entrepreneurial Government Environment." Teal gagged, but skimmed the speech and read the accompanying profile of the speaker.

William Carroll joined Governor Weld's administration in 1990. The policy of squeezing education, infrastructure and social services as a necessary business solution to "save the state" brought later charges of government negligence, but, by then, Carroll had joined the Kennedy School of Government. He instructed students in the nuances of a business approach to government.

The profile implied that Carroll's current position was no more than an accommodation while he developed the political momentum necessary to enter the senatorial race. Teal didn't imagine Ted Kennedy had to watch out, but Carroll was attractive, articulate and living—quite possibly beyond his personal means—with a picture perfect family in Duxbury.

Until Sunday's *Globe*, there had been no hint linking

Carroll to corruption. He was tagged a Weld Republican who respected business solutions and individual privacy. He was a handsome man with keen, ambitious eyes. He was not a man to cross lightly.

If a threatened man, would he move to eliminate the source of the threat? Teal wondered. Political hopes had been dashed on far less than what Konstat's interest in him implied.

"But how could he have removed Konstat with, literally, no sign of foul play?" Teal wondered aloud.

She'd seen a man die and wanted to know why. Kath's buzz interrupted. Within seconds, Dan Malley entered the office.

"Cream and two sugars, Detective?" Kathy confirmed from the doorway.

Dan Malley looked up, impressed. "Yes, thank you. You'd be some w-w-witness."

Kathy winked an eyelid over one twinkling green eye as she left.

"Detective—all right, Dan," Teal said in response to his objecting hand, "you didn't call the *Globe*'s story nonsense this morning."

Her tilted head asked why.

"I'm, uh, we're not ready to conclude or dismiss anything. The coroner's preliminary report contained a few unusual observations, that's all. Ah, thanks—"

"Kathy." The secretary handed him his coffee.

"Thanks, Kathy," Dan finished as she left. He decided not to mention the coroner's preliminary report had been an informal conversation about the corpse or the "we" was him.

"Unusual observations?" Teal said.

41

Dan had wanted this interest. He couldn't resist. "As I understand it, bruising. It may be evidence of a fight."

"And is that suspicious?" Teal asked. "You were leaning to heart attack."

"Possibly."

"Possibly suspicious or possibly a heart attack?" she persisted.

"Possibly both."

Teal waited a beat, but Dan didn't fall into the trap.

"Well, enough of my questions," she said. "They can't be much help."

"No, I like talking with you." Dan colored. "The department thinks it's going to end up a guy who died of heart failure. The official message is spend the minimum and move on." He grinned. "I'd like to prove them wrong. That's why I wanted to question you again. And, your coffee's good."

He raised his cup as Teal laughed.

"Let's start at the beginning. What did you see from the minute you entered the building? You drove in and—"

"Yes, that day, although I usually walk," Teal said.

"You live in Boston?" Dan asked.

"Um. Beacon Hill. I walk through the Public Garden and Boston Common to get here most days."

"Oh, Beacon H-h-hill." Dan raised his eyes to the ceiling for a mere second.

Teal laughed and shook her head. "Aren't cops required to live in the city?"

"Southie," Dan said. "So you drove that day?"

"Yes. I'd spent the morning with a client on Route 128. The parking rates here are crazy; but I needed a few things from my office, and I planned to lunch with a friend before I left. But that's not important."

"Did you see anyone in the garage?"

"The attendant."

"Nothing out of the ordinary?" Dan persisted.

"No. I went up to the lobby and waited for an elevator along with three men." Teal pushed back the stray chestnut hairs escaping from the coil at her nape. "The weirdest thing was that only one person got out when the car arrived. Or fell," she amended.

"What do you mean?" Dan asked.

"I've never seen an empty elevator at noon. The moment the doors open, everyone steps back automatically for the crowd to exit. We did this time, only there wasn't a crowd—just him, falling."

"The elevators have to come down empty sometimes."

"Sure," Teal agreed. "But not at noon."

"Was he holding anything? A syringe maybe? Or did anything fall out with him?" Dan prompted.

"Not that I saw."

Teal detailed her actions and observations regarding Mark Konstat. Only the absence of passengers struck her as unusual.

"Thanks, Teal," Dan said and stood.

He vacillated between an urge to ask for her professional assessment of the possibility of underworld involvement with the bank and a surety that he should keep Teal Stewart out of it. The *Alt* said Konstat had been tracking some unpleasant folks.

"Please contact me if you have anything to add. I appreciate the cooperation."

"Cooperation? It's as much curiosity. I plan to watch

the elevators at lunch. If another one comes down with only one person this month . . ." Teal shrugged and spread her hands.

"I think you will," Dan said. He grinned.

"Really," she added, "it may not seem important to you, but I'd love to know how that elevator managed to make it from the Ivy Club to the lobby without stopping to pick up passengers at every floor!"

ChapтеR Five

"Life is going a little like this," Teal wrote in her journal one week later:

"better pick up my shoes before 7:30 tomorrow
need to get cash from bank machine first
hope machine is working
hope no one's sleeping beneath the machine
should address ironing board issue
have to do laundry
need to return those library books
might meet interesting people at the library
interesting people?
Averill Cunningham, interesting person
need to get some sleep
want to read awhile before sleeping
want to get up early
sleep early? up early?
need to list things to do, must do
damn, this is a list"

Teal slammed her pen to the table. Anger and irritation filled her head. The irritation came from letting daily chores slip; the anger, over the five years she had hidden from any enduring romantic relationship. She twisted a strand of hair, its luster dulled to brown in the twilight, and inspected a nail. They needed a file and buff. Her mind circled back to men.

Oh, there had been a few: casual encounters on airplanes, profound encounters on Martha's Vineyard ending with ennui and remorse, men who wanted to marry her and other men she might have considered. There had been the good, the bad and the boring. Good sex, boring conversation. Indifferent passion, stimulating discussions. When anyone remained attractive for too long, Teal fled.

She stood, anxious with introspection, Earlier, skimming the *Globe Calendar,* she saw Cheryl Wheeler listed as appearing at Nightstage. On impulse, Teal decided to go—forget reading, forget sleep. The Cambridge nightspot did not have the desperate, oppressive atmosphere of a dating bar, although casual conversations might ensue table to table at the end of a set.

The room was crowded for a Thursday, but not jammed. Teal slid her long legs under the small table and fiddled with her beer. *What if someone approaches me,* she worried. *What if no one approaches me?* The announcer on stage saved her from either thought.

". . . and now, Cheryl Wheeler."

Cheryl Wheeler. Teal leaned into the smooth and grating voice. *It's going to be fine,* Teal decided, *just fine.*

* * *

46

But Friday morning came, disastrous with client problems on top of her late-night exhaustion. At twelve-thirty Teal realized her only chance of fitting in a bite for lunch was the deli across the street. Ugh! She rode down in a packed elevator and hustled through the lobby to step bang into a man's well-suited chest.

"Pardon me," Teal said, breathless and embarrassed.

She composed her five-foot-seven frame, five-nine in heels, and saw her target stood a solid six-foot-three or more. Then she registered the face and blushed.

"Averill! Please, excuse me."

"Well, I'm delighted to meet again, even if literally." Averill laughed. "Are you on your way to lunch? Care to join me up above?"

"Ooh, what a lovely idea, but it's impossible. Demanding clients and deadlines moved up. I'm trying to pummel everything into submission before my weekend is ruined entirely. Another day?" Teal crossed her fingers.

Averill did her one better. "Start the weekend with me after work. I'm downtown all afternoon, captive to the capital demands of a growing business. My co-owners and I hope to persuade Bank of Boston to increase our credit line. Your yes will promise a good end to the day. Say six-thirty?"

He worked fast. Teal liked her friends to be decisive.

"Perfect. Six-thirty," she assented.

"Why don't we meet at the Bostonian Hotel's bar and discuss our options for a decent dinner then. Unless you're tied up later tonight." Averill finished with the implied question.

"The Bostonian is a wonderful choice and dinner

47

sounds lovely. Six-thirty, see you there.'' Teal started to move away.

"Fine." Averill lifted his curved lips to a broad smile.

Teal crossed the street thinking about his style, weaving dinner out of an after-work drink. Mark Konstat hadn't been mentioned, his death not relevant to this time together. Teal hated her anxiety. How could she be the master of her professional life and yet insecure about a few hours with an interesting man? Too ridiculous.

At the deli's crowded counter, she fretted over the appeal of her plum-colored dress. Italian, tiny pleats and chic, she decided. Had she anything in her office to touch up her cheeks? Teal left the deli shaking her head.

The first crush of after-business socializers had already moved on to Quincy Market across the street when Teal arrived at six-twenty. She entered the room with her stride long and her carriage erect, the dress swishing with each step. The Bostonian's piano player stroked Cole Porter tunes from the baby grand to mute the din.

The host motioned Teal to the front where the window gave view of the market and street. She sank into the well-stuffed chair and looked around. The Bostonian balanced decorum with comfort. Intimate groups of couches and armchairs around low tables under flattering lights created a comfortable formality which also served to legitimize the premium prices.

Averill arrived minutes after Teal, his step energetic with success. The conversation started with his negotiations which he described with excitement and wit. The lure of business, Teal thought, of money and its movement and power. Her interest compelled and repelled her in about equal measure, as it had throughout her career. Tonight, she enjoyed Averill's recounting his deal.

He explained he and his partners, Nick White and George Henderson, ran a retail business, Climb On Up. The company had stores around Boston and an experimental one in New York City.

"Climb On Up? I've been there," Teal said.

"That's because although we say we sell premium equipment and clothing to mountain climbing, cross country skiing and other outdoor sports enthusiasts, we really make our money from people who live in cities," Averill explained.

Teal laughed. Averill was right. Goods from Climb held great panache among her peers. Merchandise intended for utilitarian purpose, like their mountaineer's belt in brilliant, fluorescent colors, had achieved cult status with more than the Harvard Square crowd.

"Nick dazzled the bank with our history of growth," Averill continued. "They loved that it's been controlled."

"And Nick's position?" Teal interrupted to ask.

"The money man, our senior vice president and chief financial officer. Nick is the ultimate CFO, cautious in daily operations, daring in his vision and committed to Climb. To a fault—he works all the time. The other thing is, he's a computer wizard. His reports would convince the most skeptical banker on looks alone."

Teal didn't mention how much neat reports worried her as an auditor. She wasn't a CPA tonight.

"And George Henderson is what, the president?" she asked.

Averill nodded. "And designer of the piton that

launched Climb. George remains our technical purist and is in charge of product purchase and design. They started the company three years before I joined. I've been the vice president of marketing and retail expansion for four years.

"The titles sound more specialized than we operate. George looks after the local stores because they still cater to athletes. I'm running our beta site in New York to test expanding market share with the upscale consumer. The loan will fund a rollout of the concept beyond New York."

"And the bank was impressed?" Teal prompted.

"Yes, particularly with our caution. Uncontrolled growth brings problems. You can see that with the other specialty retailers. Flat same-store sales and unprofitable expansion."

"What spared Climb?" Teal asked.

"I think success comes from timing and product and ego control. What will be hot when? How long to carry how much. I helped my partners understand these considerations. They opened the first store out of a passion for mountain climbing. They never claimed to be business people. While ego and product weren't their problems, the need for merchandising and expansion expertise was. I fit into a good team."

"And"—Teal took in Averill's patrician profile—"will product sensibility be a problem of yours?"

"I don't think so. I'm smart enough to defer to my partners on technical questions, and I understand targeted selection. They're damned skilled at evaluating the athletes in this market. We may disagree at the margin, but not in the way which causes harm."

"Ego?" Teal prompted.

Averill's gray eyes focused on some point in the distance. "Ego is harder, isn't it? I think it's fair to say that no one of us feels threatened by compromise. We've all won and lost points to the benefit of the company. Its success will be a personal victory for each one of us, I think, although I admit we've had our moments."

"I interrupted your narrative," Teal said. *But liked your response,* she thought.

"It was a reasonable question. I can get carried away."

"Believe me, I have times when I go on and on. I hope you'll see, but, please, continue," Teal said.

A lovely star of good-humor lines crinkled the corner by Averill's mouth. Teal enjoyed the rapport with someone who understood business. Hunt certainly didn't.

"Well, the bank was satisfied with our numbers and presentation. I can finance expansion through the Big Apple." Averill grinned. "There won't be a baby-boomer or buster in the world who doesn't feel more *themselves* wearing Climb products. We'll encourage them to dream of Everest from base camp Wall Street."

"Well," Teal said, raising her glass, "here's to you."

Averill's gray eyes met hers, assured and probing. "Here's to us."

Teal recognized the danger he represented in her present state of emotional restlessness. But why not live a little?

They ate at Season's, the Bostonian's superb restaurant. Over the espresso, Averill watched her, his expression an enigma.

"Your place or mine?" Humor tinted his voice. "Or the Boston Ballet's mandatory Christmas performance of the *Nutcracker* in a few weeks? With dinner of course."

Teal tensed, her heart beating too fast.

"Of the options presented," she said carefully, "I'll have to go with Christmas. I would be Scrooge not to."

They meandered through the city en route to Teal's home. Past the Common, they lingered in the Public Garden where trees and shrubs glowed in the chill night. Branches etched dark and graceful lines against the moonlit sky; dry leaves chattered underfoot. Teal linked her arm with Averill's. She tried to pretend to herself that she only used him to buffer the sharp wind. But the fit worked as he tucked her elbow to his side.

She turned at her doorway. "You've done wonders in dispelling the frenzy of my day. Thanks."

Averill pulled off a glove and raised his hand to brush aside the loose hairs blown across her face by the wind. He traced a gentle line down her forehead and nose before he touched the curve of her lips.

"You are a lovely companion, a good conversationalist, and, I suspect, a shrewd businesswoman. Don't thank me. Simply kiss me quickly and I'm away."

His hand touched her cheek and cupped around to the back of her neck. He leaned over to press his lips against hers.

Drawing back, he said, "I'll call. Trust me."

He slid her keys from her hand and unlocked the door. When she stepped through, he shut it with a gentle pull. Teal watched him move down the steps to the street.

Damn, she thought, *why didn't I say "my place"?* There was, at least, the expectation of the *Nutcracker* in a couple of weeks.

Chapter Six

Life never runs as simply as well-laid plans.

Teal threw a toothbrush in the bag. Why had Clayborne Whittier volunteered her to speak at the Bowdoin College symposium? Well, at least it gave her an opportunity to visit friends. Business travel seldom yielded that pleasure. The expectation of a Saturday in Maine with Robert and Margret followed by Sunday night's *Nutcracker* with Averill set her to humming as she zipped shut her suitcase.

The flight attendant tapped Teal's shoulder. "Would you care for a magazine? Is your seat belt buckled?"

Teal shook her head and nodded as they exchanged wan smiles. She watched the attendant bend to the next row of seats. The woman in the slightly crumpled uniform moved across the aisle to greet another passenger uninterested in her proffered reading. The third individual she approached greeted her attention with a hand extended for the magazine and a smile. Teal shifted her eyes to him.

His face tickled her memory as he leaned back into his seat. Teal squinted at the profile and tried to match it with a name. William Carroll! Teal remembered his picture in the *Manufacturers' Monthly*. The coincidence of that research and his appearance on the plane made her shrink in her seat.

"How odd," she murmured and disturbed the man beside her. She smiled an apology.

The flight from Boston's Logan Airport to Portland, Maine, was too short to enjoy a good book and too long for the view to be a diversion. Today the sky blanketed the ground with a dull gray, anyway. Teal reached for her briefcase and found the envelope Kath had slipped her as she left the office. Teal pulled out a typed page and found the symposium agenda. She read:

Tuesday, December 12th: afternoon arrival, registration, 5:00 P.M. welcoming cocktail party and dinner.

Wednesday, December 13th: 10:00 A.M. speeches by John Shepler, State of Maine Business Liaison Officer; Richard Stebbins, State of New Hampshire Assistant to the Governor for State Business and Resource Development; William Carroll, businessman, Commonwealth of Massachusetts; Ben Bailey, specialty farmer, Vermont; and Susan Coltrera, State of Rhode Island Development Office, 12:00 noon lunch.

So, Teal sighed to herself, that explained Mr. Carroll.

Wednesday 1:30-4:00 P.M. presentations by the
panel of experts.

Kathy's largely drawn star beside the line referred to
her note in the margin. "Called Bowdoin. You are a
'panel of experts' member, speech subject up to you,
but guess what—they hope about women in business, as
talent, as consumers, etc. (What else is new???) About
twenty minutes. Break a leg." Teal smiled. Kathy, so
different from her, remained a staunch support.

Wednesday, 6:00 P.M. evening cocktails and dinner.
Thursday, December 14th: 10:00-11:45 A.M. panel
discussion, 12:00 noon lunch, 1:30-4:00 break
out groups with individual panel members, 6:00
evening cocktails and dinner. Speeches by the
governors of Massachusetts and Vermont.
Friday, December 15th: morning break up coffee,
checkout and departure.

The fasten seat belt sign flashed on. The attendant
made a last pass through the plane to glance at belts
before she buckled into her own. The landing was com-
petent and smooth despite the fog and strong cross wind.
William Carroll preceded Teal down the steps. She
still gripped the rail against the wind as he rushed to the
terminal. Two people followed him with a mike and
camera. Teal recognized one as a Boston television reporter. Had the rumors brought them? she wondered.
No. His participation in the conference must have at-
tracted media coverage.

* * *

The symposium included vague allusions to state support for small businesses and special considerations for large enterprises, a discussion of the unique human resources in New England and the area's access to a long intellectual tradition. As Kathy had predicted, Teal presented the merits to women in staying east.

In the first fifteen minutes of the first cocktail party, Teal ran into William Carroll. More precisely, he sought her out. After he introduced himself, he steered her from the crowd.

"I understand from the *Globe* that you knew Mark Konstat." Carroll's flat voice matched an unblinking stare.

His jaw squared up, tight and hostile. This was no amicable candidate glad-handing a vote from her.

"You read the story wrong," Teal replied, curious to understand what was going on.

"He hadn't been talking to you before he died?" Carroll persisted.

"I never knew the man," Teal said. "Bad luck put me in the way of his fall. I hardly qualify as a confidant."

Konstat's smack against the tiles returned to mind, his last twitch. Teal recoiled from the memory.

"I'm sorry. My behavior must seem inexcusable. This death is consuming my life all because of unfounded rumor. The damn press hounds me, I hound you—it's ridiculous. I imagined you followed me to Bowdoin." Carroll snorted. "Forgive me. You're with Clayborne Whittier, aren't you? I know your senior partner, Don Clarke, quite well."

William Carroll stood silently for a full half minute, Teal trapped beside him.

"I need help," he said suddenly. "I'm opening my records to the *Alt Paper* this weekend to put an end to the lies. God knows, aside from a normal personal loan, I have no interest in University Savings. I thought giving the paper access to my documents should settle the issue, but my wife is furious. She believes the press will misinterpret an ant as an elephant. If I had an expert, someone impartial—someone like you—to referee . . ."

Teal waited, but for the moment William Carroll was finished.

"Questions are still being raised?" she asked.

"The fourth estate! Muck rakers fishing for another Watergate. Every one of them knows I want to run for the senate, so add rumored bank improprieties and sudden death and you bet they're being raised. All crap, pardon my direct language, but crap can kill my future. Well, will you help?"

Teal didn't say she was stunned he would turn to a complete stranger. People at parties expected all manner of intimate financial advice from her when they learned she was a CPA. She'd been asked to approve questionable tax strategies and primed for insider information. She had thought she was immune to being surprised.

She choked back her annoyance and put on a social smile. "I'm sorry, I have plans here in Maine for the weekend. Anyway, I don't think Clayborne Whittier would be comfortable if I participated."

"Nonsense. You can be identified as a volunteer from an unnamed firm, someone independent of all parties. I need an advocate for truth, not for me or the *Alt*. Look, I'll call Don Clarke myself to explain."

Teal's elevated mood in anticipation of a companionable weekend sank.

"Of course if Don approves the idea—"

"Great. I'll call him right now," Carroll said.

"Fine." Teal raised her hands in the universal gesture of defeat and tried to keep up the social smile.

Friday noon, Carroll told Teal her participation in the review of his records had been arranged. Saturday and Sunday would be spent at the *Alt Paper* with their business editor, the reporter assuming Konstat's investigation, and William Carroll. The *Alt* accepted Teal as she remained impartial, and, according to Carroll, Don Clarke expressed only pleasure at the idea Teal could help.

Teal wanted to hear that for herself. She called the partner in charge directly. The story stayed the same.

"Remember, Teal," Don admonished before the conversation ended, "you do not represent Clayborne Whittier. And, although I trust Bill is in the clear, draw no conclusions. This could be a little tricky for the firm; we don't want to alienate anyone. Your job is expertise, not evaluation."

Damn, Teal thought as she murmured resigned agreement, *it's my weekend that's being ruined, not his.* Sunday evening at the *Nutcracker* was some consolation, but she'd wanted to catch up with Robert and Margret. Robert, the son of one of her mother's friends and as woven into her childhood memories as anyone, had invited her to the party where she'd met Hunt when she moved to Massachuetts. Robert and Margret had been graduate students at MIT and married even back then. Now she wanted to tell them all about Averill, about how often she saw him, and how wonderful it felt to be in love again. She never expected this—two days on a special and unwelcome assignment.

Robert and Margret received the news politely, but with a disappointment as strong as hers. They insisted on driving her to the airport Friday night. Margret, her round face straining with artificial good cheer, tried to keep the mood light as they waited for Teal's flight.

"You take care and come down to see us soon," she said. "We'll steam up a pot of lobsters and talk—"

"About how weird it is of this guy to want you to look over his check stubs." Robert grinned. "Don't you think?"

Teal wanted to say she didn't want to think about William Carroll or his check stubs. She wanted that pot of lobsters and a long weekend with Robert and Margret now. She wanted to tell them they hadn't changed a bit. Robert still reminded her of a distracted stork as he patted his pockets for the keys he held in his hand while Margret remained the practical one by gently tapping her husband's hand.

"Oh, right. Here they are. So, you haven't opined on this guy's weird request," Robert said as he refocused on Teal.

"It's not that weird actually. His wife was smart to realize he'd made himself a vulnerable target. I just wish I hadn't been there when he decided to do something about it. I could almost see it register in his eyes—a CPA working for his good friend Don Clarke. I didn't have a chance."

"And it's not making you very happy," Margret said.

"No," Teal agreed.

60

"Do you think you'll find evidence of cleverly disguised financial skulduggery? He may rue the day . . ." Robert held a hand to his throat and widened his dark eyes in a pantomime of choking.

"Enough, Robert," Margret snapped. "Stop trying to upset our guest."

He flashed his devilish smile from his wife to Teal. "Come on, isn't it rather exciting? Best take care you don't learn too much, Teal. This Konstat fellow ended up dead. Who knows who will be next?"

Chapter Seven

Averill sent a contribution to the Arts and Letters Fellowship established by the Konstat family in memory of Mark. He did not go to the funeral; after writing the check, he forced the matter out of mind. Climb On Up monopolized his attention.

Buying into Climb four years earlier had been the opportunity he needed after the three bad jobs following business school. Each had come with all the promises made to and all the promise of a B-school graduate. Each had ended in disillusion. Climb had promised to be different.

At thirty-eight years old, Averill realized that his ideas for developing a business, viewed by his previous employers as too impatient and daring, hit the target for Climb. And Climb hit the target for Averill.

"It's my canvas," he had explained to Teal once, after they viewed an exhibit at the Museum of Fine Arts, "my forum for creativity."

"Was it difficult for you? Joining such a risky venture?" Teal had asked, curious and not a little jealous.

"Not really. My other options presented a greater, if

different, risk. The old family name, you know." He shrugged and pinched his voice into the most Brahmin, nasal tone. "Possibilities for a pleasant position with a fiduciary trust managing dwindling estates. Entree into a stuffy bank, don't you know. Being a Cunningham still counts for something," his voice changed, "but not that way. Not for me."

Averill did not tell her that his grandfather had been too incompetent to be entrusted with the bulk of the family fortune, and his father too weak and dissipated to conserve what had remained.

Oh, Averill understood his was a rarified impoverishment. He had danced until dawn at New York debutante balls at eighteen, learned to swing at a golf ball as a member of the exclusive country club. A tidy, compact trust had funded the years at Yale before Harvard and a charge at Brooks Brothers. But the family estate in Manchester-by-the-Sea, the fifty-foot Hinckley yacht and the option to live on one's interest? Those had been lost to history.

"Family name," Teal had mused. "I'm not sure what to make of the concept. Our house was a disaster of kids and Mother disappearing into the piano room and Father beside himself with nerves before every lecture to a new class. Family name meant, 'Oh, you're one of *those* Stewarts.' I think it's why I surprised them all, choosing pragmatism over romanticism, getting an MBA and then my CPA. No one would have pegged one of *those* Stewarts for business school. Did family have a contrary effect on you?"

"Probably." Then Averill had moved the discussion back to art.

But Teal's innocent question had pulled the past uncomfortably to mind, memories of his mother buying alpaca coats and marabou-trimmed lingerie, his father's hopelessly amiable smile, clock-patterned socks and drinking. Averill recoiled at a long-repressed image of his father weeping impotently as his mother demanded they use Averill's trust for a European tour.

"But, Marion," his father pleaded, his tone a culmination of years of alcohol and frustration, "can't you understand? You married into a tradition, a certain place in the community. You didn't marry millions!"

"I married like a fool and a children," she had yelled back in a grammar still confused by a European childhood. "I believe in your big house and fancy promises. I hate you, Everett Harte Cunningham. You and your precious mother and your father so pathetic. But I am the stupidest."

She disintegrated into a rage, strong with anger and seductive with the charm of her accent and wiles.

The scene was Averill's most vivid memory of his mother, a woman he had trained himself to blank from his life. But that afternoon, just home from Choate for the summer holidays, when he stood at the entrance to his parents' bedroom, the ugly image had etched irrevocably in his adolescent mind. No one needed to tell him that his mother was an embarrassment. He knew instinctively and willed at every parents' weekend that his father alone visit him at school.

His father was acceptable, another pallid Yankee joining of the last exhausted genes—a familiar breed among Choate fathers of Averill's generation. His mother was entirely different. Beyond her birth in Belgium and her startling, soft beauty, Averill knew and wanted to know nothing about her.

He never asked his father where they had met or why they married. On his twelfth birthday, Averill counted out his fingers, one for each month between that marriage and his birth. Passing eleven, he folded his hands and cried.

This Friday the future, not the past, occupied his thoughts. Climb and Teal intertwined through the fabric of his life. The notion pleased him.

Teal was not from the world of Choate boys and Miss Porter's girls. The only women available to Averill from those confines orbited the outer circle. They bored and frustrated him with their Fair Isle sweaters and wide, unadorned eyes, their fear of their tenuous status visceral. In this he understood, if vaguely, his father's choice of Marion.

Teal was different from all his previous attachments. The difference wasn't simply the clarity of her direct gaze, or her reluctance to assume intimacy too quickly; it was in her effect on him. He felt vulnerable to emotion again, to the sweep of joy and the unexpected tenor of sorrow. He looked forward to Sunday evening, the *Nutcracker*. Part of him wished her back from Maine; another savored the wait.

And he had work to accomplish before their date. Averill turned to the financial projections for Climb's expansion in New York.

Teal had been right to question his comfort with risk. He hadn't been entirely candid with her about the problems at Climb when he had joined. The company could hardly survive from one quarter to the next.

Marketing relied exclusively on word of mouth among

a limited group of techno-fanatic climbers, and sales were low. Pathetically low. But Nick White and George Henderson didn't know how to run the business any other way. They welcomed Averill and his business school strategies. Nick, particularly, wanted the company to accomplish more.

The first year Averill focused them on survival; the second and third, on marketing the superiority of Climb's line. Each partner was delighted when the company began to prosper and to grow. Now they even planned a "Climb On Up" private label for a downhill ski line. The business relationship had been a good one all around.

Averill now drew the projections to the center of his desk. He knew that growth of the "New York concept" would change the subtle balance of power and responsibility among the partners.

Nick, the vice president finance, handled that end of the business and assisted George on product selection and private label designs. Nominally president, George preferred engineering new products and running the Boston and Cambridge stores. He sought consensus for every decision. Averill was responsible for marketing strategies and store expansion. He split his weeks between the office in Cambridge and the new concept store in New York City.

Changing the number and mix of stores could challenge the corporate harmony.

Already the partners disagreed on the issue of decentralization. George believed New York should be more autonomous than the local stores. Nick vehemently disagreed. He considered independent managers an invitation to financial disaster despite all the arguments about market sensitivity. Nick worried about losing control.

Averill shrugged his impatience with these thoughts, but he knew where they came from—the image of his father eased by underlings from the center of authority. He intended no such fate. Anyway, the issue was moot. George had come round to accept Nick's position. Averill had concurred from the start.

That argument had been the first serious disagreement among the three. Growth was sure to bring other disruptions.

He dropped the expansion data and forced himself to think about the board of directors' meeting scheduled for Monday. The board expected him to report on the use of the company's new credit. Nick would address Climb's continuing relationship with Bank of Boston.

Averill remembered when the bank had required Climb to add at least one independent director to the board. George had resisted the idea of permitting an outsider to join their board, but the bank had refused to yield. Nick had proposed William Carroll, his regular squash partner and a well-qualified candidate, to defuse the conflict.

Averill knew Carroll as an acquaintance from business school. Carroll's name and political connections promised the company clout. Thinking back to the deliberations, Averill had to laugh. After all the arguing and discussion, Carroll had only reluctantly agreed to join. He'd insisted from his first meeting that the company search for his replacement.

Averill planned to present a candidate for consideration on Monday. But he appreciated the value of Carroll's participation during the development of the New York store and the recent bank negotiations. Ironically, Carroll's rumored troubles now made replacement the best course for all concerned.

The telephone interrupted Averill's thoughts.

The opening pleasantries were brief.

As Averill listened, he tapped his restless fingers to the desk. The speaker could not hear the impatient drum beat.

"I don't think you understand," Averill said.

Words rushed unabated across the line.

"Of course, I appreciate your concern. There's absolutely nothing . . . all right, then. I'll be there. I, . . . yes, fine, this should satisfy you . . . No, perfectly . . . until then." Averill hung up with care.

He made a steeple with his fingers on which he rested his chin. The sounds of the office thundered in his ears, or maybe it was his thoughts. He glanced at the papers spread across his desk. They were finished. He searched his drawer for one more document and swept the rest into a pile.

Outside his office, he stopped at his secretary's desk.

"I'm off. Copy these for Monday's meeting, please, and leave any messages on my desk. Thanks." He pointed to the clock and smiled. "I don't think I'll be back today."

Nick White watched out his office window as Averill walked across the parking lot. Casual dress and early departure were the Friday norm. Nick never left before seven, himself. He liked the office quiet and dark. He liked the privacy. No interruptions and none of the chaos he'd find at home.

Thirteen years ago he had married his wife Sara, right out of college. High school sweethearts, they had promised to write each other every day and to date no one else. Through four years of college, they kept the faith. A small, family wedding marked their graduation; then Nick pursued a graduate degree while Sara taught school. The plan was an exchange. Once he had his advanced degree, he would work while she studied for her education Ph.D.

Sara became pregnant with Jane after four months. She fell in love with the baby and stopped dreaming of another sheepskin. In rapid succession, three more girls followed. Nick found them, all of the girls, strangers to him still.

First, his wife tut-tutted as he fumbled through his first change of Jane's diaper. She demonstrated his inability to pour Kim's juice the right way. At Tanya's pre-K parent-teacher meeting, Sara shushed him to embarrassed silence when he asked about the events in his daughter's day out of turn of the other mothers.

So all right. Sara won the children. Hers, all hers, and she could have them, he had concluded, the quiet, uneasy ghouls. How could he have fathered four children who couldn't ski, wouldn't climb a hill, cried every time they scraped a knee?

Nick hit his forehead with a fist and wallowed in a mist of memory and despair. He recalled the party when the distinct sound of the women's voices drifted from the kitchen to where he had stood. He remembered that silly bucket of ice freezing the palms of his hands. One year ago today, Sara's birthday.

He had listened to the rising voice.

"I never would have said it in high school. Gosh, they seemed made for each other. You know, the sweet types. But now, my God, how can he stand it? He's actually grown into someone interesting, and he's much better looking than I'd remembered; but she hasn't changed one whit, poor soul."

"What is Justice Holmes' wife supposed to have said?" a second voice chimed in. " 'Washington is full of brilliant men and the women they married when they were young.' Do you think Nick feels prematurely dead?"

"I wonder if he plays—"

"Around?" Everyone giggled.

Nick had retreated back into the living room then, a smile glued to his face, but the conversation never left him. That's why it came to mind today. Sara's next birthday.

Averill's secretary, Nick observed, did not stay long behind, only long enough to let the boss get well away. Nick rose and leaned around his door. He smiled at his assistant.

"Make it a short day if you like. I expect to be around a good while," he said.

His assistant nodded and smiled.

In his office, Nick studied the data from New York. An adjustment here and a bookkeeping entry there and it should look all right. He flipped on his computer and waved to his assistant as she left. He settled in front of the screen, keyed in his password and set to mastering the world. His imagination soared at a universe without Sara. The thought brought him alive with hope.

Chapter Eight

Dan read the autopsy report more than once or twice in the weeks after he received it. He spent time to underline sentences and pencil questions in the margin. Death hadn't been due to heart failure. Or embarrassment at losing a fight. Mark Konstat had died from eating a peanut. A chocolate covered peanut, actually.

How did someone fatally allergic to the legume eat one? Dan wondered. Did Konstat pop a heedless handful in his mouth and give the perfunctory chew? Did he know before he swallowed?

However the peanut entered his mouth, immediately his nose began to clog. His head lightened in response to the rapid blood pressure drop as his immune system went berserk in a frenzied production of antibodies and histamines. Like Don Quixote, they tilted at their windmills, mistaking the trifling seed for a bacteria, virus or aberrant cell growth. But Konstat harbored no such lethal dose of foreign activity, just the masticated legume. Complicated by a congenitally weak heart, life's failure took only minutes.

Mark Konstat died from anaphylactic shock, straight and simple, after chasing his pretty complete lunch of veal, roast potatoes, salad and an abundance of coffee with the innocent and complimentary chocolate coated sweet.

Dan had enjoyed seven or so himself the day Konstat died. He had appreciated the nicety of club life. The complimentary sweet offered a sop to his hungry stomach. Not that the members agreed. More than one petulant complaint entertained his wait in the club's anteroom. Police ranked low among the club's priorities.

One corpulent and red-faced speaker particularly broadcast his pique. "Peanuts? What's this? Rotten damned substitute for our mint."

The gentlemen spouted "women next, you'll see" as a solicitous club functionary eased the fellow to the foyer.

Dan thought nothing of the incident except to ask, as he knew he would, why the peanuts and not mints? The maitre d', when he finally came, explained an order, delivered wrong, left the club to use up ten pounds of chocolate peanuts.

Thus, in a sense, did Ivy kill Konstat. The conclusion struck Dan as ironic, considering the poor bastard had refused to join.

The detective now forced his attention back to the report. He read again that no puncture marks pierced Konstat's hairy body. No signs of immediate foul play marred the corpse. The coroner stood right on one act: Konstat's beating was at least a week old when his life came to its sudden close.

73

"No puncture marks . . . no signs of immediate foul play," Dan reread aloud.

The bald statements rubbed against his grain. And against the claims of Konstat's grieving mother. She insisted her son carried a syringe loaded with epinephrine everywhere, every day. One shot was all he had needed to live. One shot that her son could deliver to himself in his sleep, she protested. He had practiced from age three when the family learned of his vulnerability to anaphylactic shock.

"So where was the syringe?" Mrs. Konstat had asked. And worse, "Who killed my son?"

Because that's what she believed when Dan assured her the medication had not been on or near her boy. She had raised her limp hands to overflowing eyes and broken down completely. Dan wondered if she was sort of crazy to rant about adrenaline and epinephrine.

He paged to epinephrine in the *Physician's Guide*. *Adrenaline*. It made interesting reading.

Dan set the book on his desk and leaned back to stare sightlessly at the near wall. Mother had known best. Konstat would have been a fool to leave his house without a loaded syringe. So where was it?

One other fact troubled Dan: that beating within seven days of the journalist's death.

Two cracked ribs, enlarged spleen, damaged kidneys and extensive bruising from his chest to his thighs indicated the use of undue force. The careful confinement of each blow nagged Dan's imagination. The pattern was familiar to a cop. It screamed spouse abuse, except that Konstat was no girl friend or wife. Dan littered that section of the report with more notes.

As evident as the damage to Konstat was the lack of

74

damage to his assailant. Konstat's hands, unblemished, proved he had not given as good as he got. In fact, the journalist likely had not given anything. Was Konstat a lover who had incurred the jealous wrath of a mate? Dan planned to clear up that question today.

He considered the interplay of testosterone and fate, sex and war. He mused on the havoc wrought by Helen of Troy. *The Iliad*. Parochial school had its recompense for too many years of boxed ears and a fixation with orderly rows. The compensation had been in the solace Dan sought in the home of his friend, the son of a Unitarian minister and scholar. That man had given Dan his first introduction to Homer, and Dan had read the poet in each new translation ever since.

Konstat's unprepossessing mien curtailed Dan's extended indulgence in speculation. Dan couldn't imagine Mark Konstat attracting any Helen of Troy, but perhaps Francesca Mettafora would know. Allowing for the Friday morning traffic, she should arrive at his desk within ten minutes.

"Lover? Mark Konstat a lover?" Francesca Mettafora's small frame doubled over with an indecorous howl of laughter. "Oh, God, how awful of me. Don't think ill of the dead and all, but Mark a lover? Obsessed with work, yes. The most boorish man I knew, yes. But a lover? God no! He made neither love nor war—one too messy, the other too dangerous. Or maybe vice versa. Anyway, he blamed his mother. She caught him touching his weenie as a kid and permanently scarred his psyche blah, blah, blah. But not his intellect. The man was an emotional midget, but fearless reporter. Look—" she hesitated.

Dan could imagine the reason for her internal debate. How much should she tell a cop? Anyone he ever talked to who had something to tell had first to answer this. Dan tried to assess the woman without staring. Luminous brown eyes looked back at him from a face that radiated intelligence and skepticism. He would have called her delicate except for the steely hold of her gaze and the tight curve of her otherwise generous lips. She was tiny and fit and tough enough to be a help or a hindrance. This was the critical moment. He made his decision and arranged his expression into a look of neutral receptivity.

Francesca Mettafora had called him on her return from vacation. She had requested this meeting. And she was troubled by Konstat's death. She wanted to help.

"Look, I've just started on Mark's work, so don't get all excited; I don't have any big revelation. But something is weird. His notes are terrible, and I'm finding zippo in his computer."

Francesca sat back in the chair. Dan gave it two beats. Nothing.

"I'm not sure I'm f-f-following."

"Mark was a computer nut. He documented every aspect of his investigations. He didn't give a damn for paranoia. Never locked a drawer. I mean, Mark even taped his password to his machine. We shared a few stories, but this time he's left me zippo. He was nervous." Francesca's eyes belied her flippant tone.

"What could have scared him? Make a guess—you knew him pretty well," Dan suggested. He wanted anything she could give.

"Speculation—no strings—and no later bullshit about right or wrong?"

76

"I, uh, understand you're s-s-speculating. Everything interests me at this point." Dan did not add *because I have nothing,* but unless that changed soon, *his* case would vaporize. He needed Ms. Mettafora.

"I used to have a nervous verbal tick," Francesca said. "An incessant 'you know' or 'ya know' in a down-home phase. Anyway, it's hell for a reporter, makes people think you're a jerk. It can't be much fun for a cop. Now I say 'you know' three times before I go into an interview, and that's it." She looked at him and shrugged. "Works for me."

He dropped his eyes. Her comment conjured up the impatience of the nuns who had exacerbated his stutter. The old humiliation heated his face. One young nun had tried to help. He remembered what she said, that his mind was a private and able place. That nun now ran the order.

Minds don't stutter, Dan thought. *Or shrink from blows.* So what had been in Konstat's mind?

"So, wild-ass guess? Mark knew he had touched more than just another business scam. Something emotional. Someone out there really wanted University Savings Bank, like it was a personal thing."

"Do you think Mark knew who the someone was?"

"I can't tell. The crazy notes he left include the names of a couple of underworld figures and then William Carroll. Mark never liked Carroll. He thought the guy was a phony. I do know Carroll stiffed Mark on a story years ago. Mark was the kind of reporter who never forgot. He wasn't above jerking Carroll around a little. I don't know. My work's cut out for me." Francesca rolled her eyes.

"You should be careful, Ms. Mettafora. Your

colleague wasn't a pretty sight when he died," Dan said.

He couldn't say more, but he didn't want this slip of a woman to misconstrue a verdict of death by natural causes. However Konstat had died, he had inspired a powerful burst of someone's ire.

"I always am. And I have a very different style. My subjects can't tell what hit them until the article is in print; then it's too late. Well, I hope I've helped with whatever you can investigate when the guy died naturally." Francesca's face sharpened with a reporter's hunger.

Dan didn't respond, the "whatever you can investigate," slapping at his ego. She had hit the spot. Whatever he could investigate was—nothing. University Savings' problems, if any, fell to a state regulatory board, not the Boston police. Mark Konstat was about to disappear under "file closed." Even if the journalist had been onto a story that goaded someone into beating him blue, eating a peanut wasn't murder.

"Good luck, Ms. Mettafora. Please keep me informed."

He accompanied her to the far door.

"Oh." Dan stopped. He, at least, would dignify the case with a complete set of notes. "Were you aware that Konstat had allergies?"

A laugh originated in Francesca's chest and rumbled up her throat. It sounded incongruous from so small a body.

"Was I aware he had allergies? Who wasn't! He took different shots for every season, he carried a Japanese oxygen spritzer from some department store in Tokyo, and, of course, his ever-ready syringe. Mark loved the attention. Believe me, the entire newsroom knew. Before I switched to free lance, I don't think we were ever at a loss on his birthday. A play doctor kit, a subscription to *Prevention Magazine,* a blow-up nurse doll; well, you name it, he got it. And more, I suppose, after I'd gone off on my own.''

"Did you ever see him use the syringe?''

"Fortunately, considering its purpose, no. I saw it once. A junkie's dream, a clean needle. I think he carried it as a matter of routine, but what do I know? Good luck.''

Dan watched her leave. End of case.

Teal Stewart had asked for a call when the autopsy came in. She hoped to bring closure to the experience, Dan realized, while he faced the case's end with reluctance. But he had no excuse to delay the call longer.

"Ms. Stewart's office,'' Kathy answered.

"It's Dan Malley. Is she in?''

"Sorry, Detective, she's out until Monday. If it's important, I can reach her with your message.''

"Please don't bother. I can wait. Uh.'' Dan fought his tongue. "Just leave the message I called. It looks like the Konstat case is about done and, uh, any c-c-chance we could have dinner tonight?''

He was as surprised as Kathy and happier than surprised when she said yes. Konstat might be over, but the case had introduced him to the pretty, dark-haired woman. He filed the coroner's report in his desk, and his smile dimmed. The beating still worried him. Francesca Mettafora expected to take up University Savings where Konstat had left off. Threatened ambitions had a pattern of striking back against the living.

Dan shook his head and told himself to let up. The case was finished.

Chapter Nine

Mornings like this made Teal wish she still drank coffee. The sky was low and overcast in that particularly New England gloom that made her long to return to California, and the barometric pressure was dropping. Days that began with a falling barometer made her want to stay in bed. She tried to cheer herself with the thought that parking should be easy on a Saturday.

Her Mercedes didn't act any happier with the weather. The idle threatened to stall out the motor at every stoplight, and she hit red on each one. The old 190SL sport coupe didn't like the cold or damp any more than she did.

Teal eased from the gas and engaged the clutch as the last light turned green. One more block and she'd have to put on her professional face. She drove past the front of the *Alt* and turned onto Hampshire Street. The dashboard clock reminded her that she was late. She glanced at the side door of the newspaper. No one waited. Good. He was late, too.

Parking was as easy as she expected. She locked the car in a legal space just half a block up and across the street. When she realized he might be inside, she picked up her pace to a run, eyes up and forward on the door. She would have missed him entirely if her stumble on the curb hadn't made her look down.

Then she threw up.

"Dan, he's dead." Teal rested her forehead against the top of the public telephone. The cold metal bit into her nausea with a jolt of cold.

"Start again, Teal. S-s-slow down." Detective Malley heard agony in her voice. "Who is dead?"

"He's such a mess. Oh, God."

Her teeth clicked a tattoo over the line. She could not let go of the image. She could not forget the viscous darkening of the blood, the lumps of pulp dotting a half-shredded, half-perfectly furled ear. The gun still in his hand. No wonder women chose to kill themselves with pills.

"Okay. Teal, listen. Tell me—who is dead?"

"He's near the side doorway of the *Alt*. Cambridge, on Hampshire Street, I forget the number," Teal whispered.

She sucked in a lungful of air. Oxygen. Breathe. She had to get more oxygen. She wanted to throw up all over again.

"Are you there, Teal?"

"Across the street. Don't hang up. Not yet. Please."

"I have to, Teal. I have to call the Cambridge police; then I will meet you there. Did you drive? Can you go to your car and wait?" Dan no longer hoped to get more over the telephone.

"Yes, I drove. It's half a block from here. Dan, it's so horrible."

How could he know? Her right hand rattled against the booth's glass door. She curved her fingers into a fist, then shook them free. The fear did not dissipate.

"Come quickly, please. I don't want to be alone with the Cambridge police. Don't say anything more or I won't be able to hang up the phone. I'll be in my car. It's a 1959 Mercedes 190SL. She's cream with a gray hardtop. You won't miss her. Sorry, Dan. You were the only person I could think to call."

Teal hung up carefully, concentrating on every movement. Her jaw muscles pulled into the shape that preceded a scream. Bile flooded her throat. She dropped her face to her palms, but nothing could massage the horror away. A tremor racked her body as she shuffled from the booth.

Finally, she was beside her aged sports coupe. The passenger door opened when she turned the key. She lowered herself to the seat and tugged the handle until the heavy door swung closed.

"I'll play the radio," she said aloud to comfort herself.

An awkward maneuver slid her over the stick shift and into the driver's seat. With familiar precision, she turned the ignition and hit the starter button.

WBUR offered Weekend Edition: an interview with an East African ivory poacher and, coming up, a piece on the growth of the Antarctic ozone hole. Tears coursed down Teal's cheeks to merge at her chin. Each splatter marked a wet blotch on the leather steering wheel.

Then the storm ended. The sick feeling in her stomach, the constriction around her heart and the crying

stopped to leave her empty. She foraged a handker-
chief from her purse and raised a circle of mirror to
her face.

Blue mascara trailed down each cheek. Scrubbing
brought up false color. The glass reflected her rueful
excuse for a smile.

"What's your grief?" she asked the pale image. "You
hardly knew the man."

But you knew him, she acknowledged, and the sick
feeling rose again to clog her throat. Her mind's eye saw
the figure broken and still—and the gun. She should have
arrived earlier. On time. If she had . . .

"Oh, God." Teal moved her lips. "I don't want this
guilt."

The sharp rap made her jump as Dan bent to the window.

"Would you rather wait there?" he asked.

Teal shook her head and opened the door. He took
her hand and helped her step out beside him.

"Thanks. No sign of police." Her voice held level.

"Except for me." Dan smiled. "Listen. They should
be here any minute."

Sirens shrilled in the distance.

"Let's meet them at the *Alt,*" he suggested.

They walked the block without speaking.

"Who is it, Teal?" Dan prompted when they stopped.

Who indeed, Teal wondered. She couldn't recall the
color of his eyes or sound of his voice. Did he love
Mozart or the Rolling Stones? What did he feel as the
bullet blasted flesh and bone? Did he give a name to his
despair?

In the moment before death, had ambitions unrealized
filled his mind? Had he eaten breakfast, kissed his wife,

84

hugged his kids before he turned to go? Suddenly it seemed imperative to know. But her only sure knowledge was that he had died.

"He's a was, not an is. 'Who was it?' would be right." Teal could not look down. "He was William Carroll. Hard to see, isn't it? No face at all, really. He was lying in it."

She knew a vision of the hideous mess could terrorize every night of her life. What a joke on the woman who closed her eyes to avoid violence in movies. She'd missed whole films that way, like *Alien*. She sensed Dan beside her, waiting.

"He asked me to participate in a review of his records at the *Alt*. We agreed to meet here half an hour before the start. He wanted to talk with me alone."

Teal looked up the street. The sirens had stopped, but not the rotating blue lights. A man in uniform headed for them; another stopped at the body. She shifted her eyes.

"Anyway, that's about it. I arrived a few minutes late, and he was there, on the ground. I didn't notice anything else, just that he'd made such a mess of himself. What a way to want to die."

She repeated the same story to the Cambridge police. More blue-and-whites, an ambulance and unmarked cars brought further commotion. They cordoned off William Carroll's body. Every passing vehicle slowed; every driver pointed and stared. Dan stood to the side. Cambridge's curiosity at his presence in their jurisdiction was masked by a show of fellowship. Everyone expected to talk later.

The police were questioning Teal when writers from the *Alt* realized something big was happening outside.

They flooded the sidewalk to express shock and dismay and pulled out their notebooks and pens. The police ignored their antics. When the first television action-cam van arrived, Teal sought out the officer in charge.

"May I go? I've told all I know. You have my home and work numbers."

"Fine, Ms. Stewart. I can understand you'd rather stay out of their way." The officer gestured at the cluster of reporters.

Teal hurried away from the cameras.

"It's only sheer, rotten luck," Hunt said into the telephone. He didn't confuse the unexpected Saturday call with anything but Teal's need to distract her mind. "You haven't been singled out by the fates."

"If you'd seen him . . . . I'm not sure you'd find it easy to dismiss."

"Perhaps you're right. Meet me at the office. Oh, and watch out for Argyle—he'll be all over you after all this time." Hunt cringed at his jibe.

"I know," Teal retorted. "I used to live with him."

One hour later Teal looked up from her calculations. "I'm fighting back."

"Fighting what?" Hunt asked.

"The furies, or fate, or whatever."

"They aren't picking on you. Mark Konstat and William Carroll are dead, not Teal Stewart. And they're people you didn't even know."

"Maybe, but too many bodies are turning up in front of me." Teal sighed. "I don't like it, Hunt. I don't like these feelings."

"But aside from the general unfairness of you happening to be there—"

"Twice!"

"Yes, twice, but nothing has happened to you even if it feels that way now."

"But something has, Hunt. I've become afraid. Sure, these deaths belonged to strangers, you're right. Still . . ."

When would her heart slam to a stop? Teal wondered. Could her finger pull the trigger on herself? Nothing was certain.

"Still, I need to make some sense of them."

"And how, exactly, do you plan to start?"

"I don't know."

Teal scratched Argyle's head and gazed past Hunt. His partner, BG, worked at the other end of the floor.

"I hate to break into the reverie," Hunt said after a minute. "But any comment on the calculations?"

"They look fine, Hunt. You and BG should win on cost control alone. Look, I think I'll go home now—unpack properly, unwind."

"Okay. And thanks. I know you've had a hell of a morning, but this, too, will pass." Hunt touched her arm. "Let's go out after we finish with the bid tomorrow. Maybe see *Jules and Jim* for the hundredth time?"

"I didn't plan to work on this Sunday. Just make sure you consider every alteration to the plan and materials."

"And a film?" Hunt persisted.

"Sorry, I'm off to the *Nutcracker* in the evening. Thanks for the thought, though. I'll call midweek." Teal waved from the door. "I'm sure you'll win! Hey, BG, *ciao.*"

Teal heard the phone ring as she unlocked her door. She dumped her keys on the hall table and pulled free of her coat as she ran to catch the call.

"Hello?" Teal said.

The sleeve tangled on her right arm, and she tried to shake it off.

"It's Dan Malley, Teal. I've been trying you all afternoon. I talked with Cambridge this morning. Are you up to more questions?"

Teal stopped wrestling with the coat.

"You mean now, don't you?" Teal said.

"Yes. Observations are best when fresh. Boston believes Carroll could be related to the Konstat matter, and Cambridge offered to share information. So, on this side of the river, it's mine." Dan tried to strain the excitement from his voice.

Teal gave him directions and replaced the receiver.

She unpacked Maine's optimistic complement of weekend clothes, and she waited for Dan. Each garment hung in the closet reassured her with the ordinariness of life. Hunt was right. Life went on.

But the shock of William Carroll roiled her stomach and raced her pulse. Teal left her unpacking for a cup of peppermint tea. The bell rang as she sat, the hot mug in her hand.

Down two flights, the front door still needed a new deadbolt. Dan noticed.

"That's it? That's all the security you have?" Dan asked.

"Well, the apartments have front doors with their individual locks. If you are done with the inspection, follow me up. We can talk in the library. I'm having tea. If you'll excuse me a minute, I'll fetch a mug for you."

Dan sniffed the peppermint with suspicion as Teal described her first meeting with William Carroll at Bowdoin College. Why did she find him dead? No answer satisfied the question.

"He accused you of following him, then changed his mind and asked for help? Fast turnaround," Dan puzzled. "He was eager for you to join the review, not noticeably agitated?"

"No, not after I swore I hadn't known Konstat. I think he had realized he was leaving himself awfully wide open to the *Alt*. I looked like someone who could protect him, I guess."

"Konstat—Carroll—University Savings. I'd hate to jump on the obvious and draw the wrong conclusion. Konstat may have died from anaphylactic shock, but indications are that the preceding week he suffered one hell of a beating. Now Carroll turns up a suicide one month later. Where's the sense of it?" Malley lifted his eyebrows.

Teal spread her palms. "I'd give anything to know."

"Well," Dan continued, "the favor. Are you still willing to go over those records? Carroll's?"

Teal rocked forward and back as much as nodded. "I won't say I'd be happy to, given the circumstance, but I will."

"I'll arrange something after Christmas. This can't be fun for you, Teal." Dan stood. "I hope helping doesn't add to your burden."

"No. I don't think it will."

Teal didn't admit that Dan Malley's needs in this met

89

hers. Hunt had asked a question she couldn't answer. How would she start? Well, now she knew—with Dan Malley's request.

Chapter Ten

Hunt never speculated about Mark Konstat after Konstat's death. He thought about Teal and the distance growing between them. The subtle shift still signalled a change in the rules. Her behavior this weekend particularly annoyed him.

Competition in the affordable housing bid had narrowed to his firm, Huntington, BG and Associates, and a prestigious Boston collaborative. Final revisions to the plans were due Monday, and Hunt had assumed Teal would assist. She often vetted his cost calculations. But she had declined, "other commitments" the limp explanation.

The fact that she had ended up at the office for half of this Saturday didn't count. She had come in need for herself. How could she ignore the importance of this contract to him?

Hunt had risen rapidly as an architect in a competitive, crowded field. His success reflected brilliance tempered by pragmatism. Clients appreciated his realistic plans and sensitivity to a budget, but clear, creative purity had won him the critical acclaim.

He had worked hard to achieve the recognition his father, a builder in Western Massachusetts, had never received. Hunt worked for his father every summer of high school. By the second summer, Hunt was offering suggestions to modify the homes they built.

"And can we build it, now, for the dollars we have and have maybe a dollar more at the end?" his father would roar at each proposed change.

The first time, the teenager froze, and his ideas were ignored. By the time he was fifteen, he knew enough to approach his father with building plans in one hand and a financial analysis in the other. The technique gained his father's respect, and sometimes the alterations were made. The day Hunt turned sixteen, his father took him for a walk.

"I grew up in Ireland, you know, and when I came to America I found a good life. I never expected what I have to give you wouldn't be good enough."

"It is, Dad. I love the business, you know that. It's fine for me," Hunt replied.

"Had you grown up in Ireland, I don't know but you'd have become a painter with your eye. That's what I'm trying to tell you. I want you to learn more about the plans and ideas in your head. The ones I'll never build. You should be an architect, son." His father watched to measure the boy's response.

"Why do I need to be an architect to be in business with you?" Hunt asked. The weight of failing his father cracked his voice.

"No, I'll not let you make a decision you'll regret. You will come to resent me, and by God, it's my business until I die, not yours. Hunt?" His father gentled his voice. "You'll come to want to use all those designs

I could never approve. I've talked to your school. You aren't to be wasting your time. Harvard's Graduate School of Design, the GSD, is the place to go after you start with college at Harvard.''

Hunt hated what he was hearing. He kicked at the curb and spoke to the asphalt.

"I'll never be accepted, Dad. They take the top kids from my school. I'd never make it." Hunt looked at his father then, embarrassed.

"You've got two years. You're going to Harvard or you'll be my junior partner for the rest of my life. And don't go thinking you could start your own construction company. It wouldn't do for you, son; it wouldn't be enough."

His father took Hunt's hand, and shook on it.

Hunt studied and worked. He had no time for friends. Late spring of his senior year, Huntington Erin Huston was accepted by Harvard College. Within three years he entered GSD. Two years later, his first competitive design was under construction.

"So, is she coming by to help tomorrow?" BG swung his torso around the door frame and took aim on his partner's forehead, right between the eyes.

"No. And for Christ's sake, throw that beast out. Damn you." Hunt wiped the water from his face.

BG lowered the hippopotamus water pistol. "Nasty, nasty mood. She's not coming to give the dollar signs one last little kiss? Unlike our thorough Teal." BG slid to the chair. "I need you on the floor."

"She said to make sure we 'consider every alteration to the plan or the materials.' No kidding! Our first bid

93

for production housing and she does this." Hunt snorted. "Okay, what's our problem?"

Hunt and BG had been friends for eleven years, partners for seven. BG's antics masked intellect and talent. He specialized in landscape, Hunt in structures, and they shared an aesthetic vision.

BG had known Hunt and Teal through their many metamorphoses. They had known him through three marriages and three Dominican Republic divorces. A fourth marriage was in the offing. She was petite and dark and adored BG, who resembled a large, fair St. Bernard.

"Hunt, maybe she's really leaving. I know, I know— the two independent lives rap." BG lifted his arms in mock defense. "But she could be tired of a tie that doesn't quite bind even if you aren't. No one ever said 'see you around' categorically. It'll hurt when either one of you does, whatever you believe. Christ, I've passed three fabulous weeks in the sunny Republic in near as many consecutive years to dissolve rotten marriages, but even good endings smart. Anyway, if you suspect she's moving on, you're feeling like shit."

BG whipped the hippo to his own head, fired at his ear and dropped to the floor.

Hunt had to smile. Reverting to sophomoric humor was characteristic of his partner. BG pretended artistic legitimacy. He called himself the last of the dadaists. Call it what he would, it worked. Hunt fought a spasm of resigned laughter. He stood.

"Thanks for the counseling, Beeje. What's up out there?"

BG rolled to his knees and bound upright, grinning like a fool.

"Sorry, Hunt, I had to. Couldn't have stood my own sincerity much longer" He paused to breathe. "That latest addition to the corner lots—either we're off scale or the damned earth shrank."

"Do you have revised drawings?" Hunt asked.

BG nodded.

"Let's take a look."

Hunt submerged himself in his work to avoid emotional stress. When his dad told him to get into Harvard, he studied. When his younger sister was killed in a car accident his first college summer, Hunt and his father built the best development of his dad's career. Work was his instinctive cover.

It had driven Teal wild.

"Good lord, Hunt, relax. Breathe slowly and deeply and let yourself drift," Teal would admonish with ill-concealed annoyance when he woke her, unable to sleep.

On other days, she ignored his compulsion. "All right, I'll ski alone. You stay in Boston and obsess."

Slowly, he came to set work issues aside to ferment, to resolve, to diminish. Oddly, the metamorphosis angered Teal.

"Great," she once said when Hunt mentioned he was off to sail around Nantucket with a friend. "Just great. So nice to know you're finally relaxing. So very nice."

Teal's anger was palpable in the shrug with which she gave a parting kiss, her eyes cool.

"What's your problem?" Hunt had asked. "I expected hurrahs. Instead—I get this."

It took BG to explain. "Jealousy, Hunt. She wanted this time with you years ago. She did the heavy lifting, and now that she's gone, you let go. She's pleased for you and sorry for herself.''

This latest change in Teal pushed Hunt back into the arms of his oldest succor and torment—work.

Hunt and BG labored the remainder of the Saturday as if driven. They wanted to win. Hunt recalled his father's earlier telephone call.

"So, with this you'll be back at developing, son. All the education, all the years, and now you try to do your old dad one better." Hunt's father had chortled parental pride across the line.

"Ah, but Dad, all that education, all those years, and I'm likely not to win the development," Hunt had replied.

"And why not? You're famous, you're good, and I know myself that you can build a house that stands and makes a dollar."

Hunt could imagine his father nodding happily at the thought. He hadn't had the heart to explain the first two probably made winning harder and no one but his father really knew the third.

"Sure, Dad," he had said.

Just as he was saying "Sure, BG," now, despite his lack of enthusiasm. A blind date? BG's pushing made acquiescence easy. Anyway, Hunt couldn't stand the idea of coping with BG's ragging about Teal if he refused.

"The chick's adorable, Hunt. Cute little ass and loves to give head. Look at it this way, another hour of work and we'll undo all that's still good. There is such a thing as ruining a plan, pal. And this lovely is out there, just panting to meet you. Be flattered and come." BG drove the banter at Hunt.

Hunt straightened from the drawing board, arms up in surrender. "I'll go. I'll go."

"Great! Then, any chance of a little enthusiasm?" BG asked.

"No." Hunt shook his head. "Not much."

Chapter Eleven

"I woke you, didn't I?"

"No, of course not." A groggy voice belied Teal's denial. "Kath?"

"You aren't even sure it's me."

Laughter snapped in Teal's ear.

"You've jolted me thoroughly awake now," Teal said peevishly. She stopped complaining to focus. Kathy calling on a Sunday morning? "What's up?"

"I just came in with the paper, Teal. I don't sleep late, even on the weekend."

Teal didn't want to explain her night of bad memories and worse dreams. Not of life and death, but of death alone. Corpses curled at her feet, blood swirling in the road.

"The paper," Kathy interrupted. "You're in it, big time. I thought you should know."

"No . . ." Teal sat up. "What do you mean I'm in it? The paper? Tell me they didn't use my name, Kath."

Teal rubbed her knuckles across her forehead. She covered her eyes. The memory remained: William Carroll dead by the side of the road.

"You and CW."

"Clayborne Whittier? Oh, great!"

"Was it awful finding the body?" Kathy blurted out the question.

"Yes. Awful. I can't believe it's in the paper. Damn, Kath. Do you think I should pull the telephone jack for a few hours?"

"I wanted to satisfy my morbid curiosity. I'm not going to be the only one. I've told you to buy an answering machine—"

"And this just might make me agree, but I don't have one right now." Testiness raised Teal's voice. "Anyway, thanks for the warning."

Teal hung up. Storrow Drive hummed busy with Sunday traffic: residents escaping and tourists entering the city. She watched a pack of weekend athletes braving the chill on roller blades along the bike path beside the Charles. Sunlight bounced off the water in a shimmer of blinding light. The telephone sounded.

She swiveled from the view. Ring number six, then seven, filled the room. Teal unclipped the line from the wall. Silence.

She stood under the shower's hot, pounding water as long as she could. Old white painters' pants, a faded black sweatshirt and neon bright socks cheered her mood. No carefully crafted dress, no high heels, no waist-wrapping pantyhose constrained a Sunday.

Teal tousled her shoulder-length hair. Wet, the chestnut mass fell straight as a rule. Dry, each strand would buckle in undisciplined curves. Her hair would freeze outside unless she spent the time to blow and comb it dry. Curiosity propelled her to the door. She opted for freezing.

Blessed are those who practice moderation, Teal thought, *for theirs is the peace of a quiet Sunday morning. Or maybe theirs is the compensation for a dead social life*. She couldn't decide. Church of the Advent's bells pealed a call to worship.

The sky shone a brilliant, hard blue while wind stiffened and crackled her hair. She sped her pace over uneven brick sidewalks and arrived breathless at Deluca's Market on Charles Street. She bought the paper.

The Coffee Connection on the corner of Revere and Charles bustled with steamy heat and a noisy neighborhood crowd. Teal shifted foot to foot, jammed at the end of the line. The four tiny tables were full; then a man motioned from his table wedged by the window. He stood.

"I'm leaving," he mouthed to the crowd.

Everyone in front of her shook their heads and said, "Take out."

"Yes, thanks," Teal pantomimed.

She bought a plain croissant and cappucino, frothy with milk and hot espresso. The paper and drink and pastry overfilled the table. She held the metropolitan news on her lap to read. Not one, but two front page articles reported William Carroll's death. Teal was identified in both. Clayborne Whittier appeared once, in one. She skimmed, then slowed her eyes on the second paragraph.

"The body was discovered by Boston resident Teal Stewart. Ms. Stewart, a CPA, is one of a number of financial pros in the metropolitan area available to prominent individuals, government agencies, and companies to interpret the financial

100

dealings of powerful individuals and institutions. Clayborne Whittier, an international accounting and auditing firm, loaned Ms. Stewart to William Carroll to help protect his interests.''

What crap, Teal fumed.

The second column indulged in even greater creativity. The story hinted at a nefarious reason for Teal's rendezvous with Carroll. Here she was the ''unknown CPA'' assigned to either investigate underworld activity or be the instrument of its cover. The ludicrous options left Teal furious and laughing.

She returned home along the smaller streets at the flat of Beacon Hill. Bayberry wreaths and holly chains adorned the doorways of an eclectic mixture of structures. The flat, more modest than the Hill's grand front slope, boasted a diversity of converted carriage houses and stables, solid apartment buildings and single-family brick homes. Charming urban gardens hid behind many of the simple facades.

Her own town house was like many on her block. Built in the eighteen hundreds, it faced the Church of the Advent and backed onto Storrow Drive and the Charles River. The parlor level entrance topped a flight of exterior stairs.

The ground floor, once a kitchen, had been converted before Teal's ownership into a studio apartment. Her renovation gave it access to a walled garden. The prior owner, greedy to make rental units, had stripped the second and third floors of their ornate cherry panelling and plaster moldings and cut the large, formal rooms into a rabbit warren. Teal bargained the destruction to her advantage in the purchase. Hunt advised her to gut and join the levels in a spacious duplex apartment.

The fourth and fifth floors, with the lower ceilings and simple detail of space meant for children and servants, were opened by Teal into the airy space she now occupied. She loved her expansive views of the river and enjoyed Fourth of July fireworks from her roof deck.

Pale pastel washes colored the walls. Wide pine floors creaked underfoot, and rooms shifted and merged throughout the house. She worked on black granite counters and stood on a thick rubber floor to cushion her feet in the kitchen. Her freezer held homemade soups and sour dough for pizza. The bathroom she used was modelled on one in the Hotel de Crillon in Paris. A deep European tub dissolved her tension at the end of particularly bad days. The separate shower behind a thick glass door got her going in the morning.

Teal loved the place she called home. She had been lucky; she bought the building before prices soared free of economic sense. The years of eating construction dust and vacationing on a ladder had been rewarded. It felt good to come home.

"Yes." She grinned as she shucked her old bomber jacket.

She'd curled up with a good book. Forget the paper. Forget William Carroll. She started for the library with plans to build a fire.

"Odd," she murmured as she pushed aside the room's French doors. "I shut these."

"No, lady, you didn't. I didn't wanna be surprised."

Teal froze. She believed in the most childlike part of her soul that stillness would make her invisible. One shaking hand gripped a door for support.

102

"Come in, hava seat. Nice room you got here. I said, come in. Come in." The voice moved from bland to bullying.

Teal averted her eyes and stumbled into a chair. *If I don't look,* she affirmed, *this won't be true.* She groped for understanding in her mind. Should she fight this intrusion? How? And from what?

The thought startled her.

"Did I interrupt you in the middle of ripping me off?" she blurted out.

She glared at the interloper, shocked at her boldness.

He was maybe early twenties, maybe not. Perhaps Mediterranean. Nothing pronounced, except for eyes that stared back a large, soft brown. Dark hair waved from his sensuous face. His boots made him tall, or maybe it was her fear. He appeared as surprised by her challenge as she; then he laughed.

"Christ, what a question. You're a gutsy broad. Of course I forgit, you don't know me. Mosta my people, they know me when I come. I collect. Loans and other stuff."

"And what do you hope to collect from me?" Teal interjected all the challenge she could muster into her voice.

"My, my, still ballsy. Don't have too many balls. That's what I'm here to say. Too many balls on a pretty girl like you make people uncomfortable. Especially about bankers, see. You don't want that. My friends hope you're too smart to do anything stupid, but they thought maybe someone needed to point stupid out to you. It's poking around uninvited. You get me?"

"I believe I do." She forced herself to speak. "Did your friends think Mark Konstat was poking around too

103

much? Is that how your friends hope to silence me? Or were they thinking along the lines of William Carroll?"

Teal had an urge to slap her hand over her mouth. This was no time to be clever. She wanted to say, "I'm sorry, forget what I said," but her tongue lay dead in her mouth.

The stranger looked at her and shrugged.

"The world is full of A1 nuts, know what I mean? My friends didn't do nothing. Carroll hadda be crazy to trigger himself. So listen, my friends don't want to get messed up in this. No way. They're outta it. Where you should stay."

He turned to inspect a row of books.

"Nice library, but all these paperbacks are a little ratty, ya know? You read Shakespeare?"

Teal sat, stunned. Stay out of it. Out of what? She couldn't think. What was she in?

Of course, the newspaper. The silly stories. A manic urge to laugh threatened her.

"Hey, you read Shakespeare, I asked!"

"Yes." *Now what*, Teal wondered.

"What d'you have?"

"The plays and sonnets are somewhere." Her eyes drifted, sightless, along the shelves.

"Can I borrow a few plays?"

Teal wanted to ask what she could do to stop him. She didn't. She said, "Sure."

"Good. I've read the big ones, you know, the movie ones. Like *Romeo and Juliet* or *Anthony and Cleopatra*, which bombed with Burton and Taylor acting like asses. I saw it on T.V. The play was better. Do you have the one about the real twisted little guy, the king?"

"Richard III?"

"Yeah, that's it. What do you think of Lear? He shoulda stuffed his two bitchy daughters. He acted old, and they just nailed him. He should have, you know, kept his dignity at least."

Teal nodded automatic assent. Sure, keep his dignity, why not. Unreality surrounded her morning. The paper. The cold. The stranger in her library. What was she supposed to do. Did someone keeping their dignity scream? Her builder's accommodation to a desire for perfect sound insulation would mute to silence the most frenetic yell. Kick the guy's groin? He'd catch her foot the instant she raised it and slam her, not him, to the floor.

"Hey, you thinking about some fast move? Forgit it. I ain't about to hurt you. Just fill you with a little healthy respect, see. Get those plays, will you? I wanna get outta here."

Teal moved quickly. Everyone exhibited certain compulsions in arranging books. She knew height people, color people, alphabet people. The traditional organization by subject and author governed her. She found *Richard III* and *Julius Caesar*. Why not? She handed them to the uninvited guest.

He hesitated and smiled. "My name's Shag causa the shag rugs at my pad. Anyway, put your coat on—and get a hat or something, we gotta split."

"Where?" Teal stiffened with resistance.

"Hey, lady, don't push your luck. You ain't gonna get hurt; I'm trying to keep you from getting cold. The plays I'll shove through your mail slot one day, so get a coat."

Teal retrieved the bomber from a chair, Shag close behind. He pulled a scarf off a hook and jerked it around her neck.

105

They exited together. Close together, like any happy couple the morning after an intimate night at home. Shag laced his arm around her waist and leaned into her clean hair.

"Don't do anything stupid, sweetheart. Nothing. Smile." He grinned at the family turning for the church.

No one noticed him push Teal through the driver's side door of the Bronco illegally parked at the curb. A permanent lock barred the passenger door. Teal considered screaming as an old man shuffled past, but what if he couldn't hear?

"Where are you taking me?" she asked, feeling helpless and a fool.

"A little Sunday ride. I'm sure you like fresh air. See, this is nothing. But you gotta understand unless you stop poking around, life will be no fun. You get me? This is a taste, right, and you won't want any more. So shut up now. Look, I don't want to do this, but . . ."

Shag shrugged as he pressed against her mouth and nose with the chloroform rag hidden in his glove. She slumped. He arranged her like a lover sitting close. No one noticed. When he pulled from the curb, she shifted away from his side.

"Shit."

He braked and backed up. He pulled Teal's head to lie in his lap. Better, he decided. Even if she came to, she wouldn't see nothing. He laughed. He preferred assignments that required ingenuity. The daily routine of busting furniture, or worse—that was no fun.

He tapped Teal's nose. She was sorta pretty for a professional broad, and she hadn't hesitated about the books even though she showed plenty of spunk. He hoped she'd

106

take his message and be all right. He hoped she'd repair her front door lock. The city could be dangerous.

He steered the Bronco back into the street.

Chapter Twelve

Traffic in the rain. No. A vacuum cleaner. The cleaning crew in the hall. *I'll have to call for repairs,* Teal thought, *the sound insulation must be going. God it's cold.*

She rolled over to find a comfortable position.

"Ouch."

Teal smacked against something sharp and hard. Her eyes opened to blink against the bright gray light. Where was she? Where was her bed? Her home? Disoriented thoughts circled her mind.

Kathy's call. The Sunday paper and that hood in her library—panic began to heave through her stomach. The vacuum cleaner transformed into wind. This desolate concrete slab wasn't her bed. She was not at home.

Teal wobbled to her feet amid the jumble of construction and saw water and a distant skyline. Rain drizzled from the sky and wet her face. She struggled to orient herself. A dull ocean licked a misty shore. And Boston's profile rose straight across the harbor ahead.

Inland a nest of buildings, low and high, large and

small, signalled people. Around Teal, the earth bunched into mud banks and dipped into hollows full of stagnant water. The site was deserted.

Sheets of black plastic flapped against a pile of reinforcing rods. The rain thickened. Teal navigated across a concrete surface pitted with holes. Fear had penetrated as deeply as the cold.

"Help," she screamed. "Help."

The wind broke her voice into meaningless pieces. No one was around, anyway. No savior.

"I'll get out of here on my own," she yelled at a dead tree.

But how? She raised a hand to block the raindrops while she squinted. Three old trailers and a guard hut stood by a gate. She set out full of hope.

Her watch registered two-thirty. Averill would collect her for the ballet close to eight. She need not be late. It was a comforting thought, the ballet and Averill. It propelled her to run.

The torn-up ground had become slick with rain. Teal stepped over a sodden sweater, half-buried in mud. Next, she circumvented the tip of a boot. How did random clothing arrive in empty lots? beside the road? at this desolate site? How had she?

Her head ached like she'd been hit with a two-by-four, or worse. The Shag person took shape in her mind, standing in her library, walking to a Bronco, raising a soaked rag to her nose. No. How wasn't the question. Why had she been dumped here—that's what Teal really wanted to know.

The shack contained a heap of trash, but no other sign of human occupancy. A padlock barred the chain-link gate.

She rubbed her hand down a cold post and peered through the metal weave. The geography began to gel in her mind. The Boston skyline, the buildings past the fence, this was close to the site of the former Columbia Point projects, next to the University of Massachusetts Boston and the Kennedy Library. On a clear day, the view of land and water would be considered beautiful. Not today.

She looked left and inland. Columbia Point, a legacy of poor city planning in the 1960s, had been replaced by Harbor Point, a mixed-income, mixed-use community. But the cost of conversion, the loss of public housing units to middle class occupancy and the whispers of suspicious use of government funds had raised new objections to the treatment of the disadvantaged. Then there was the Kennedy Library.

That monument to the slain president had become the old project's unexpected abutter in the 1970s. The City of Cambridge had refused the memorial building on the excuse it would increase traffic in Harvard Square. That was said in public. Teal suspected a different truth. The good folks of Cambridge harbored a greater fear—the fear of motley tourists wearing polyester pants and drip-dry shirts.

The Boston campus of the University of Massachusetts was pleased to accept the library.

Teal turned her mind to her present situation. A telephone call would be easier than scaling the metal mesh and trudging through muck to the university. She hoped to find a telephone in one of the trailers.

The first offered a locked and barred door, as did number two. The third lay gutted. Teal considered screaming, or crying, but returned to contemplate the fence. All the destruction around her, and her last obstacle to flight showed no breaks or openings.

Teal hated heights. She hated physical pain. The chain link represented a vision of fingers jammed tight into diamond-shaped wedges, toes struggling to stabilize her climb and trousers split as she straddled the top.

The effort transpired about as she foresaw it would.

What a pain-in-the-ass place to abandon someone you wanted to scare, Teal thought as she fell to the ground. She flexed numbed fingers and sighed. The campus and a telephone were just through the mud and rain ahead.

Teal reflected on her task-oriented response to danger as she walked. Her focused energy repressed fear, not anger. She grew madder as the university drew closer. Mad at her vulnerability. Mad at that rotten hood who had so easily violated her privacy, her home and her life. Mostly mad at herself for pretending that she could remain safe while other people died.

Teal waved and yelled at an approaching campus guard. "I'm glad to see you."

She bent over panting and wobbling with relief. How could she explain? She smiled at the aging guard.

He inventoried her muddy clothes and snarled hair with a expression of deep skepticism. A morning-after wreck if he had ever seen one, his face said. Now she acted like she wanted his help. He sighed.

Teal tried to act nonchalant. "May I use your phone?"

"I'm not supposed to allow that except for emergencies."

"This is one, sort of, and only for a short, local

call, please. I need to ask someone to pick me up. I have no money for a cab.''

The guard pressed his door open with reluctance. Teal didn't care that he watched with suspicion as she dialed Hunt. The telephone rang and rang and rang. The guard motioned her to hurry. He wasn't very friendly. She couldn't risk his tolerance for another call. She hung on and implored Hunt to answer the phone. Twelve rings and she began to lower the receiver.

''Hello?'' said a tiny voice.

Teal snapped the instrument back to her ear. ''Hunt, oh, thank God you're home! Look, I need you to come get me at U. Mass.''

''Amherst?'' Hunt boomed his incredulity.

Teal could hear a woman's voice call to him. ''Hunt, honey, why couldn't you ignore that mean old telephone?''

Teal knew just how the voice felt. Hunt's compulsion to answer the phone when it rang used to drive her nuts. No more. She actually smiled.

''Amherst?'' he repeated.

''No, Boston.'' *And please agree,* Teal prayed, *whoever she is.*

''Why the hell are you down there?''

''To take an exclusive look at Harbor Point, a tour of the Kennedy Library—look, it's long story. Are you going to come or not?'' Teal asked, drained of sweet persuasion.

''How'd you get there? Where's your car? Did it finally do your bank account a favor and break down for good?''

''No. Hunt, I'm sort of holding myself together with

112

rubber bands right now. Come before they snap, will you?'' Teal counted heartbeats and listened to the plane overhead. The guard began to motion her out.

''Give me five to dress, ten or fifteen to get there.'' Hunt banged off.

It seemed to Teal a definitive click, a click utterly and irreparably cutting away her world. She felt more abandoned.

''Safe enough to fear,'' she mumbled.

''What? You finally done? I can't have you here.''

''Sure. Thanks for letting me use the phone.'' Teal was tired.

The guard looked pretty tired himself. His thin, gray hair, combed that morning across a bald crown, straggled over his left ear. He shifted his paunch to let Teal sidle by. She crossed the drive and sat on the curb. She faced him, unable to allow the sight of humanity, if not civilization, out of view.

The guard returned a sullen gaze. He bent, and Teal saw light bounce off a metallic surface. Her body stiffened and ducked. The second flash showed the side of the pint. A bottle of liquor, that's what he had raised. Teal shifted to stare at Morrissey Boulevard. That represented humanity, albeit farther away.

Hunt arrived thirty-five minutes later. Teal didn't complain. She didn't ask him how he had explained his sudden departure to his friend.

He watched her as they turned onto Morrissey. ''Are you going to tell me what happened or am I supposed to guess?''

113

"I'm not sure you could. But it's hard to know where to begin without sounding crazy."

"I won't think that, Teal. You look pretty bad."

Teal told him then, neither condensing nor embellishing. She talked as they parked, as they entered his now-empty loft. She talked over Argyle's insistent barks. She ignored the strange perfume lingering in the air and repeated the story.

"I keep thinking that if I go over everything in detail, I'll understand, get control. God, Hunt, will I be afraid of the dark tonight?"

"Hey, kid—spend it with us." Hunt handed her a tumbler of wine. The deerhound panted happily at her feet.

"No. No, I can't. What time is it?"

"Four-thirty."

"I guess I'm in good enough shape now to go."

Hunt snorted disbelief.

"Well, as close as I can get. Give me a break!"

"Shag and Shakespeare—maybe you are pulling my leg." Hunt leaned to kiss her cheek. "But fool that I am, I believe you." His expression sobered. "Call the police, Teal."

"I don't know. I don't know that I really believe all of this. Maybe I'll call Malley. Maybe I won't." Teal shrugged. "I'm going to start by learning what I can about Carroll, the bank and the mob."

"Start with the police, Teal. Give them a chance to nail the guy."

The suggestion made her cringe. "What good will that do? With Shag I know one face of the enemy. If the police find him, his friends may get really angry—and I

114

can't recognize them. Maybe I'll call Malley tomorrow, but not now.''

They sat quietly.

''I should go,'' Teal said a few minutes later.

Hunt took her slim hand. ''I have a police lock. BG gave it to me as a joke. For the freight elevator, wouldn't you know. I can find it in a minute.''

''Naw.'' Teal shook her head. ''I'm tough; I don't need your police lock. I do need the front hall deadbolt replaced sometime, remember?''

''I insist, Teal.'' Hunt rummaged through a storage bin. ''It's easy to be confident now, with me and Argyle and a glass of wine. When you are alone tonight, it will be different. I'm not keen on a two A.M. call. That's if you are alone tonight.''

''Should be, unless Shaggola drops by.'' Teal ignored the jibe. ''All right. Find your damn lock.''

Hunt attached the hardware to her door easily; then he waited for the shower to stop.

''Teal?''

''Um?'' The bathroom door cracked ajar.

''Well, it's set. The key is on the hall table, and I'm off. Check that the lock caught as soon as you're dry.''

''Hang on.''

Teal stepped through the door, her hair wrapped in a towel turban. Her old chenille robe fell to show deep cleavage from broad shoulders. She drew it closed.

Hunt turned away. ''Take care.''

''I will. I don't know what to say. You're always there when I ask for help. I do appreciate it. Thanks.''

Hunt grunted a combination of embarrassment, disbelief and resignation.

Teal followed him with her voice. "I'll be fine, Hunt. Really I will."

Who was she trying to convince? Herself?

Chapter Thirteen

Teal's independent words rang hollow in the empty house. She slipped a black silk sheath over her head as her legs threatened to buckle. Soft fabric tangled against her face; a thin strap caught around her ear. Wrestling free, she tried to laugh. The sound emerged a scream.

"Stop it!" Teal stamped the floor with a foot.

An earring slid from her fingers and struck the tile with a ping. She flinched. Imagination put Shag lurking behind the bedroom door. Every door. Waiting. She drew in a slow breath and brushed fingers through her hair.

Vanity eclipsed fear as she regarded her image in the mirror. The random freckles bridged across her nose didn't make her look like any girl next door. Charles Jordan slippers, a steal from Filene's Basement, added chic gaiety. Bright red flashed on her nails. The woman in the glass reflected courage.

Dressed and still, she experienced a moment of resistance to going. The doorbell's shrill buzz sent her tripping against a chair in her sudden turn. Lovely, she thought as she straightened, poise and paranoia.

* * *

The ballet diverted Teal from fear. Then the dance of fantasy and dream was over. Averill negotiated them through the crowded Wang Center lobby which glittered with refurbished gilt as families, festive in holiday finery, pressed for the doors. Averill's hand rested so lightly on her shoulder, she had to smile.

"The Ritz, perhaps, for supper at the Cafe?" Averill asked as they stepped outside.

"What a wonderful idea! Precisely what I need."

To avoid returning home, Teal did not say. He could think she was hungry. She was.

"You look tired, Teal." Averill stopped at the curb and faced her. His hand grazed her temple, a second's touch. "Very tired."

"It's been quite a day." Teal enjoyed the understatement.

Averill held her in the curve of his arm as their taxi moved through the theater traffic and down Charles Street between the Common and Public Garden.

"I don't want to pry, but if I can help—I'd like to know."

Averill's breath tickled her ear. She responded to the sympathy with talk. About *Alt* and Carroll. About finding the body. About reading the paper to see her name. About Shag. Averill pulled her closer.

"I had a busy morning; I didn't read—well, that's not important to you. I am so sorry. How perfectly horrible." His voice remained even, but he tucked her gloved hand into his own.

"Yes, but it's past." Teal tried to shrug.

"I didn't know you knew Bill Carroll."

118

"I'm not sure I knew him. I met him Thursday at the symposium. Was he a friend of yours?"

"I knew Bill professionally and a little socially. I had no idea you found him. How awful." Averill's attention to Teal was absolute. "Suicide—the family must be distraught. It's such a waste. He was on our board at Climb, you know. A good man—smart, ambitious, honest. I think your review would have proven that without doubt."

"The *Alt*'s review," Teal corrected.

"Their's, then," Averill said.

"Maybe you should call it mine." Teal sighed. "I guess I am going to be looking through his files. Do you remember the Detective Malley on Konstat's death? He asked me to do that review. The University Savings connection, I guess; anyway, I want to do it for myself."

Teal stared into the dense night. She had not imagined that other people, his family and his friends, would need to react to Carroll's death. Would have a reaction. She'd thought only of herself. She turned her face up to Averill.

"His death must be much worse for you. I never really knew him, but he was your friend," she said.

She leaned in for a hug when the taxi jerked right and slammed to a stop at the Ritz. She tumbled against Averill. He returned the embrace with unexpected passion, and they emerged laughing and heated.

Teal stood aside as Averill paid the driver. *Caught in time, frozen in a still photograph,* she thought, *we are the picture of a carefree couple. Tall and energetic, decked out and festive—irony of life.*

"No more talk of death or policemen tonight, fair?" she said when Averill returned to her side.

"More than fair, Teal."

The supper was appropriately tasty, the wine properly chilled and the conversation engaging, like makeup applied to disguise an aging face, and no more successful. The evening was drawing to a close. She shifted, tense and anxious.

"What's the matter, Teal? You're scared, aren't you?"

"No. Yes, well . . ." Teal blushed shell pink in confusion. "The contrast between the past two days and sitting here . . ."

Her face twisted, the tears hot behind her eyes. "I don't want to go home. The fear . . . I have a fancy new lock," she finished.

"Then, why go? The Ritz isn't just good for a meal, you know. And if you prefer solitude, I will see you settled and depart." Averill smiled.

"Seriously?" Teal raised her eyebrows over luminous blue eyes.

"Quite, quite serious. Accept this night as my Christmas gift. The respite will do wonders for you, and where better than a great hotel?" Averill spoke calmly, gentle in tone and generous in affection.

Teal fiddled with her fork, round and round in her long fingers. The proposition sounded simple, to accept or reject the unexpected gift. But if she gave an affirmative answer, the more complex issue remained. Should she invite Averill to stay? Yes.

Juvenile apprehension flooded her body. There was getting along over dinner, and there was getting along in bed. Did she want the answer?

"You're too quiet. You can tell me the idea doesn't appeal. Or are you torn between a foolish notion of bravery and the urge to escape?"

Teal held his eyes like a lifeline. "It's a wonderful idea. And I'd like you to stay. Yes, please, join me for a night at the Ritz. There." She grinned. "Let's hope they have a room."

They did. A suite with the birch log fire laid and a view of Beacon Hill rising from the far corner of the Garden. The honor bar offered five star brandy to be poured in crystal snifters. Uniformed staff delivered the toothbrushes, razor, comb and brush Averill requested at registration. The desk attendant hadn't blinked.

Now, after the brandy and before sleep, Teal stood in a bathroom the size of a grand hall scouring her teeth and trying to ignore the clash of emotions within her. It had been a long, long time. She returned to the bedroom in her slip, dress draped across a shoulder.

"I don't have anything appropriate for tomorrow morning," Teal said.

Even to her, the complaint sounded like a stall.

"We can play hooky." Averill winked and disappeared to wash himself.

Teal hung the black silk shift in the empty closet. Its magnitude of unused space and the vacant hangers accelerated her confusion. What did she want here? What was she doing? She sank to the edge of the vast bed and eyed the sheer panty hose clutched in her hand. She didn't hear Averill return.

"Suddenly dejected by this idea?"

Teal started. "No!"

"No?"

She shrugged reluctant assent. "Well, maybe a little. Any suggestions for how I can be seductive without a French garter?"

"Um, an equally grave problem with Brooks Brothers

121

boxers and English lisle socks." Averill snapped the elastic at his waist as he wriggled hose-clad toes. "I quite see what you mean."

Teal thanked Averill with the smile that illuminated her face.

After that, the medium of their communication changed. No more words. No more looks across big spaces.

Averill's body was lean and cool and muscular. He smelled like Pear's soap and the memory of ballet dust. Teal was lithe and smooth, her silk underwear weightless and skillfully removed.

They leaned back into the pillows piled on the bed. Teal drew away, teasing the edge of his mouth with a light tongue, drawing a finger across his parted lips. She traced the line curved around his ear and sliding down his spine. He stilled her hands with a grip like a vise and kissed her from eyelids to knees. One kiss turned into a bite of mock ferocity. They explored each other as new territory.

Toes curled at being tickled; desire became an urgency. Bodies opened and bloomed, receptive, driven. Arrhythmic play became rhythmic, became imperative motion. Such pleasure.

"Well," he said minutes later when his heart no longer pounded the ribs of his chest.

"Well," she said and swept her arm in an arc, taking in the room, their lives.

"A brandy and a shower, perhaps?" Averill suggested.

"A shower and a brandy."

* * *

The water ran for forty minutes. They emerged giggling and wet. Averill stood them before the window and proposed a toast.

"To this magnificent evening!"

"And look, Averill, it's snowing!"

"Then, to the snow, the *Nutcracker* and you."

Teal butted his shoulder with her head, and they drank the last of the brandy. In bed, arranged like strangers with a decent interval between them, sleep came quickly. Once in the night, Teal kicked out fretfully as chloroform choked her dream. Averill slept through the sharp jerk of her foot.

They woke late to a clear, high sun. Averill ordered breakfast. In the wait, Teal called Kathy. The conversation snapped her back to reality.

"Where are you, Teal? Don Clarke just threatened to rouse the police. I can't tell if he's concerned about you or mad, but those stories in the newspaper have everyone shaken."

"Great."

"Don's not the only one who's wired. I'm not happy with you myself."

Teal dodged the accusation. "I'll be in after lunch."

"Can people reach you now?"

"No."

"Are you interested in your messages?" Kathy asked after a long pause.

"I'll see them soon enough."

"Fine. Look, between now and then stay out of trouble, Sherlock."

Teal smiled. "Thanks."

"I'm too good to you, you know," Kathy said before she hung up.

Teal relaxed in the plush yards of hotel robe wrapped around her body. A knock announced room service at the door. Breakfast rolled in, laid out in linen and flowers.

Teal ate dressed in her slip. Averill sported boxer shorts. They could have been adolescent.

The love they made after breakfast certainly was. She, coltish and sly, flirting from his touch. Her lashes lowered like a coquette until he shifted to pin her down with the force of his weight. She strained to meet his kiss with a laughing mouth.

Frolicking and passion subsided, Averill pulled her to his side.

"I could come to love you very much," he said with quiet and sober intention.

Teal tried to fight old fears, but the fear won.

"Please, don't let's promise each other anything. This freedom is enough. Really and truly. We are at the beginning, you and I. I don't need to know more."

He tapped her nose and looked at her with appraising eyes.

Departure was uneventful, the day staff courteous and efficient.

High heels made the short walk to her house a hazard, and she leaned into Averill like a familiar drunk. He accompanied her inside to inspect each room and assure her no one lurked hidden behind a chair. At the door, he took her lower lip lightly between his teeth, his eyes tender and his breathing hoarse. He held still for a long beat before the kiss.

Funny, Teal thought as Averill walked down the steps, *I feel like a violin string left quivering and vibrating after the bow has passed.*

Chapter Fourteen

Kathy greeted Teal with a motion of her thumb and one raised eyebrow.

"He's in there, with Detective Malley."

"Oh, great," Teal mouthed. What protocol applied to meeting with the senior partner and a detective? She shook her shoulders square.

"Good to see that you're all right," the senior partner of Clayborne Whittier said.

Teal found his face impossible to read.

"Thank you, Don." She nodded. "And Dan."

"Well." Don Clarke pressed his hands against the arms of her desk chair and rose. "I'll leave you two together to work out the attack. Teal, I've approved Detective Malley's request for your assistance. I understand you've already agreed. A disturbing mess, this. Carroll could have been good for the state, understood the needs of the business community. And hounded to such a dreadful act by the media—utter irresponsibility. I'm glad to see you survived their first attack, Teal. I worried yesterday."

He patted her shoulder like a father. Teal's teeth set on edge. He would never understand.

"Detective, you're getting our best." Don Clarke clasped the detective's hand and pumped.

Teal shut the door as the partner in charge left.

"So, I'm to be an official loan," she said.

She didn't want to discuss yesterday's events, but Dan was more than a nice guy; he had a professional right to know. For the third time in two days she recounted Shag's visit. Her expert audience listened, then probed. Question followed question.

"Shag? Describe him again.

"How long were you out?

"Is anything about the U. Mass location s-s-special to you? To Clayborne Whittier?"

Teal shook her head and tried to rub away the growing ache. The young detective with sandy hair and the nice, boyish face was wringing her dry, and he hadn't even come to last night. What would she say?

"No need to describe last night," Dan said as if he could read her mind.

Teal wondered if she imagined the emphasis on night.

"Okay, Shag one more time. Build, voice, hair, car— the works."

Dan shook his affirmation when she finished. "Sounds like Shag."

"You know him?" Teal asked, incredulous.

She stared at Malley. He acted so matter-of-fact about her ordeal.

"Sure. Brian Viccaro, but the punk calls himself Shag. Petty enforcer for the mob, no special family alliance or history. He's a part-time beef-boy with one of the health club chains and never been pinned with any-

127

thing big.'' Malley steepled his fingers. ''It's sort of strange.''

''Strange?''

''Unless the mob boys are so, uh, chauvinistic that they really thought this child's play would scare you.'' Malley rearranged the steeple until he could look inside and see all the people. He wriggled his fingers. ''But they aren't that dumb or that polite.''

''Maybe they can't decide how much I know, if anything. Maybe all they intended was to keep me from acting on my natural human curiosity—''

''Curiosity killed the cat?'' Dan said.

''Maybe that's what they wanted me to see. Of course, satisfaction brought it back. They must have forgotten that.'' Teal grinned.

''Possibly,'' Dan agreed. ''The writer on Konstat's investigation believes University Savings must be a personal goal for someone. Anytime these guys get personal, it means trouble. But using Shag?'' Dan's pale face wrinkled in disgust. ''He's a lightweight.''

''Hey, Shag's good enough for me. More concerned treatment and I might not be here.'' Teal spoke with false jocularity.

''True enough.'' Dan hesitated. ''Look, for now this information stays confidential, but you have a right to know. Carroll wasn't a suicide.''

''Wasn't a suicide?'' Sweat beaded Teal's palms. ''What do you mean?''

Nothing prepared her for Dan's reply.

''Murder.''

''Murder? You're joking?'' Teal scrutinized Dan's face. ''You're not joking.''

"The physical evidence is conclusive. I know this changes the situation. And with the episode yesterday—maybe you should back out. We can tell your boss I decided the investigation didn't need an accountant."

Dan had debated with himself endlessly on the request. Teal Stewart could be put at serious risk. He never expected the swift repercussion from her limited exposure to public view. The run-in with Shag had to be enough to scare her out of her wits. He wasn't too happy about it, himself. Now he was telling her Carroll had been murdered.

Dan wouldn't blame her for a refusal, but he could control the project. No one outside need learn of her participation. He held his breath.

Teal shifted in her chair as though she hoped to shake off the burden of fear. The fear remained. Denial was no answer.

"I want to help. I found him, remember. No one should die like he died. But don't you have your own financial experts?" Teal asked.

Yes, she had vowed to confront the fates—before the episode with Shag and knowledge of murder. She was fishing for an honorable retreat. If the fates offered an easy out, she would take it.

"Two people buried in work. Without you, the d-d-digging will wait." Dan twisted his hands.

Teal couldn't believe how quickly the "okay" came out of her mouth. "When do I start?"

He raised his eyes. "Thanks."

For the next forty-five minutes they established a strategy. Kathy brought in bottles of mineral water and

129

sandwiches. Neither Dan nor Teal had a clear vision of the best approach, but, gradually, a plan evolved.

"You're right, Teal, I'll check the University Savings' board of directors and officers against police data and pull the file on Shag's employers. Mrs. Carroll has given the permission for you to look in her husband's records. I'll make the same request of Konstat's estate," Dan said.

He bent to add the last task to his notes. The felt tip squeaked against the paper as it ran dry. He shook it, hard.

"Dead?" Teal opened her middle drawer and pulled out a pen.

Dan made a face. "I don't use ballpoints."

Teal laughed. "They're the standard issue, right?"

She dropped the gold-toned instrument with the tell tale clicker on top back into the drawer. She wasn't that crazy about ballpoints, herself.

"Yep. And so cheap they skip from the start. I buy the felt tips myself, even though they get clipped. That's the police for you."

Teal fished up a narrow felt tip. "This better?"

Dan nodded contentment.

"I'd like to talk with the people at the *Alt* since I would have met them with Carroll," Teal said.

"No, I don't want you talking with anyone. Your job is with the documents, out of sight and out of trouble. Don Clarke suggested you might be freer after the New Year. I need time to get things together, so that's good for me. Then you can puzzle through the numbers—and no conversations with anyone. Agreed?"

"Sounds fine." Teal smiled.

She neglected to mention the more hands-on approach she had worked out. Why upset Dan? Her alternative promised to keep "Teal Stewart" hidden and safe.

Chapter Fifteen

Teal glanced over the wineglass rim to study Averill's partners and each spouse.

Nick and Sara White. The woman perched on the edge of her chair as though prepared to take flight. A mother most at ease with her peers in the park or with an over-tired child, Teal decided. The path she had not taken in life. Not yet.

Teal watched Sara pluck a loose thread from Nick's jacket. Then Sara raised hazel eyes glazed with anger. A startled second held the two women locked together before Sara White turned her attention to Averill. A wan smile illuminated her face, and her eyes only looked tired. Teal shook her head in confusion. What was truth and what illusion?

Nick smiled at her from across the table. He seemed an ordinary guy and attractive enough with his velvet brown eyes and brush cut hair. His body was an athlete's trim. Averill had said Nick still did a good bit of climbing in his spare time.

Bare rock-face climbing struck Teal as somewhat less than ordinary after all, and she grinned. Nick White shot back a broader, amused smile, and for no account, they laughed. Sara was on Nick immediately, plumping up his napkin, brushing a stray crumb off his chin. Nick's grin dissolved to a compressed line.

Then Nancy Henderson sat down beside him.

"George has about wrestled the roast from the pan, won't be a minute. Sara, I hope you appreciate I've seated you next to your husband." Nancy winked and addressed Teal. "I prefer the old etiquette, but Sara can't abide losing Nick to another—"

"That's not fair," Sara whispered. "It's me I worry about with a stranger. I'm shy."

Nancy shrugged. "Whatever. I need the stimulation of conversation with a man who's not my mate after all these years. Not that you're a bit dull, dear."

Nancy winked at George as he entered the dining room with the platter. Everyone admired the handsome roast as he set it before his place. He raised the carving knife as Nancy turned to Teal.

"Of course, you unmarried folks only have eyes for each other. That's how love should start."

Nancy struck Teal as able and sharp. Earlier in the evening when the guests met the three Henderson children, Teal had envied Nancy's quiet pride in their poise. Despite the common bond of motherhood, Nancy and Sara engaged in little conversation. Teal had noticed.

"I'll get the salad. You're doing a wonderful job, dear," Nancy said as the tiny woman passed her husband.

George beamed, and the expression softened his rough face. He could have been the giant at the top of the beanstalk, Teal decided, or Paul Bunyan's cousin if only

133

he'd been tall. He wasn't. He was very small, and very able.

That he could balance on a minuscule rock ledge, or rappel a cliff supported by mere rope, seemed quite possible. The pictures of George atop McKinley, traversing Tibet and making camp on the Matterhorn lined the dining room walls. Nancy stood beside him in two, glowing flush and happy with exertion.

George had greeted Teal at the door with an unexpected hug before he grasped her strong, slender hand in his smaller one. Teal had warmed to him immediately. Now he finished laying slices of the pink roast on the serving plate. The dinner began in earnest.

"To friends old and new, a merry, merry Christmas!" George said after the group left the table to resettle in the living room.

He poured champagne, and Nancy sliced the impressive bûche de Noel.

Teal viewed the dessert with respect and envy. Nancy must have spent the better part of a day making sponge and beating up vanilla and chocolate butter creams. She confessed to purchasing the meringue mushrooms growing from the buttery bark, thank God.

Averill waited beside Nancy, ready to hand out full plates. Smart, tall, blond, a twinkle in his eyes—Teal liked what she saw. Better, she liked what she felt.

"It can't be a very merry Christmas for Ellen Carroll," Sara said to the room.

Chatter trailed to silence.

"No," George agreed. "I don't suppose it is. Carroll was a decent fellow, if a little too Republican for me. Nick, you—well, all of us here knew him, except for Teal—"

"I'd met him, George, though I hardly claim to be a friend."

"Since we all knew him, I think Nick should say a few words." George turned from Nick to Teal. "On the mountain, Nick and I have had occasion to say goodbye to a comrade. The mountain is not a bad way to go, not like this."

Nick's grip tightened on his plate. "I'm not sure what I can say."

Everyone stared at the floor, and no one spoke. Nick's hand began to shake, and his slice of chocolate log slid across the plate to the edge. Even Sara couldn't move.

Averill saved the moment from unbearable tension. He bowed his head. "In our hearts, may we cherish the memory of our loyal friend William Carroll, and may his wife find peace."

They murmured amen.

"Didn't another friend of yours die this year?" Sara asked Averill in a clear and carrying voice.

He nodded. "My roommate from Yale. You may have read his stuff. Mark Konstat. He was a renowned journalist. With the *Alt.*"

Sara pet her husband's arm. "You knew him, didn't you, Nick honey?"

He glared back at his wife. "No. I never met the man."

His hand shook. The plate dipped. Chocolate and meringue splattered to the floor.

"Thanks for coming this evening. Not too bad for you, I hope?" Averill kept his eyes on the road.

"No," Teal replied. "Not bad at all. I like meeting the important people in your life."

"And I wanted them to meet the most important person—you."

Christmas Day began with the doorbell ringing. Teal ran down the three flights to the outside door. A young man sporting a ponytail and three earrings shifted foot to foot on the other side of the glass. He held up a white box.

Teal turned the lock and pushed. "Yes?"

He thrust the package into her arms.

"Don't worry about the tip," he called at a sprint to his double-parked van. "It's all taken care of."

Adrenaline burst into Teal's veins. She cradled the package motionless against her body. Could it be from Shag? Could it be a bomb?

I'm being paranoid, she thought, but she had to will herself to move. She had never been so careful mounting the stairs. She eased the box to the kitchen counter. Mr. Ponytail wasn't Shag, she reminded herself.

The crisp, white rectangle looked like any florist's box. She used the longest scissors she owned to cut the ribbon. A wooden spoon served to flip off the lid as she stepped back. White peonies burst into view.

Twenty-five peonies when she counted. Each nestled in purple tissue, showing a vivid white against the shadowy paper. Teal bent her face to revel in the beauty.

Thick ink curved across the accompanying card. "You aren't a rose, Teal, you are more beautiful and more rare. Averill."

Her gasp of joy rippled the petals. She replaced the

bunch to lift the individual stems. A red freckle marked each center. Averill had returned her home to her, a lovely, safe haven.

Am I being wooed? Teal wondered.

She settled the flowers in a cylindrical vase. Sunlight dappled the surface of the clear glass and water. A rainbow shimmered on the kitchen wall. How marvelous to be wooed.

Ah, blest Christmas morn, Teal thought.

Chapter Sixteen

Malley called her the day after New Year's.

"I'm sitting with a stack of material for you. Some courtesy of the Attorney G-G-General's office. I'll send it over tomorrow."

"Great. Dan, is there any problem if I work on this out of town? I've been asked to house-sit for friends who live in Dover. I can work without distraction and—"

"I don't care where you are, just don't tell *anyone* what you're doing. Do you understand?"

"Promise," Teal agreed.

"I appreciate this," Dan said and hung up.

He leaned back in his chair, elated. His first death as lead, and only, detective was supposed to be a cake walk. Dull. Routine. But evidence of a beating and a collateral murder was changing the view of the brass. Of course, they didn't know about Teal, his financial expert. The case was going somewhere; he could feel it.

Teal stuffed Dan's package into her briefcase the next day, prepared to leave her office at three. She wouldn't miss this environment for a week. On the way out, she stopped at Kathy's desk.

"Well, I'm off. Call when you must, but please don't pass out the number—"

"Don't worry. The hush-hush mission is safe with me." Kathy waved her boss out.

House-sitting or running away, Teal wondered as she climbed into her lovely, old 190SL Mercedes. Who could say? Why not take a break from Boston and the apprehension that clicked into place with the police lock at night? Why not take time to sort out her emotions? Early January brought an annual reduction in client activity, the period of calm after a hectic fall and before the demands of year-end audits later in the month. Even the time drain of the BiMedics' initial public offering was on hold while the company waited for a better market.

Dover, fifty minutes from Boston in the worst traffic and thirty in the best, still remained a world apart. Tidy forests and fields surrounded Federal period estates. Open space and generational wealth had spared Dover the stigma of suburbia. Her friends occupied a Greek revival farmhouse on seventeen acres inherited from an unmarried aunt who despised charity slightly more than her only niece. It had been an unexpected windfall.

A note on the hall table welcomed Teal. "Bar's stocked, freezer and fridge are full, remote on top of the VCR. Enjoy!"

Enjoy? The following afternoon Teal wondered at the word. She looked around from where she worked at the couch. Polished woodwork, a crackling fire and bright

139

drapes in chintz presented a life where the uneven edges were folded and tucked out of sight as neatly as hospital corners on a bed. A deep depression weighed against her chest.

Teal flung her notes off her lap and kicked at the piles of documents spread at her feet.

"Damn it to hell," she said to the room.

She rubbed the tension banding her head. Surely her Dover friends felt as vulnerable and incomplete as she, at least now and then. The thought did nothing to assuage the envy. Teal wondered if she, of all the world, had been robbed of a real life. Husband, hearth and home—bull.

"But with Averill," she resumed aloud.

With Averill what? A house with a lawn, children underfoot, some sort of hunting dog and good neighbors down the road?

"Come on, Teal. Back to work and real issues." She smiled and bent to retrieve the clipboard.

The morning had started with sun streaks across the kitchen floor and a languorous perusal of *The Wall Street Journal*. The afternoon's labors turned from the enjoyable to the tedious. Her notes, messy and profuse, detailed a tangle of overlapped relationships and murky dealings. Question marks punctuated the margins.

Teal signed in frustration.

Oh, certain names appeared and reappeared, certain connections became evident, but little stood out as remarkable. The first excitement had been Nick White's name in Konstat's file. Then she read further.

White showed up as one of a squash tournament pair listed on a page Konstat had clipped to a tear sheet of an *Alt* article written by him. The piece followed a game

140

between an African American and European American man, point by point, as Konstat analyzed each man's life in a psycho-socialist context. Teal enjoyed the commentary, but found no link between Konstat and Nick White.

The stack of University Savings financial statements disclosed the dollar total of their loans but did not reveal to whom the monies had been lent. How the bank evaluated an applicant or the integrity of bank personnel was not made evident.

University Savings provided one surprise.

Vinnie Rollano, senior vice president, Lending, might know Shag, at least according to the latter's police file. They frequented the same in-town bar. Did they carouse the town together looking for a fast pick-up or to pick up fast bucks? Was it a Big deal! Or big deal? Teal couldn't tell.

Then there was Mark Cohen, Boston's publicized and publicity-seeking lawyer. His name turned up more than once. One of Shag's known employers counted among Cohen's clients. Cohen had served as an outside counsel to the *Alt*, years ago.

Teal remembered finger painting in kindergarten. She always used too many colors. Most of them ended up adorning her and her dress. The few painted pieces of paper that ended tacked to the kitchen wall looked gray. Her mother praised them as art.

Teal cast as appraising eye over the welter of information spread around . . . but like with her muddy smears, she couldn't find the art. She was lost in a forest of Shags, Marks and Vinnies.

* * *

"Enough of this," Teal said aloud, hours later.

She stretched her arms over her head, and the Carroll file in her lap flipped to the floor. Papers scattered across the Navajo rug. Teal rolled her eyes and laughed. Her vaunted organizational abilities had come this, a game of pick-up.

She bent to gather the mess. Mrs. Carroll's cover letter to Dan Malley caught her eye. Teal knelt and read. The widow assured the detective of her responsiveness to his request. She had noted her husband's affiliations on the attached. Teal skimmed the list. Climb On Up was on it, of course.

Teal collected the spread-out copies of the Carrolls' tax returns and investment records. She stopped at a Climb directors' resolution signed by Carroll to authorize bank borrowing—but not with University Savings. The authorization went back in the file.

Climb, Teal realized, was the only name that excited her. And that gut reaction wasn't relevant to Dan's case. She grinned.

Low clouds obscured the weak afternoon sun as she started her walk. Rain cut it short. Teal returned more disgruntled with her progress. There was her alternative strategy. She considered calling Malley. No, she decided, and made three other calls instead.

Number one was easy. This friend headed a division in the city's housing department.

"Clyde," she interjected into his chatter, "I need a favor, a sort of shortcut for some research. I want to pretend I work for you, or, actually, a Dee Shore works for you. Nothing underhanded, and it would really help. Just confirm her employment and describe me if anyone calls."

Teal listened before she responded. "I won't get the department in trouble, I promise. And, yes, I'll be careful. Thanks."

Teal dialed the second number on her list.

"David Morgan, please."

Teal considered the male secretary's frosty grilling. "No, just Teal . . . No, no stated business."

He'll talk with me, you snip, Teal was tempted to say, but the secretary passed her to David.

"Teal, Jesus! Sorry but this new guy is tough. He fancies himself a gatekeeper. So how the hell are you? Not calling because you've changed your mind? I can't be that lucky."

"You're not; sorry, David." They laughed uneasily.

David's wife lived in an alcoholic stupor. Nothing, not money or specialists or sanitariums, could cure her longing for a husband who chose his work over her. She found solace in the bottle. David accepted the condition as penance for too many good years, fast deals and excessive financial success. He would not divorce her—the act he considered abandonment—and he could not love her.

He once promised to reward Teal's career with contacts. He didn't promise more. Teal's answer had been deliberate. No. The tension retreated into an awkward joke between them.

"I need some information and your support. Are you still fighting the city over the tax delinquency you discovered on your Bowdoin Street block?" Teal asked.

David was, among many pursuits, an aggressive developer.

"Knock wood, a settlement is in the works," he said.

"Great. Well, let me ask this. How quickly will the claim be off the city's books?"

"You don't want to hear what I think of Boston's real estate tax files, but half my time has been spent settling the red tape on this issue. That means, it's not off yet and damned if I know when, Teal!"

"Then, the records at City Hall still look pretty bad for you?" Teal crossed her fingers.

David let off a stream of invectives that ended with a "yes."

"Last thing, David. If I happened to pass along a rumor that the city is about to foreclose, would it trouble you?"

"Shit, you want to ruin me, Teal?" David let out a sharp hoot. "Actually, I'd love you to do it. I'm negotiating for a deal right now where I want to catch the bastards off guard. Lie away. But I have the feeling I don't want to know more about what you're up to."

"Thanks, David. And you don't," Teal agreed.

Her last call was brief and pointed.

"Mark Cohen, please," Teal said.

"I'm sorry, Mr. Cohen is in a meeting. May I ask who's calling and the nature of the call?"

"Dee Shore. D-E-E S-H-O-R-E. I understand Mr. Cohen is a terrific real estate lawyer. Anyway, I'd like to set up an appointment to discuss a property. I need professional advice on how to proceed."

"I'm sorry, Miss Shore, Mr. Cohen does very little real estate work. You'll have to be more specific before I can book an appointment." The woman was cool.

"Sure, I understand. I need to move quickly and heard Mr. Cohen can appreciate urgency. Due to certain connections of mine, I may be able to move on a parcel up for foreclosure before the public auction, if you understand me. I'd be happy to introduce my connections to Mr. Cohen if his advice is useful. He may be unhappy if I fail to get through.''

Silence burned the line. Teal pressed a thumb against her front teeth. Say anything, please, she prayed.

''I don't like muscle, Miss Shore, particularly female muscle, and I doubt very much that Mr. Cohen will be interested. However, I will let him make the decision. I hope eight-thirty tomorrow morning is no inconvenience.''

The click cut Teal's response short. She didn't care. The lure had dropped and the bait been taken.

Chapter Seventeen

Oh, my, which is more blinding—the signature belt buckle, the chunky gold link bracelet or the diamond pinky ring? Teal blinked the glare from her eyes as she rose.

"Dee Shore."

"Mark Cohen. What can I do for you, Miss Shore?"

"Please, Dee."

"Well then, Dee, perhaps our discussion would be more comfortable in my office. Sorry about the wait. I'm afraid my secretary misread my calendar."

"No problem, no trouble at all. I don't mind waiting for help," Teal said. That Mark Cohen loved to keep people cooling their heels in his oh-so-post-modern waiting room, she left unspoken.

Cohen indicated the visitor chairs with a flip of his trigger finger. Teal sank into one of the red leather circles. They looked like a carnivore's lips after a feed.

"You referred to help, Dee. Are you in some trouble? It may be outside my specialty."

"No. I need advice, and a friend who once worked

146

at the *Alt* told me about you. I guess you're one smart lawyer.''

Counselor Cohen issued a deprecating cough from his squat, tanned throat. His gold necklace shifted under the two-hundred-dollar custom silk shirt that could not make him svelte or tall. Expressionless eyes watched Teal from beneath manicured, brown brows. He was short and ugly and powerful, and used all three with a certain seductive charm.

''You put me on the spot. You may have been misled by a fool,'' he said and smiled an amusement that did not move past the stiff curl of his fleshy lips.

''I doubt it.'' Teal accentuated the edge of deferential whine in her voice. ''I work for the City of Boston's housing department. Anyway, we're about to take a row of three fronts, six units each, on Beacon Hill's Bowdoin Street on a claim of tax delinquency. No mortgages or liens are outstanding except the tax default. I checked.''

''How much in back taxes?''

''About a hundred thousand.''

''Could be a nice opportunity for someone, but I don't see where you need me. Are you interested in it for yourself?''

''Yes.'' Teal bobbed her head.

''Then, I suggest you bid when the city auctions the property. You may have stiff competition for that location. Good luck.'' His hand gestured, a cool and professional dismissal.

Keep talking, Teal thought.

His face remained blank. Surely he picked up on the innuendo. Clyde would kill her if he heard about this, Teal knew. Of course, these deals happened. A few plums for the boys.

Mark Cohen returned her glances with dead flat eyes. He drummed his buffed nails on the gold tool of his leather desk top. He swivelled in his black leather chair. It towered above his head like a throne.

"I'm afraid I can't see how you think this would interest me. And I can't understand what brought you here when you've already explained that you have, well, access, Miss, Miss—?"

"Shore. Dee Shore."

"Of course. Dee."

"It's simple. I run into great deals all the time, but I don't have the money. I mean," Teal softened her voice, "all the time. So I thought, with you being connected in real estate and all, you might like a regular report from me on the city's activities. Sort of a trade of information."

"A trade of information." Mark Cohen chuckled as his eyes narrowed. "But I don't see what you are trading, Miss Shore."

"Well, I guess I'm not with this one since I want the property. But I run into these situations every day; that's the thing. They could make someone rich—"

"Someone like me?" Mark Cohen asked. "In the future?"

"Well, yes. But I expect to pay your normal fee right now for help finding a bank officer who can understand my position."

"In other words, you need a mortgage?"

"Yes."

"This is a very strange approach, Miss Shore. If you need a mortgage, your morning would have been more profitable talking to bankers. I do admire your unabashed approach, however, so, contrary to instinct, I'll hear you out.''

Teal almost collapsed with gratitude. ''Thanks! Well, as I said, I work for the city and I've had friends in the assessor's office for years. Kids I went to school with in Southie and all.''

Please, Teal prayed, *don't be from Southie.*

''I'm an assistant to Clyde Sloan. Anyway, about these buildings. The thing is, sometimes the city is so anxious to unload the real estate that it never gets to an auction if you know what I mean.''

''Who owns the property now?'' Mark Cohen asked.

''Some wheel named Morgan. He filed for abatements, but didn't pay, which you have to do to get a review. Rumor is, he didn't have the cash. People say he got in too deep.''

''Morgan's property on Bowdoin,'' Mark Cohen mused. ''I thought that could be it. Nice—for somebody.''

''Yeah, I'm thinking condos at an average of one hundred thousand plus a unit can gross one point eight million with maybe half profit. With those numbers, I'll make good on a loan easily. I just need the start-up cash for my initial construction.''

''You've developed properties before?''

Teal nodded a general assent. ''In a small way.''

It wasn't a lie, exactly. She had developed the building on Brimmer Street into her home and two rental units. She understood sweat equity. She understood debt.

Cohen smiled genially. ''Sometimes, Dee, you have to spend money to make money. Or even borrow it. Have you considered that?''

The smile did not warm Teal's heart. The bottom of

the chair bit into the back of her knees, and the top lip pressed at her back. The jaws were tightening.

"Hey, I'm not into illegal. I mean this whole deal is because I hear about things, that's all. I appreciate your fees are high."

"You catch on. I'm hoping you're a generous girl," Mark Cohen said.

Teal fought the urge to laugh. Instead, she squirmed out of the chair. Mark Cohen did not rise to meet her.

"I think we understand each other," he said.

"Oh, thank you. Call me at this number, and if I'm not in, leave a message." Teal wrote down Clyde's extension. "I need to line something up fast."

"I'm not promising anything big," Mark Cohen said.

He did not see her to the door.

Teal drove back to Dover in a state of agitated triumph. A little creativity sure beat her dutiful plodding of the days before. She thought of the documents on the living room floor. Research was no match for an appeal to greed. Teal grinned.

Mark Cohen methodically reviewed his conversation with Dee Shore. What the hell was the little bitch after? A mortgage, she said. Could be true, of course, he had heard about Dave Morgan. But this Dee had been a little too cute on how she came to him. He didn't like the direct approach. Direct meant no connections. But if she didn't have the connections, who told her about him? Mark Cohen kept his relationship to University Savings very, very quiet. And that was the kind of deal she wanted to make.

Disturbed, he lifted the telephone.

"Excuse me, I have an appointment with Mr. Rollano."

"Your name?" The gum snapping stopped long enough to set the indifferent words in the air.

"Miss Shore. Dee Shore."

"Sure. You can wait there."

Sure. Sure what? Sure you have an appointment? Sure you're Dee Shore? Sure Rollano will see you? Sure drop dead for all I care? Teal smoothed the short, black-checked skirt that matched her bright purple jacket for lack of taste and leafed nervously through the *Banker and Tradesman*. She saw the mortgage for four hundred thousand plus in Charlestown. Now there was a greater fool.

"Hey, he can see you now."

"Great, thanks."

"Yeah." Staccato snapping and sporadic typing resumed.

Rollano diminished Teal by his flagrant size and volume. His hips draped over his chair. His belly rested on his thighs. His voice boomed through the room. The only sign of restraint was his covert, thorough scrutiny of her.

"Dee Shore. Good to meet you and glad to know you. Any client recommendation by MC is one hell of a find. What's the proposal? Need a loan, I take it? You hope all the way to the bank, ha ha!"

The patter drummed against Teal. Splashes of sound. Excitement made her dizzy.

She hoped her story sounded plausible as she repeated the lie one more time. She waved newly lacquered red nails to cause a small distraction. How would a female opportunist behave, exactly? Like this, Teal hoped.

One thing she realized the second she extended her hand to Rollano: if the veneer was too thin, he'd see right through it. But he listened with interest to her story.

Teal hardly had believed her good fortune when a message came from Clyde only two hours after she left Cohen's office. A Mr. Vinnie Rollano of University Savings expected to see Dee Shore the next day. Now Teal finished pitching her story to him.

"Sounds like a hell of a deal. And I can appreciate your interest in creative financing. Still, a loan is only as good as the property. If the property fails, you fold and we have nowhere to go. So let's take a look!" Rollano pumped his head up and down.

"Take a look?" Teal asked. She thought she'd considered every possible reaction, but she never imagined this.

"Sure thing." Rollano stood. "My car's a nice fat Caddie designed for a buffalo like me. Let's check this out."

Later Teal could not pinpoint when she realized the careful scenario had gone awry—or was awry from the start. Sometime, she came to believe, when they walked up Bowdoin Street and discussed the loan. She had worried, even then, that Rollano accepted her story too eagerly. His questions sounded perfunctory, like a man in a play. Her play. But Teal submerged her discomfort beneath the desire to believe she had managed the trompe l'oeil.

"Hell of an opportunity. Of course, I'll have to work my butt off selling this to the loan committee. They are tough! I'm sure you'll make the effort easy for me."

"Sure thing," Teal agreed.

Her face burned. Was this a veiled reference to his cut? Or the expectation she would take on partners? Or something more? She hoped not. All she wanted from him was the proof that all was not right at University Savings. Not a big scene. Teal prepared to negotiate cautiously.

Rollano surprised her. He didn't push, but changed the direction of their conversation with alacrity.

"Let's hop back in the car. I'll give you a ride."

"Oh, no need, thanks. I didn't drive to the bank," Teal lied. "My office in City Hall is only a block from here. It's silly not to walk."

"Now, now, I won't have it rumored that I've deserted a girl as pretty as you." He took a firm grip of her arm as he steered her to his car. "In you go."

They started off in silence.

"You can drop me off here." Teal pointed to the vast brick plaza surrounding City Hall. A wasteland according to Hunt. She did not agree.

"Sure would appreciate it if you'd hang on a minute and let me detour to Hanover Street first. Hell of a street for parking. You'd be making my life a lot easier if you'd sit in the car while I pop into Modern Pastry. Modern's the reason I'm the great hulk I am, ha ha."

"Sure. Anything for the man with the money," Teal said, but her heart sank with the intuited dread.

It wasn't an entirely odd request. Modern Pastry in the North End sold the best cannolis and cioccolata torrone in Boston. Rollano could be a fan. His girth proved that. And legal parking was impossible to find, he did not exaggerate.

They doubled beside another sedan like everyone else on the street.

"Won't be a minute, sweetie." Rollano heaved his bulk out of the car.

Teal watched him enter the crowded shop. The minutes passed, and her anxiety mounted. She fiddled with the radio until it came on. Opera. The soprano's big, Wagnerian voice drowned out all thought. Teal closed her eyes.

She heard the car door open, and, as her eyelids flew up, a hand clapped them shut. The opera stopped. She heard doors slam shut and the motor roar. She rocked as the engine turned over and the car pulled into the street.

"Sorry to inconvenience you, Miss Stewart, but, you see, you have inconvenienced me far more." The voice quavered, high and thin, the voice of an old man.

"Oh, don't deny the Miss Stewart. Dee Shore hardly suits you. Nor do the clothes and silly bouffant hair."

Teal heard the din of traffic and lurched as the car stopped and started. Traffic lights, she decided.

"I will be very direct, very simple. Your dangerous game could involve me with inconsequential men. Men who posed no threat to me. That radical reporter. The overreaching politician. They were harmless. But the tragedy of their deaths—and how I hate wasted life—that tragedy could hurt me because of your persistence."

Air whistled and wheezed into the old lungs. Teal was, herself, almost unable to breathe. She couldn't move her lips to speak. Fear made her hyperattentive.

"You behave foolishly, Miss Stewart. The boy should have been deterrent enough, but no, you continue. What am I to do? I cannot kill you and encourage the false

154

notion that these men troubled me. I have decided, instead, to talk with you. You must see how lucky you are, that I chose to talk. I am sure you realize what a problem you have become.''

In one swift motion cloth replaced the hand. Her sight blackened beneath the press of a blindfold. She regretted the loss of pink filtered light.

"Do not try to turn, Miss Stewart. Do not allow your animal instinct to succeed. It would only jeopardize your chances of walking away from this car alive.''

Chapter Eighteen

The nausea of terror heightened. Teal experienced every sound as an assault. She shrank from the shrill of a voice outside the car. "Do as you're told, John! Hold my hand!" a woman yelled.

Teal cringed as the transmission whined when the impatient driver cocked the wheel too tightly in a turn. Her isolation deepened despite a collage of human noise. The blindfold cut behind her ear, and her body plunged forward at each sudden stop. Every sensation distorted her efforts to monitor and to measure.

I must do something, Teal decided in a panic of sweat and terror. *Open the door! Roll to freedom!* But the image of a leg mangled as she flung herself from the car, her roll to freedom ended by truck—no. Her willful mind pressed on the notion of time, but time ticked on. She could not edit or erase the events of this day.

Would that I could, she prayed. Her skin, stretched over muscle, vein and bone, was both enclosure and impediment. Trapped in herself, captive to the car, she struggled to remain sane.

Her rapid, claustrophobic thoughts paced the bucking

automobile. When the motion finally stopped, her mind emptied of distraction and noise. Fear and confusion left her drained.

"You have been thinking during our ride. Thinking of yourself. How precious you are, the body vulnerable, the mind so ashamed. Both impotent. What you must have learned about yourself. Do not answer—"

Teal sensed the lifted, protesting palm.

"I don't want to know the petty vanities twisting in your heart. The ride was to acquaint you with the limits of your youth. Death scares even you." The voice flattened with the weight of irony. "Feel your heart's beat, Miss Stewart, the blood pressed through your veins. I have only to tighten my hands"—dry hands stroked Teal's throat—"to squeeze out the life you so want to sustain."

The stiff fingers slid away. She could feel the effort he had made to shift his balance back in his seat. She heard the rasping breath.

"I appreciate your will to survive because I know I am dying. They say if I am lucky it will be a year. What do they mean, lucky?" He snorted. "You do not know. You do not accept that death could come today, tomorrow. The ego of the young and the vanity of good health delude you. But mortality is not cerebral, my dear. Do you appreciate that, Miss Stewart? Do you appreciate the implication?"

The voice died. It died in a small, audible expulsion of air, exhausted with the homily. Teal felt the old man's effort to resume.

"I hope you feel the impact of my words. I have nothing to lose killing you. I would have had nothing to lose in killing those men whose deaths obsess you and brought you, most unfortunately, to this meeting with me. But I have certain pride and vanities, too. Vanities of dying. I wish to be remembered well by my children, my grandchildren, my community. I wish, most of all, to be remembered unsullied.

"Stop prodding, Miss Stewart. Stop poking and provoking. Should your interference, however speciously, lead to me, I will silence you without hesitation. I have nothing to lose. Believe me, Miss Stewart. Believe me and stop."

The car stopped and doors opened. Many hands now, younger hands, guided her exit. Tape was wrapped around her wrists. Big bodies sandwiched her on the right and left to form a trio that moved as one. Then strong arms pressed Teal down, inside another car. They slammed the door, and their footsteps receded.

A pungent, leather odor stopped Teal cold. She sniffed the familiar smell of her 190SL. The restraining wrist tape stretched and gave just enough to allow her purchase with her teeth. She bit until the nick ripped wider and she was almost free. She did not hear the sound of acceleration as the old man was chauffeured away.

The tape separated; the blindfold slipped over her head. Fear caught in Teal's throat as she made herself look around. Things were vaguely familiar. Where was she?

She picked out the curve of the ramp, the size of the lot. This was the Aquarium Garage, not six blocks from Modern Pastry. In another lifetime, before this day, she had parked here herself between the Aquarium and Quincy Market. From here she had shopped for Christmas. Had visited the seals frolicking in their cold pool.

Had walked to Christopher Columbus Park to watch tall ships. In another lifetime she had been safe.

Indignation lit through her. And to think the old man had moved her precious Mercedes as a simple expedient. She wanted to cry at her loss of faith.

Teal rubbed at the tacky streak of adhesive on her wrist, traced a slow finger around the circle of steering wheel. She could not bring herself to start the car. The afternoon had left her body unbruised and her mind a mess. She could hear his struggling breath, could imagine his thin, veined hands like a claw at her throat. Her stomach heaved fear into her throat.

She knew who he was. An important man, she had learned from her research in Dover. A man with an interest in University Savings.

His plea had been so simple: the ironic hubris of man, the ego of reproduction, the pride of progeny. For the sake of his offsprung genes, he wished to pass untainted a legacy accrued from other people's desperation and despair. The old man aspired to have grim legacy become cherished heritage, the culpable ancestor recast as treasured relic, the old sport, the wily patriarch.

His children, the graduates of Northeastern University, would have children even now hurrying to classes at Boston College. The great-grandchildren, even more fortunate, would attend Groton or the Windsor School before Princeton or Harvard.

Teal snorted. *What a chain*, she thought, *what a chain that ruthless old fraud expects to forge. And how it will weaken and dissipate from his brutal founding strength.*

She imagined in another generation the angry adolescent unearthing facts about Great-Grandfather, facts to jolt the decorum, the world of privilege and acquired antiques.

"Oh, old man," Teal whispered.

She twisted her key in the ignition and depressed the starter button. She shifted the grand dowager of sports cars into reverse and eased the clutch. The low, heavy vehicle handled easily. It swung back and around. Teal braked to raise her shoulders in a shrug. Actually, she wanted to cry.

"Perhaps you win. I get the point. I believe your need to go to the grave confident your children are better people for your sins. You believe that myth." Teal's voice broke, and she relaxed the brake to start forward.

Malley hardly expressed sympathy when she called to tell him what had happened.

"Idiocy, Teal! You could have been killed in this little charade. Who do your think these guys are? The Little L-l-league?" Dan's voice rose.

"I was stupid, I know. I agree. But I am all in one piece." Teal had no desire to fuel his anger with an argument.

"Damned stupid. Where are you? Dover?"

"Yes and about packed to go."

"Meet me at my office in two hours." Dan invited no discussion, and Teal proposed none.

She gathered strewn papers, watered plants and locked every window and door. She left a note on the kitchen table.

"Thanks for the house. Take care, call soon."

The message reflected a certain creative bankruptcy. Too bad it hadn't happened sooner.

"I didn't want to tell you. I didn't think it was risky, but I knew you'd say no." Teal levelled with Dan. "The research had confirmed my suspicion that University was involved with some pretty high flyers. Big-time borrowers with close ties to organized crime. But the research couldn't tell me how, exactly, or who. Mark Cohen offered a link. Maybe it wasn't smart, but I struck a nerve. Do you think the old man is behind Carroll's—"

"Murder? Is that what you think? And you didn't consider your actions a risk! You're lucky to be sitting here. Leave the investigation of individuals to the police. Now let's go over what you found in the data."

Teal talked Dan through her notes, the web of people and deals.

"It may prove to mean nothing, but that bank is in big trouble. Carroll had overextended himself badly, the old man is lurking behind the scenes, and I think Konstat was close to figuring out just who was up to what. I only wish he'd left us a few clues," Teal said.

"We are looking. We the police, Teal. Not you." Dan glared.

She glared back. "I understand why you don't want me talking with people, but if I could meet with someone at the *Alt*—"

"Forget it. I've spoken to Konstat's r-r-replacement; there's nothing more there. Uh, I hate to say you've done a great job on this after today, but you have. I know we'll get our answer—"

"But drop it for now, right?" Teal finished.

"Right. You will drop it. No fooling around."

They parted amicably. Teal did not blame Dan for his pique; she had been rash to go off alone to stir up trouble. Still, it had brought a result—a result she wished she'd prefer to forget. Sliding into her car, her heart began to jump in her chest.

Dan pondered the information synthesized by Teal from the disparate data. University Savings was in trouble, and she was probably right on the individual behind the trouble—her old man. Dan had never heard that name for him before.

The media called Boston's senior underworld boss, "the Chameleon," because for all the activity rumored to be under his control, he remained invisible. There wasn't a single charge on his record. That fact didn't improve Dan's mood.

None of what Teal had unearthed established a direct link to Carroll's murder. The aspiring politician had been killed with his own gun in the daylight on a city street. No one had seen anything. Suicide had been assumed from the placement of the gun, as though it had dropped from Carroll's hand, and the proximity of the shot to his head wound. The theory had been mistaken.

Dan knew the department would have let the case stay under his direction if not for the prominence of the victim. As it was, Dan had been joined by a more senior detective. Boston wanted to show that it took William Carroll's death seriously. Dan's situation could be worse. His "co-equal" colleague had acted with sensitivity to his pride, and Dan was, after all, a cop's son. He understood. Still, if the department learned of Teal Stewart's shenanigans, he could lose the case entirely.

Homemade whole wheat bread, lentil soup, a salad of greens and a glass of red wine graced the table. Teal sat down with an appetite. She enjoyed eating. The day's events made tonight no different.

She ate and considered her antics with the bank. Kathy would have questions, and Teal considered how to deflect them. Of course, Kathy might not have the time. The backlog of Clayborne Whittier work could make next week an ordeal. Anyway, Kathy hadn't been asking her usual quotient of questions, Teal realized. Which seemed odd. She broke off a chunk of bread and followed with more wine. Why not forget the whole mess for one night?

After dinner, she carried her tea to the library. A good book, a small fire and quiet was what she needed.

Then the doorbell sounded.

"Get lost!" Teal shouted from the other side of the glass beside the building's front door. "I got the point!"

Her hostility bounced off an impervious and grinning face. Shag gestured and laughed. Teal's left eyelid began to twitch.

"Lost! Get lost!" She stomped backward into the hall.

"Hey, waita minute." Shag rattled the knob. "Come on, I'm not here on any mission to, like, do anything. The old man scared you, huh? Anyways, I just want to return Shakespeare. And to, like, thank you." He held a book up. "See."

Exasperation overwhelmed Teal's fear. "So, you're welcome. Leave them there."

"Excellent stuff," Shag said, undaunted by talking through glass.

"I hope you haven't planned to drop me into the Charles."

"Hey, I mean it, this isn't business. This is to give back your books. I saw your light on up there and all." Shag shrugged.

"How considerate," Teal said through clenched teeth.

"Yeah, well bye." With odd grace, Shag made a show of placing the books on the top step. He started down.

"Since you are here—" Teal cracked the door and called out, "tell your friend he has little to fear from me and I, I hope, as little from him."

"I'll pass it on. I didn't scare you, huh? You hadda keep pushing where you weren't wanted and I look like a wimp."

"No, Shag, you scared me good and proper. It's just fear isn't always the most effective weapon."

"Yeah. Well, that's the way it goes." He faced her from the sidewalk. "But all my customers? They pay what they owe in the end. You would, too, if I'd come on a debt."

"I'm sure I would have."

Averill was more reassuring when he called after she had watched Shag disappear into the night. "Put it behind you. No broken bones and even Shakespeare back unscathed."

"No, only me with a bruised ego. I felt so foolish telling Dan. I wanted to run away." Teal wrinkled her nose at the telephone.

"And if you were to run away, where would you go?

What would you do?'' Averill asked across the miles between them, having called from New York City to say hello. She knew her precarious state kept him on the line. He was kind.

"Anything and anywhere I want?" Teal asked. She liked fantasizing. "A pied-à-terre in Paris and a villa on St. Barts. The life of contemplation—"

"Luxurious contemplation!"

"Well, yes," she conceded. She loved his laugh. "And you?"

"Me? No question—a big boat and the seven seas. If my obituary could say 'he sailed the world solo,' I would be dying fulfilled. Whenever things go wrong or I get really mad, I take out my navigation maps and plot a course."

"When did that habit start?" Teal asked. "Sounds like hard work."

"Not at all! Oh, I guess when Father gave me the Wee Scott. She was one yare little boat."

Teal imagined a determined young Averill at the tiller, running with the wind. "Did you ever make the break for it? Use the charts?"

"I did at twelve, and made it from Southwest Harbor on Mount Desert to the end of the Cranberry Isles before they caught up with me. Actually, Father put the yacht club on alert, and I was hauled in by the commodore. Seaman that he was, he applauded my skill and still managed a royal chewing out. I loved that boat."

Teal felt loved herself.

"Teal, promise there will be no running off to Paris tonight. Read a good book, then sleep long and well. Leave the bank and Carroll to the police. Deal?"

"Deal."

And it was, with dreams of sailing through Paris filling her night and not a dead body in sight.

Chapter Nineteen

In mid-March Averill was not thinking about sailing; he was thinking about skiing, and he was thinking about Teal.

The telephone rang as Teal entered her house. She dropped her briefcase inside and slammed the door in one motion of hand and foot and rounded the corner to the library. She grabbed the receiver.

"Hello," she said.

"What do you say to skiing next week?" Averill asked.

"It's almost spring!" Teal laughed.

"It's almost spring and the biggest snow storm of the year is heading across the Midwest ready to cover two-thirds of Vermont. Which, on the current four-foot base, should mean good skiing. We're doing a trial of our new equipment. The last test before committing to full production. You need the break and I need you."

Teal did a rapid series of *if* calculations. *If I finish the acquisition work by Friday, if I give New York a final draft, if . . .*

"If you don't say yes, I'll feel awfully lonely on those gorgeous slopes," Averill persisted.

"Y-e-s," Teal answered as she reassessed each if. "Yes. I'll make the time."

"Wonderful! I fly into Logan Friday on a six-thirty shuttle. Meet me there at seven-thirty for the flight to Burlington."

"Seven-thirty, the shuttle, you—I wouldn't miss it for the world."

"Nor would I, love, nor would I."

Averill had not lied. Vermont reflected car headlights off new snow and into the night sky. Teal pressed her nose against the scratched airplane window. A bright pool spilled from a farmhouse window not far below.

"I think we're almost there," she said, and fogged her view.

Averill grinned. "Then it's meet up with Nick and George, the car rental desk, the drive, the lodge—"

"Dinner with everyone and being polite before we can escape to bed." Teal laughed. "So, who among the partners is the best skier?"

Averill shrugged. "We're all pretty good."

"You mean expert good, don't you?" Teal asked.

Averill shrugged modest assent.

"Then, I think I'll ski on my own."

"No one will blame you," he said. "We all like to take off solo once in a while."

The plane bounced up on the first touchdown, then settled to the ground.

"Ready?" Averill asked.

"Umm." Teal smiled. "Ready."

The temperature dropped as the chairlift ascended the mountain. Weak rays of a setting sun cast long, dense shadows off trees and rocks below. He decided to take this last run down the most difficult face of the mountain. He wanted to put the skis and his skill through a final test. His partners dangled in the chairs above him, each intent on a different trail.

He slid off the lift at the top and swung across flat terrain to the lip of his trail. The empty drop left him the last fool on the mountain. He liked the isolation, the chance to hit unconscionable speeds as he screamed down alone and free. No one to complain to the ski patrol.

He knelt to adjust his bindings and check the release. He liked the feeling of the boot against his ankle. He was cautious and methodical about everything in life. Smoking an open slope required attentive preparation. It had been years since he skied Stowe, and it felt good, very good, to beat down the mountain's side.

He could visualize his route. Where the trail narrowed between two sheer-sided granite cliffs and the squeeze made traversing a challenge. One other tricky spot required a series of sharp turns through a pine forest above the last quarter of the run. Nothing difficult for him, but habit made him review the options. There were a few should he tire—junctions with a path to an easier trail, connections devised to accommodate those who panicked mid-run. Not him.

He pushed off, looking to check for anyone who might be starting with him. No one, and the slope below still clear. *Great,* he thought, and indulged in a hot dog jump. *It's mine.*

He sped downward, traversing, crouching for speed, tilting his body to keep the edge, playing downhill racer. The sun dropped with his descent. Skimming along the narrowing trail, he saw the granite-lined pass below lay in deep shadow. A single flash of light, an impression of blue, faded so immediately against a distant wall, he hardly registered the movement.

He had intended to check his speed as the granite rose above him; but with the slope empty, the snow powder and the skis responsive, he decided not to hesitate. He cut back and forth in diagonal sweeps of mounting speed. He loved the blown-up wall as he sped closer, the blur as he cut away.

The granite was growing right now. He saw the upper lip disappear, the rock face fill the horizon, the veins of gray and pink burst into focus. He felt that odd thump of panic and adrenaline as he set his body to shift. Facing the cliff excited him. And in a moment, he would be safely away.

He began to lean forward, collecting his balance to make the turn. A sudden distraction pierced his concentration, and in that instant he felt the shudder, the flood of all his adrenaline, all his strength. He prepared his lungs to scream when the rock face did not disappear, but time ran out. He met the granite without realizing this time the slope won.

Death was instantaneous.

Teal pushed into the packed bar and shimmied onto a high stool. She shouted her order over the noisy, elated crowd. Averill, Nick and George were still at it, winging down their final runs, but she had opted to quit over an hour ago. They agreed to meet here, the "Rusty" something. Fatigue made her slow. She relaxed and looked around.

Two vivacious young women seated at a table across from the bar flashed bright fingernails and day-glow apres-ski outfits. They scanned the room for someone promising and male. Teal watched a paunchy man zero back. The women cooed at each other, keenly aware of his interest as the aging Lothario edged closer. They laughed at a remark he tossed to them as he pulled a chair between them.

Giggles and whispers ensued as hands rested heavily on willing shoulders. Teal marvelled at the instant sexual byplay, the automatic physical intimacy. She shifted away.

Where were Averill and crew? The blast of continuous music began to irritate her. Someone tapped her arm, and she jumped.

"Teal?"

The someone tapped harder and she turned.

"There's been an . . . a problem. We have to answer a few questions."

"Oh, sorry—you startled me," Teal said.

"There's been an accident. The police need to talk to us."

"What do you mean, an accident? How bad? It wasn't . . ." But it was too noisy to ask as they threaded across to the door.

He gripped her shoulders as they stood in the snowy drive.

"It was bad, Teal. Very bad. George." Nick's voice cracked. "He's dead."

"Oh, no, Nick. No." She shook her head in denial and clung to his arm to comfort him, to comfort herself. "What happened?"

She was aware of the inanity of the question, the pointlessness of detail as though the answer could be analyzed, the flaws isolated, the outcome reversed. As though with death it was not already too late.

"I don't know. I'm so exhausted, I just don't know." Nick's voice faltered.

"The new skis?"

"Maybe. I keep wondering about them, and some rotten part of my brain is hoping that it wasn't the skis. An accident would be the end of them. I'm disgusted at myself." Nick trembled.

"Hey, that's not unnatural. Not pleasant, but not unnatural." Teal patted his arm.

"Sure."

"Where do we have to go?" she asked.

"The station. Averill is waiting for us there."

Nick moved like an old man burdened by the lethargy of his despair. His step slurred as they walked in silence to his car.

Teal remembered her conversation with George just that morning. He stopped her after breakfast with a few questions on the management letter Climb's auditors proposed to issue. Accounting issues left him flummoxed. *You might think it a science,* he said, *but to an engineer it's hocus-pocus.* He refused to be on the defensive with the auditors, or his partners for that matter, so he hoped for a little tutoring from her. If she would.

172

Teal was happy to agree, and he flattened a copy of the draft on the table.

Auditors always shared a draft with management for discussion before issuance to the board. The inventory particularly disturbed George. He did not understand how accounting records could differ from a physical count of stock. Teal had assured him that the difference fell within normal for a retail operation, but it took a lot of discussion before George relaxed.

All day Teal had enjoyed her memory. Averill's partner seeking her out and showing his trust. How could it be their last discussion?

"When did you last see George Henderson, miss?"

Teal stared at her hands. They clenched and unclenched in her lap. Another body—how could that be?

"When did you last see Mr. Henderson?" the officer prompted.

"Around three o'clock, I guess. I knew if I kept skiing, I'd end up in trouble. I'm not that good and the advanced trails really challenge me. After I made the decision to quit, I waited at the bottom for Averill. Nick arrived first, and we talked about mostly nothing."

"And did he comment on the new skis you all are trying out?"

"Not me. I rented, but, yes, we talked about their performance. Nick thinks they're super. Flexible but with good control. We agreed Stowe had become too crowded. He said that was part of why Climb debated entering the downhill market. You know, it was so commercial and contrived."

"Climb?"

"Well, Nick and George. Averill isn't such a purist."
Teal sighed. "George and Averill arrived maybe five minutes later. Not long anyway. George got a ribbing for wearing a jacket like mine. He's color-blind, I guess, and had grabbed purple. We all have been trying out the new downhill fashion line. I alternate between purple and fuchsia to insure being located on the mountain if I go down."

That joking reasoning sounded awful now.

"Anyway, I told them I'd had it, and we agreed to meet later at the bar next to the inn. They all wanted to get in a few more runs. I didn't see anyone until Nick found me."

"What did you do after you left the mountain?" the policeman asked.

"Oh, sat in my room exhausted and frozen for about ten minutes before I took a shower. I knew that they would be at it for at least an hour, so I wasn't in any hurry."

"Why didn't you plan to meet at the inn?"

"Because I knew that if they returned early, they'd want to talk new skis and I'd be underfoot. If they skied longer, I'd be bored waiting. The bar seemed easy and more fun. That's how we've arranged things all week. There was no reason to change today."

"Can you think of a time any one of them complained about their skis? During this tryout period or before it?"

"No. No, they all sounded excited about the product. Maybe a few comments on unexpected little things, but nothing significant enough to remember. Of course, I wasn't around during their jam sessions, but no, nothing they ever mentioned to me. Did the . . . was it the new skis that—"

"We don't know yet, miss." The officer's voice was even and sincere. "Did they complain about bindings or the edges slipping and losing control?"

"I don't remember anything like that."

"Well, thank you for your cooperation."

"How did he die?"

"We think he spun out on a turn and hit the rock wall."

Teal's face turned pale. "Oh, God no."

Teal, Averill and Nick met Nancy at the airport. George's wife arrived on the last flight from Boston. Stunned with grief and frantic with hostility, she blamed the partners and new skis for bringing George to Stowe and death. Nancy mostly blamed herself for not leaving the kids with George's folks and coming along like Teal.

Nancy did not want anyone to stay in Stowe with her. She informed them that she would make all the arrangements.

The next morning, after the police said they could go, Averill, Nick and Teal prepared to leave.

"Nancy, if I can do anything . . ." Teal poked her head around the door to Nancy's room.

"What can you do, bring him back? You can't do anything, not anything!" Nancy choked in anger and sorrow.

"I am sorry," Teal said as she withdrew.

The distraught voice followed her down the hall.

"All these big-shot downhill ideas getting George killed! Why did it have to be him?"

There was never a good answer to a question like that, Teal knew. How could you explain chance to a widow?

Teal understood. If it had been Averill, she would be the one asking why. Why him? Why me? But it was George who had died, and Teal was spared the dreadful depth of sorrow consuming Nancy.

Teal wondered what she could say to the woman to alleviate some of her grief. Nancy was right; she couldn't bring George back. Teal didn't think Nancy would be interested in the story about George and his confusion over Climb's inventory.

Teal jerked to a stop in the middle of the corridor. Nick White had reacted quite differently. He'd prodded for every detail of the conversation on their drive to the police station. What was she imagining—that murder was the answer to Nancy's questions?

How ridiculous. Nick's interest made perfect sense given his position at the company. Forget murder.

Chapter Twenty

The mood on the flight back to Boston remained somber. Each of the trio retreated into private thoughts, the week of work and play stopped by death. It had become the week that George died.

At Logan they waited together beside the luggage carousel. Teal's rolled off the chute first. Averill brushed her cheek with dry lips, and Nick squeezed her hand in a physical affirmation of connection. Then each collected their bags, and the group parted.

Teal could not stand the idea of an empty house. She decided to go to her office. She could use the day of work. She could use an escape.

"S-s-someone may have been after you, Teal!" Dan's anger sizzled the wire.

"No way. A terrible accident happened to George—I wasn't even around!" Teal shouted. "Anyway, how did you hear about it?"

"I have sources," Dan answered.

Teal did not push, not so angry with him about her call to Francesca Mettafora over a week ago. He had been furious at her when he'd found out. Or rather, when she'd told him. Who said confession was good for the soul? What was it she had said?

"I talked with the reporter at the *Alt.*" That's all, but it elicited a burst of ire.

"Teal, how many, uh, times do I have to say it? Don't play around with this. It could be dangerous!"

"Does this mean you found a link between the old man and Carroll?" Teal had pressed.

"No."

Teal believed Dan couldn't admit the case was all but close. Not then and not now.

"Are you with me, Teal?"

"Um. Yes, sorry," she said and started to pay attention.

That's when he repeated it. "Someone could have been after you!"

Teal listened to the detective defend his theory.

"Henderson wore purple yesterday; so did you. He was a small man; you are a tall woman. Dusk plays tricks on the eyes." Dan sighed.

Kathy must have tipped him to her sudden return, Teal decided.

Dan reviewed the few details he had pried from the Stowe police. They tagged the death an accident. But Dan was not so sure. He conceded his theory might be a push, but with Carroll's apparent suicide a murder— appearance and reality didn't always conform.

Two people wore purple. One ended the day laid out in the morgue. Was it the right one?

"Humor me, Teal. Leave University alone."

"I'll be careful, Dan."

That was the best she could do.

At home that night, Teal searched for a distraction from the heaviness in her heart. She unpacked Climb's financial statements from the bottom of her luggage. Would looking at these help?

She had surged with professional and personal curiosity at the time she watched Nick and George bend their heads over the report at Stowe. The habits of an auditor were heightened by an interest in Averill's life. George had noticed.

"Nick, scoot over so Teal can look," George instructed.

Teal recognized his pleasure in Climb's good year.

"Come on," he prompted Nick when the vice president of finance did not budge.

Nick moved his head. "We are, after all, a private company, and Teal isn't with our accounting firm—"

"Bother all that. What are you afraid she'll do with the information? Calculate Averill's net worth?" George chuckled at his joke.

Nick turned to Teal. "No offense. Here's an extra set."

Teal caught resistance lingering in his eyes. He held a degree in mathematics and a masters of science in accounting, but he never had worked for a public accounting firm. Perhaps he harbored some resentment that Averill's girlfriend could flaunt an MBA and CPA. As though Teal might inspect his work and find it wanting.

Such fears were groundless, if only he knew. Teal envied Nick his practical perspective. She wasn't sure she could merge the demands of a company's day-to-day operations with the strictures of arcane accounting rules. Her role as an outside expert made her familiar with the later and unhampered by the former. For Nick it was exactly the other way around.

George had urged the financial statements on her willingly. He glowed with pride over Climb's banner year. With profits up fifty percent and cash flow showing real strength, he had a right to glow.

Teal's keenness to review the data in detail had faded in view of the more active diversions in Stowe. She'd flipped the papers into her bag for a time when she was less distracted. Once she was back in Boston would do fine.

Now she turned to the income statement and considered the teamwork such impersonal numbers represented. George, Nick and Averill together had brought the company to success. Now George's untimely death would subject the numbers to divisive scrutiny.

Teal knew that unless the widow agreed to a quick settlement with the remaining partners, the company could suffer. She hoped Nancy was obligated to offer shares back to the corporation before to a third party. If such an agreement bound the widow, it would make everyone's life easier.

Valuing a private company to arrive at a stock price was a complicated task. Teal started to study the balance sheet, but she could not focus on the columns of data. Horror overcame professional curiosity. The point of her thoughts meant George was dead.

The telephone's ring jarred her from her reverie. She lifted the receiver to hear a smooth voice claim to have made her acquaintance at Bowdoin.

"You remember?" the man persisted. "We discussed

journalism at the cocktail party the last night. I'm 'Larry the reporter with *The Wall Street Journal*.' "

"Oh, right. Sorry," Teal mumbled. Larry?

"So you do remember. Good, that makes the next question much easier."

"Yes?" Teal prompted, but she remained hazy on Larry's identity.

"How about a drink tonight? I should have called weeks ago, but this new territory has me busy."

"A drink?"

"Hey, are you the same Teal Stewart who enlivened that dull Maine evening? Or have you given up good wines?" Larry paused. "I called at a bad time?"

"No."

Teal lied from a lifetime of responding to men politely even when she should have screamed no. Larry—the man took sudden shape in her mind. Maybe getting out would be a good thing, she decided.

"Yes," Teal said, "I'd love to get together."

"Say forty-five minutes, and I'll meet you at the west end of Quincy Market. I'm the handsome one, remember?"

Larry might be a bully, but Teal didn't care. He wasn't important. He was an escape from unhappy thoughts and a long night.

"Fine."

Teal hung up, torn between the desire to drop kick herself across the room for agreeing to a date she did not much want, with a man she didn't think she'd much like, and the desire for escape. In either event, she had to hurry.

* * *

181

The following morning, Teal took a closer look at the Climb statements. Larry had her puzzled. He had spent the evening pumping her for information with an undisguised interest, not in her, but in Climb On Up. She had mentioned Averill at Bowdoin.

Larry Harkin was not a reporter on *The Wall Street Journal* by chance. He was following up on rumors about Climb. That was why he had called.

As her willingness to maintain the banal conversation diminished, she had put it to him.

"Larry, I don't think you asked me out for my charm. Come clean."

He grinned with her. "Okay, so my initial motive might be suspect, but that was poor memory and bad judgement on my part."

"Cut the crap. Your motive to what?" Teal asked.

"Oh, all right." He pouted. "I want to learn more about your friend Averill Cunningham. I wasn't sure from our conversation at Bowdoin if you knew him very well. I thought taking you out might help me find out."

"Not that well then and not, I suspect, that well right now given the nature of human beings."

Teal wasn't going to discuss Averill with this ambitious turkey.

"Bankers on the street can't figure out why he kiboshed a big infusion of venture capital money into Climb. I heard Cunningham opposed the deal down the line. It sounded weird."

"Why?" she retorted, surprised and put off that Averill had never mentioned a venture offer. "What owner wants to sell their soul to that crowd unless they have to? Climb doesn't need money at the price of diluted ownership."

"I heard Cunningham's two partners didn't agree. But the crazy thing is, they refused to screw their buddy, and the deal died."

"Loyalty maybe, not some crazy thing!" Teal snapped.

Larry shrugged. "Maybe. Anyway, it ended up screwing all of them. I heard it was a damned attractive deal."

"What exactly is your interest?" Teal asked.

"My interest?" Larry pulled a long face. "My interest is to find a neat topical piece out of my new region."

"Well, if I were you, I'd check my sources."

"Aren't I?" he had responded and laughed.

The encounter may not have enhanced her social life, but it provoked her interest in the slim financial statements she had put aside to meet with Larry.

Teal plucked a dried cherry from the glass jar beside the chair. She popped the wrinkled fruit into her mouth. She worked to separate the flesh from the pit, then raised her head long enough to drop the stone into her hand and a small, silver dish. She resumed her review of the document on the desk.

On the balance sheet, her mind did a few calculations. Good ratios, moderate debt, a retailer's heavy investment in inventory—nothing unusual. She flipped to the income statement. Strong net sales and a nice gross margin, she concluded. Climb could easily attract a venture group.

And it had, big deal.

She fingered the heavy cream paper. Averill. Averill's company. Averill in her life. A relationship more intimate and more promising than her stale reliance on

Hunt. Hunt represented too much past history. Teal wanted to think about a future.

With Averill? Maybe, she acknowledged for the first time to herself.

Then, as unexpected as any emotion was, it really hit her that George Henderson wasn't worrying about tomorrow. George was dead.

Chapter Twenty-one

By April, Nancy finished with unproductive mourning.

She had three children to raise and business to settle. It was not lack of love; she had loved her husband and their marriage. Her love had been constant even when her tolerance for his foibles was not, but she refused to be devastated by his loss. Not yet. Not with so much to do.

The will had been clear. George left Nancy his third of Climb On Up. The lawyers had been clear when they explained she must tender shares back to the company before considering a sale to anyone else, but she was not required to sell. Nancy had been clear, too. She wanted to rid her life of the company she associated with her husband's death.

She made the offer through her lawyer. Nick and Averill must pay no less than ninety percent of the highest value placed on Climb by independent investment bankers within two weeks of final valuation. Unless they agreed to her terms, she would sell to any higher bid.

Nick and Averill knew of unwelcome third parties eager to own a piece of Climb's success. They accepted Nancy's terms. The deal was fair enough.

However fair, the problem of funding the purchase remained.

On book value alone, Climb's worth exceeded $9 million. Nick calculated that intangibles like market position, company name and favorable leases moved the total up to as high as $12 million. Nancy's buy out would come in between $2.7 and $3.6 million.

The company's life insurance on George was less than half the sum required. Bank of Boston had Climb at its credit limit. The partners could not expect an additional loan. They discussed a third partner, but feared a hasty choice.

Averill spoke aloud the conclusion both had avoided. "We're down to venture capital, aren't we?"

Nick wadded his set of notes one at a time into balls, then lobbed them at the waste basket. In. In. In. Out. In. Out. The paper spheres popped from his palm. Averill sat and watched. Out. Out. In. In. In. The last page, compressed in Nick's fist, dropped. In.

"Nick, you and George said it to me yourselves—their goals match ours. Profitability, growth, quality. I know I convinced you the venture vultures could be trouble, but the situation now is different. We can keep them out of daily operations, and we both know they have the cash," Averill said.

He realized the irony of the switch of position, but what could he do for Climb but this?

Nick squirmed and looked for more paper to turn into missiles. "I don't know. Endowment dollars from Princeton and Harvard, founder's money from the Xeroxes and IBMs, pension money expecting beat-the-Dow returns—these venture deals make me nervous. Half of the stiffs running around as general partners in some fancy venture firm have never operated anything more complex than their electric toothbrush. They could ruin my Climb. I mean our Climb."

"They only get one-third, Nick, not control," Averill said.

Nick snorted. "Are you sure? They'll put some guy on our board and make us change to their favorite bank. They'll make me fire our auditors for a firm that is better known because the name will help us go public. That's what they really want from Climb. To take our company public and cash themselves out. In the end, we'll be nothing more than hired help."

Nick glared at the waste basket.

"I guess I convinced you too well in the last go round," Averill said. He tried to laugh. "Look. Our alternative is to fight the valuation down, but we agreed we can't afford delay. You said it yourself, Nick. More investment bankers would turn this place upside down, and we'd pay close to the same amount and have the same problem we have now. Where to find the money."

"We don't have a choice," Nick conceded.

"No."

"I'll call the venture outfit we turned down," Nick said. "Maybe they'll still want in."

"I have a better idea." Averill paused to nod. "I know someone with Simon Brown Associates out of California. They invest West Coast money willing to take the long view. The last time we talked, she asked me about Climb. Simon Brown has a reputation as good people."

"Think it will make my life easier? Will your friend

keep her partners out of my books, because I don't have the time to babysit," Nick stormed.

"Let's hope so," Averill said. "I'll try to set up a trip to California—"

"For you, not me." Nick cracked a knuckle.

Averill frowned. "You are the v.p. finance—"

"But I need time here to prepare for their snooping and poking."

Teal decided to disregard Malley. He didn't understand that she was still frightened by every bump in the night. She had to find out why Shag had entered and disrupted her life. Unaddressed questions brought greater discord than dangerous answers. She understood the risk and planned to remain well out of sight as she sorted out the relationships among the key players. University Savings. William Carroll. The old man. Mark Konstat. She made the list.

Francesca Mettafora agreed to accept Teal's help as long as the CPA remained a backroom expert. Francesca's own technique for completing Konstat's research depended on avoiding disasters like Teal's Dee Shore.

No one ever took too much notice of Francesca. No one begrudged her an extra second of explanation. Best of all, no one stopped to consider the purpose of the questions she asked. Teal, herself, had underestimated Francesca at first.

The journalist managed to land a job as a University teller at the main branch—with Vinnie Rollano in the next office. After she started, she decided to speak with him about applying for a student loan.

That afternoon, she acted humble and reticent and receptive. She couldn't thank Mr. Rollano enough for his time. Couldn't help but hope her education would allow her someday to become a loan officer, just like him. Her flattery was overt, and from that day on, he took a special interest in his "little Francesca." He liked the role of mentor to hers as confidante.

Vinnie bragged, Francesca praised and pried, and Teal analyzed the financial implications of each finding. The nicest thing about Vinnie, Teal and Francesca agreed, was he took credit for everything.

Both jobs were about done, they had concluded over lunch the prior day.

"Ready to write the story, Francesca?" Teal asked.

"Write it and rewrite, rewrite again after the damned editor wears out his blue pencil. I'll be lucky if the bank is around by the time it's in print. Which is when I get paid." Francesca sighed. "How can I love a life with such crappy cash flow?"

"Well, you could stay with our favorite bank. Vinnie certainly figured out how to make ends meet."

"Yeah, well, after my article comes out, they'll be fitting Mr. Loose Lips with cement shoes." Francesca laughed.

Teal didn't feel as confident as her new friend. "I'm more interested in our feet. The old man isn't going to be happy when he reads your article. Not at all."

"Hey, you play in the big time, it's a risk. For him, for us. Anyway, he'll be dead soon." Francesca had developed a certain indifference.

"His friends still trouble me," Teal said.

"They'll be singing to the Feds by the time I'm through."

Teal raised her glass. "To a great job!"

Their laughter rang with satisfaction and relief.

"Now I can get down to what's really important," Francesca said.

"Oh? What's that?" Teal asked.

"Mark's fancy computer game."

"Are you telling me journalists at the *Alt* sit around playing Nintendo?" Teal asked.

Francesca flashed a gamine smile, one that promised maybe she'd tell the truth and maybe not.

"Not all of us. But Mark did. Since I inherited his desk along with the story, I get to play with his computer, too. And it's not Nintendo but one of those ridiculous fantasy games guys like. Dragons, damsels in distress—never women, mind you—and manly men. I spent yesterday trying to get out of a dungeon."

"And did you?" Teal asked.

Francesca frowned. "No. But I figure if I could break into the damn game, I should be able to escape the dungeon. The stupid thing is on a network you tap into through your modem. Mark must have been at the level against a real person as his opponent. You should see the list of player names. Mark used Beowulf, and I think his competition used Jason. Of the Golden Fleece, I suppose. Does testosterone do this to men?"

Teal rolled her eyes. "I don't like computer games, all that aggravating noise—"

"Sex stereotypical." Francesca's expression said, *Wouldn't you know.* "Men flee into fantasy while women like us are left to change the real world."

"Oh, sure." Teal groaned and shook her head.

* * *

190

Today she felt less jovial. Too many questions remained in the University Savings, William Carroll, old man and Mark Konstat equation. Some pieces fit; some were left hanging.

Yes, the mob had moved on the bank to satisfy the old man's compulsion to endow his family with respectability. He wanted a bank and contrived to buy it his way. Befriend the most corruptible loan officers.

After that, it wasn't hard to receive approval for amounts in excess of an established credit line. The rules bent for the old man's puppets. He targeted the most vulnerable bank officials. Vulnerable to the gratuities offered—dinner in New York, flight and hotel arranged. Vulnerable to the Caddie. Vulnerable to a direct deposit into their account. The old man, never evident in these transactions, concealed his investment in the bank's fate.

The stage was set for his grand finale. He was that close to his goal, Teal conceded, and she and Francesca planned to pull the curtain down prematurely. He was not going to be happy. Fear shivered Teal's arms.

Already the loan officers had been informed that significant payments would be late or skipped or short. Teal imagined each of them sweating their portfolio. "Why did I commit so much to that guy?" they would be wondering nervously. "I lost sight of the ball," they were rehearsing before their bathroom mirrors.

Already the directors had called a special meeting to discuss management's unexpected proposal to double the loan loss reserve. Already rumors buzzed between bank executives in Cambridge and Boston. "Looks like University's in trouble." Already the stock price edged down an eighth, a quarter, until today hit a full point.

The old man could wait. Teal understood that. He

could wait until the stock closed at bottom, until the board of directors became desperate, until another week would invite a bank examination. Then he would move to buy stock directly from the worried holders. He would enter the public market the whispered savior of a troubled bank, an act of service to the community.

Once he secured his target, he would issue the covert orders for delinquent loan payments to resume. The public would relax, the stock recover, and the examiners retreat as grateful directors elected the old man chairman of the board.

The family business would have its bank, a nice, clean laundry in a university town.

Oh, no, Teal realized, *he is not going to be happy to have Francesca and me ruin his plan.* Nor was she particularly happy as she reread her much fingered list. University Savings. William Carroll. Old man. Mark Konstat.

Where was the fit?

William Carroll had been a University borrower, his largest loan big enough to require his wife to cosign. The record indicated he had considered another person first. The loan file read, "July 19. Met with W. C. on $200k. Agreed to consider co by R. J. L. He is well known to me."

Some weeks later the writer concluded, "$200k granted by committee. See summary of C's personal financial statements, copies of stock certs, joint returns following. Cosigned by wife Ellen Carroll."

"R. J. L." troubled Teal. The initials matched the bank's most active borrower, active on behalf of the old man. Mrs. Carroll knew of no R. J. L. among her husband's associates. She suggested such generosity wasn't unusual for someone who hoped to influence a politician, but William had not been for sale.

Teal could believe the old man sought political clout in the quest for prominence before his departure from the world. Carroll must have seemed a logical choice. She imagined the plan, perhaps to meet Carroll in a social setting through R. J. L. after the bank dust cleared.

The old man might have planned to support Carroll's campaign as a way to open more respectable doors to his children. That would be the satisfaction, the chance to realize his dream and move the next generations away from the world of crime and blood feuds through which he had achieved the family's original power and wealth.

Teal sensed Konstat incorrectly had connected Carroll to University's problems. Francesca pointed out something else.

"If sex can't be added to a business corruption story, go for tainted politicos. Mark appreciated commercial necessity. Banks and the mob are yesterday's news."

One thing nagged at Teal. Death by bullet did not add up to benign use.

"Yes, Kathy?" Teal answered the buzz.

"Detective Malley has arrived," Kathy said.

"Send him in."

Teal stretched her arms to dispel the knots in her neck and just managed to collect herself as the door opened. She tried for an executive smile.

"Dan." Teal grinned.

"You called this meeting," he prompted.

"Um. This is going to make you a little mad, but

before I can share our conclusions, I have to confess I collaborated with Francesca Mettafora.'' Teal watched Dan's open face redden with fury. She spoke fast. ''Don't you want to hear what we found?''

''Kathy didn't tell me anything about you working with that reporter,'' Dan said, staring hard.

Kathy waited in the doorway, a mug of coffee in one hand, tea in the second. Teal cast her eyes from one person to the other.

Kathy and Dan—and it had never occurred to her.

''You didn't know about Kathy and me. I, uh, didn't know you'd been w-w-working with Francesca,'' he concluded.

''Touché.'' Teal took his point. ''I was afraid of your reaction and I guess you were—''

''Worried, too,'' Kathy said. She unloaded the drinks.

Teal faced Dan when the door shut. ''She's a terrific woman, Dan, and I'm delighted for you both. I should have guessed since she's been so deliriously happy. Not much recommendation for my skills of observation. I hope I did better with Francesca.''

Teal condensed the hours invested in research and wove fact and their conjecture into a conclusion.

''Our theory clarifies the old man's relationship to the bank and maybe to Carroll, but I can't find a direct link to Carroll's murder. Kill a man because he rebuffed a cosign for a loan? I'm not that crazy. Then there's Konstat's beating. I still suspect the old man, but—'' Teal shrugged her frustration.

''Since you're answering all the questions, is there anything else?'' Dan asked with good humor.

''The empty elevator still troubles me.''

Teal spread her hands in resignation. She didn't need to tell Dan that Konstat's fall had threatened her peace.

"I can't shake the feeling, Dan. Too much death. Konstat linked the bank to the old man and to Carroll and now two of the three are dead."

"The academy drilled me with the discipline of questioning easy conclusions, but sometimes the facts make it damned hard. There can be coincidence in life. You believe that of your friend George wearing purple just like you."

"George," Teal mused. "But that was a coincidence. So, where does the investigation of Carroll stand?"

"That's my problem. Nowhere—no leads, no suspects, no nothing."

Dan failed to mask the defeat on his face. His efforts had come to nothing despite following every lead, even Teal's discovery of a "Nick White" in Konstat's file. Dan made call after call through the list, and except for the squash players profiled by Konstat, no one admitted knowing the journalist. A call or two had yet to be returned, but he harbored little hope.

"Well, maybe Mrs. Carroll discovered he was cheating. Maybe some lunatic didn't want him to run for the senate. Maybe . . . it is the bank." Teal did not know.

Dan tapped his foot in nervous bursts against the floor. His case, his very first, had stalled, and Teal, heedless of his professional instruction, now made him fear the consequences of his bringing her into it. Going after the old man had been going way too far. Irritation tainted his voice.

"Teal, what are you planning to do when the old man reacts to this exposure? He didn't fool around when he wanted to scare you before. You've been damned stupid!"

Teal swallowed hard. "I'll be careful, Dan. I will."

She didn't lie this time. It was exactly what she meant to do.

Chapter Twenty-two

Averill lifted the Jeep's key from his bureau drawer and slipped on his boat shoes. He flipped up a thumb at his reflection in the mirror, and his smile broadened as he tossed the beribboned Tiffany & Co. box into the air. Small, precious, bright blue box. A blue that matched her eyes. He held it in his palm a minute longer, then replaced it in his top drawer. If its purchase had been precipitate, its use would not be.

His affection for Teal had grown beyond a fantasy of a wife making a home of a Cunningham estate, or raising their family, or hostessing entertainments with friends. Reality would be much more difficult with Teal and much more fulfilling. He would best the past by marrying wisely, as his father had not.

Teal pulled on and pulled off first one, then a second, then a third outfit. The indecisive frenzy did not spring from her date to watch a polo match at Myopia Hunt Club. She'd done that often enough with Hunt and a poor man's tailgate of sandwiches and beer.

What was different this time was her role as the guest of a member. She and Hunt always went as the paying public, happy to enjoy the feats of the ponies in perfect anonymity. But today, she, equally, would be on display. She wanted Averill to be proud to introduce her to his friends.

Perhaps she should wear the white tee shirt advertising Boston's Blue Diner with baggy shorts and white canvas Keds. No one went wrong in Keds, she concluded. Her thoughts returned to Averill. This afternoon was turning out to mean a great deal to her.

They were a pretty decent fit, she decided and grinned. It had been a long time since she had been vulnerable and excited with love. When the bell sounded, she lifted the picnic basket out of the refrigerator, snatched her visor from the table by the door and ran down the stairs to meet him.

"Hunt called three times." Kathy handed over a stack of pink slips.

What a start to a Monday. He answered in one ring.

"Saturday, Teal. The awards dinner starts at eight, after the reception at six-thirty. Since I'm an honoree, I think we need to arrive in time. If we can get together earlier, I want to show you—"

"Ooh," Teal exclaimed and took a deep breath. "Sorry, Hunt, I'm flying out to San Francisco Friday night."

"Work?" Hunt asked after an awkward pause.

"Not exactly. I plan to visit friends while Averill completes some business—" Teal about bit her tongue. "I am sorry."

"You're not coming to my big dinner; you're going to California."

It wasn't a question. And it wasn't fair. He'd won awards before. She had accompanied him to more than one big dinner.

"San Francisco, yes, and then a drive down the coast. I think, well, I hope, Averill and I are testing the odds for . . . oh, who knows? Well, marriage. And, Hunt"—Teal wanted to be gentle on the point—"you never actually invited me to this thing."

"I told you when BG and I won the contract. I told you about the dinner." His anger spilled over the telephone.

"You told me. You never asked and I didn't agree. It's so like you to think things are settled. Well, not so, obviously. I'm sorry!"

The conversation ended with two receivers going down with a bang.

Nothing improved over the course of the day. At four-thirty, the senior auditor on the Fruiers account called Teal from the building's lobby.

"I have our work paper trunk in the garage, but the guard tells me the freight elevator is tied up for hours carrying partitions to forty-one. He won't let me use a passenger elevator. Any suggestions?"

"Are they enforcing that stupid rule?" Teal didn't need this today.

"No argument from me, but the guard here doesn't agree."

"Okay. I'll go talk to our office manager. But I bet even money it will be at least an hour before the trunk is up here."

"I'll pass on that bet. Good luck." The staff was resigned to his fate as keeper of the papers.

"I'll be there with a dolly as soon as I sort things out," Teal said.

One hour and ten minutes later, Teal and the senior auditor wheeled the trunk into the one passenger elevator that could be specially keyed to open in the garage.

The construction crew using the freight elevator stopped their work to help. Lots of "Hey, Bert, she's too smart for you" and "Look out, Tina, that kid in a suit is sure ta be a haart breaker" bantered about, but since Bert and Tina had interrupted a coffee break and heated exchange—Teal heard Bert say, "Well, he deserved to be fired. Losing his key in September was just the start of what he done" before he got up—she was particularly tolerant and grateful.

At the other end she broke a fingernail and banged a hole in her hose as she wrestled the trunk off the dolly.

The significance of Bert and Tina's argument struck her in her office. The elevators could be controlled by a special key! She hurried back down to the garage to catch Bert and Tina. They were loading the last of the partitions, about done.

"You guys saved us earlier, thanks. Look, I have this stupid bet with a friend and hoped you could help. Back in the fall, say September, could anyone have exited the elevator at forty-one without being seen by your crew?"

"Off at forty-one in the fall?" Bert asked. He and Tina exchanged looks. This-woman-is-crazy looks.

"Floor was ripped open for wiring, but sure, the elevator made the stop. Unless you jumped right back on, we'd have noticed you weren't crew. No hiding that,"

Tina said. She pointed to Teal's stiletto heels and laughed. "Cripplers."

"You're right," Teal agreed. "But couldn't I have made it at lunch time, maybe between one and two, if I headed straight for the fire stairs?"

"Well, then you'd a been an A1 nuts-o. Forty-one floors does worse than your shoes to cripple the pins. Fire doors prevent you from exiting before you get here to the garage. But sure, maybe with the crew at lunch." Bert looked at her like she was the nuts-o one.

"This dumb bet." Teal shrugged like it meant nothing. "You've helped again. Thanks."

Malley responded less enthusiastically when she called him. "I get how it could have happened, but why? The guy died of complications from his allergy and a crummy heart. Sure it's no f-f-fun to ride around with a corpse, but why get off before the lobby?"

"Panic. Panic if that person didn't know how to help. Or to avoid the questions. If that fired construction guy's key was still in the control panel, it would make it easy to lock out the other stops. Averill told me Konstat ran into someone just before he left the club. That's who you want."

"Thanks for pointing that out to me," Dan said in a voice devoid of expression. "I'll think about it."

Teal suspected the thought wouldn't take long.

Kathy brought in more messages that did nothing to improve Teal's spirits: BiMedics' chief executive officer needed a return call ASAP, and the partner on the account wanted her to stop by his office.

Certain days Teal enjoyed her profession and certain days were . . . like today. She tried to take a calm, centering breath, but the meditation did not come. Kathy's delivery of peppermint tea and two chocolate chip cookies from the bakery across the street cheered her more successfully.

"Angel of mercy," Teal said. "Something is up with BiMedics, and I can tell our week isn't going to be any fun."

"Hey, I can play once you're away. We'll get you on your Friday flight. With Averill, uh?" Kathy grinned.

"Yes, with Averill. And stop smirking."

Teal and the partner together called BiMedics' CEO. Teal understood the pecking order. And she had been right; it was going to be a tough week.

Last fall when BiMedics put its initial public offering on hold, Teal knew it would come to life in the spring. And spring's improved stock market did resurrect the IPO. The CEO wanted to alert Clayborne Whittier to the Securities and Exchange Commission's question on certain accounting policies disclosed in the preliminary prospectus. Another potential delay, Teal thought, and frowned.

Everyone understood time cost money in a volatile market. Everyone concurred the SEC staff had misunderstood the facts, but steps needed to be taken. Teal and the partner planned to consult Clayborne Whittier's national SEC practice and help the company craft a response. They hoped to clear the matter in a telephone conference to keep to the Wednesday target for issuing public stock.

Teal crossed her fingers for BiMedics to have good luck and let her make the Friday plane.

The company's luck ran out during the telephone call among BiMedics, Clayborne Whittier and the SEC.

Management described the transactions behind the disputed accounting; then the Clayborne Whittier partner detailed a complex analogy in an effort to illuminate the nuances in their discussion. Unfortunately, he used a most condescending tone. The young SEC staffer brought swift retribution.

"That sounds very nice," the SEC staff said, "but I can't see it bears on the issue at hand. I'll talk it over with the chief accountant and get back to you."

In other words, "I'm bouncing it up to my boss and you can wait until we're good and ready."

Teal spoke up in the stunned pause.

"Would you hold a second?" She turned to the CEO. "There isn't a chance of making it Wednesday, but maybe next Monday if we fly down to Washington to meet with the chief accountant this week." She turned to the partner. "Maybe I should make an example using BiMedics data. The SEC fellow couldn't grasp your more conceptual framework."

Teal dropped candor for diplomacy. The partner had sounded like an ass, but the success of her proposal was more important. Once in a while, she remembered to use tact. And it worked despite everyone's grousing.

The CEO hated the delay. The partner was offended by Teal's usurpation of his role as educator. The SEC staff feared appearing ignorant in front of his boss. Teal offered to review her presentation with him alone, first, and everyone agreed to the meeting.

Thursday, midway through her illustration to support BiMedics' accounting, Teal realized that the SEC staff was bright. Neither stupidity nor resistance had motivated his refusal to agree with the company. He was simply unable to lay aside opinions formed in dealing with other companies. Teal changed her approach immediately.

The SEC reversed their objection, leaving the offering free to proceed. Honesty made Teal reluctant to accept all the credit.

"Actually, my tenth grade science teacher really won the day," she confessed to the CEO. "He wrote DBATCTO on the board every day. 'Don't be afraid to challenge the obvious.' I realized the obvious—the terms used—had blinded the SEC. When the fixation broke, understanding came easily. Anyway, it's done!"

Friday morning, Teal dictated two memoranda to close the file and reviewed the most recent prospectus when it arrived from the printer's. The partner offered to perform Sunday evening's final review. She could leave for California.

Teal skimmed her last memorandum as Kathy waited.

Teal nodded. "I'll write a cover note, and you can send this to the partner. You've been great."

Teal fished a pen from her drawer and hit the ballpoint's top. Nothing. Then she saw the cap. She pulled it off and pressed again. Liquid sprayed across her desk.

Teal and Kathy stared. No ballpoint worked like this. Like an injection pen.

"Konstat's adrenaline! I never realized what I'd picked up! Poor bastard, he had his antidote all along," Teal

204

said. "Look, can you give this to Dan? I'll miss my plane if I call now."

"No problem, Teal. Write your note and run."

Thinking about the stock market helped her to forget the unused adrenaline. What it meant. Unnecessary death.

Stocks almost never went public on a Friday, just as companies seldom released earnings on the last day of the week. Friday signalled "bad news." Well, BiMedics would do fine on Monday, Teal decided, grateful to old DBATCTO. It had saved her trip. Then the next thought clicked.

The obvious had fooled her with the injection pen.

The devise resembled an ordinary pen, a convenience to insulin-dependent diabetics and those, like Konstat, who needed a dose of adrenaline. The revolution rested in the design, not the medicine. The pen was discrete, not like something used by a junkie. It worked. Teal never questioned that she found a ballpoint pen in the elevator.

Had the obvious blinded her in the University Savings, William Carroll, old man, Mark Konstat equation?

She raised the possibility with Averill on the way to the airport.

"I'm so frustrated I can't get further than the old man's designs on the bank. University Savings is such an obvious connection. But did it kill William Carroll? Contribute to your friend Mark Konstat's death?" Teal rubbed her head, and wisps of chestnut hair curled from her chignon.

She imagined the pen lodging unused by the elevator

door. The guard's cursory search didn't find it, and she removed it before the police inspected the car again. But she couldn't burden Averill with that.

"We may never know, Teal. Leave it to the police; it's their job," Averill advised.

"They aren't getting anywhere," she objected.

"Well, you are." He chuckled. "The Top of the Mark, cable cars and, once the deal is done, Carmel to Big Sur. We're going miles away from here, and you're still chasing a connection to that old man. If he finds out, you could be in trouble. Let it go, Teal, for me."

The cab passed through the tunnel, and Logan Airport came into view.

"You're right. The obvious is to leave everything to the police. And face it, William Carroll had as much connection to Climb as the bank."

With that, she dismissed the conundrum.

Chapter Twenty-three

Teal sat on a bench in the small park between the Union Pacific Club and Grace Cathedral. The morning's soft fog had burned off to leave the intense butter yellow of sun and liquid blue of California sky. Such were the differences from Boston: the steep grade of the hills, the pastel brick, the embrace of ocean and bay. Water surprised so many views of the horizon on her morning walks.

Today she had headed down Mason to Lombard with its tight switchbacks and verdant brilliant plantings. The ascent had been so vertical that periodic intervals of steps served as the sidewalk. Teal descended on Hyde to take a cappucino and biscotti amid the bustle of Ghirardelli Square. Like any tourist, she rode the cable car back up Nob Hill.

Now she relaxed in the sun. Children chalked careful games of hop scotch across the walkways cutting through the park. Double jump ropes slapped puffs of dust from the ground while a melody of giggles rose and ebbed and rose again. Nannies chatted among themselves and eyed their charges from the safety of a painted wooden bench. Now one, now another shifted up to calm a squabble. More often, the voices of happy children punctuated the quiet of the day.

Teal's thoughts meandered, lulled by the warmth and calm. An intermittent breeze teased a chill across the air. She sighed, content to accept the benevolence of peace. No deadlines or clients disrupted her stay, and the pressures of the last week had begun to fade. Bye-bye BiMedics. There remained only one worry.

She repositioned herself on the rigid bench. Should she have said something to Malley? In any event, she hadn't. Still, she was sure her cab had been followed the night she met the BiMedics group to proof the first-draft prospectus at a printshop in South Boston. The location beside the Fort Point Channel gave her tail no place to hide.

Later she laughed at herself, until Francesca admitted a similar suspicion.

Then there was Friday. Standing beside Averill at the gate check-in for their flight, Teal caught a glimpse of a person much like Shag, powerfully muscled and dark. The man never turned full face to her, and when he boarded for Detroit, not California, she sighed with relief.

The San Francisco plane prepared for take-off jammed with quiet executives and excited families. Teal squinted at everybody on board until she thought she'd go mad. Finally, the plane lifted clear of Logan and her fears on the ground.

Today, Boston's apprehensions seemed very far away. California, home to her years in graduate school, represented safety and touched, she admitted, some quite un-New England corner of her soul—the part that had

208

stopped this morning to read the sign advertising tarot card advice. The part that had rung the bell and walked on up.

The reader, a blond and freckled twenty-five, did her consulting in a bright and airy studio. Only a mosaic of crystals arranged on a low table referred to the New Age. Teal shuffled and cut the lavish, illustrated cards as instructed. The reader dealt, her face bright with concentration.

"Oh, my. You're wrestling with the classical dilemmas, aren't you? Freud's love and work, what we need to keep us going. Don't worry the work part—this isn't the time—and you're going to do fine. Pentacles enough to assure financial security. You can take care of yourself in the material world."

The reader nodded. She pursed her lips. Teal expected the next word to be "ah." The next word was "love".

"Love. Well, yes—love. There's your conflict, the darkness and the light. Both princes in opposition, see, with you in the middle." She pointed with pink, buffed nails. "You're the fulcrum on the seesaw. You must be careful! Strong, possessive forces inhabit the darkness."

Now her finger tapped a gray and aging king. "You've crossed someone a good deal more powerful than you. You threaten to interfere with his own flirt with immortality. His anger is very dangerous—be vigilant, my friend."

Other revelations followed. Teal would travel a great distance. She would fail a friend in need and cause a child to challenge. Right now, however, she must enjoy California as a balm to her spirit. She must trust understanding to come.

Teal mused over her "twenty-dollar/thirty-minute"

consultation in the peace of the park. Her flirt with the tarot contained a hopeful curiosity. At a minimum, the twenty dollars bought an unapologetic discussion of self with a willing, if paid, partner. Not such a bad exchange.

Averill, her light prince, but the dark came harder. She couldn't imagine Hunt a threat, even with his black hair and blacker disposition. He had been dismayed and hurt by the change in their relationship. Could that make him the other prince? Teal shrugged. Hunt was as close as she could come.

The king fit the old man, but "be vigilant" offered no helpful insight.

Maybe she had yet to meet the dark prince, Teal decided. She wanted to remove that cloud from Hunt. No longer lover, he was part of the fabric woven through years of her life. No, she didn't want him to be the dark. She laughed aloud to realize California had inspired her to give such credence to a tarot reading.

Time to return to the hotel, she thought, and respond to any messages before dinner. Averill, unavailable during each of the past three days, gave their evenings the luster of a date. Each night he asked for the details of her renewed affair with the city by the bay while they evaluated the progress of his day spent wooing Simon Brown.

Averill, her light prince indeed, Teal concluded, and stirred with yearning and desire. No dead bodies, no old man and none of her defenses against emotional entanglement followed her here. California offered infinite possibility.

Averill planned to present Climb's funding request to the Simon Brown venture partners tomorrow. The final decision would free Teal and Averill to head south. The negotiation had moved from pleasant curiosity to serious discussion through the weekend meetings arranged by Averill's friend, and Teal was grateful. She wanted her time alone with Averill.

The hour chimed from Grace Cathedral's towers as Teal made herself depart the park.

The lobby of the Mark Hopkins embraced her, dim and cool. An energetic desk clerk called out to Teal and handed over messages from Kathy and Francesca. Teal dialed her secretary first.

"Hi, Kath. No disaster with BiMedics or Fruiers? Say no—I couldn't bear the thought of returning early."

Teal balanced on the plush arm of an overstuffed chair and gazed out the sixteenth-floor window past the Fairmont Hotel and down Mason Street to a tease of blue at the bottom. San Francisco Bay. No, she couldn't stand the thought of leaving California one minute prematurely.

"Nope, just good news. BiMedics went on the opening of the market, and everyone is happy with the price. Fruiers' controller called, but spoke to the senior when I said you were out for the week. There's only one sort of bad thing: Dan told me to tell you the *Globe* reported someone is buying University Savings at depressed prices. He wants you to be careful."

"That's what my tarot reader advised," Teal confided.

"Tarot?"

Teal could imagine her secretary rolling her green eyes.

"It's the Californian in me," Teal said.

"I don't think I'll share this with Dan." Kathy stopped laughing. "You were right; the pen-thing held adrenaline. The police lifted your prints and Konstat's and a bunch of smudges. The only surprise is the engraving they found on the thing. 'Beowulf.' Dan wondered if you had any idea of what that's about?"

Damn. Teal realized she never thought to mention Konstat's computer game to Dan. She explained what she knew to Kathy including the history of his computer game playing at the *Alt*. Most of Konstat's colleagues knew of his fantasy persona.

"Tell Dan to call Francesca for more," Teal suggested.

"I'll tell him. Nothing else is going on here, so you can enjoy your break from the madness. Honestly, Teal, tarot?" Kathy was laughing again.

"Hey, what can I say?" Teal said and hung up, grinning herself.

She dialed the second number to get a machine's answer on the fifth ring.

"Spill all after the beep." B-e-e-p.

"Hi, Francesca. Greetings from the sunny coast. Right now I'm looking at the building Patty Hearst is rumored to have hidden in. It's across from the side window of our suite. Pretty swank fugitive to live at the top of Nob Hill. Oh, well. I'm returning your call. I can—"

"Check out the rental rate for me. We may want to move in," Francesca's voice broke on. "I'm screening my calls."

"Because you're worried?" Teal didn't have to ask.

"No, for practice—I think the article is going in next week's *Alt*. An unprecedented record for my career. The editors on high consider it a tribute to Mark, but I'm getting worried. Maybe. Our old man isn't going to like being found out so publicly. Not our Mr. Wash The Past Clean with the new hygiene of legit money."

Francesca didn't sound her blithe self. Apprehension flushed through Teal. She squashed it down.

"Yeah, but he'll be too busy worrying about his image and disproving the allegations to bother with us."

"I'm just worried a draft will leak to him early. No number of alleges will mean anything then," Francesca said.

Teal passed on Malley's admonition to be careful along with the tarot's be vigilant. She heard Francesca's snort.

"Easy for you to say from three thousand miles away. I'm at my temporary desk right here in the middle of the paper's floor. Think I'm not feeling like a sitting duck? So, come on, what else did your cards say?" Francesca asked.

Teal ran through light and dark princes with the rest of the tarot reading.

"I don't know, Teal. 'A child will challenge'? You paid real money to hear that?" Francesca started to laugh. "Well, at least it's a break from real life. Stay out of trouble; I plan to."

"I will," Teal agreed. She smiled as she replaced the receiver. There was trouble and trouble.

Dressing was easy, the decisions having been made on Friday when she packed. She passed the time leafing through the presentation materials Averill had assembled for the Simon Brown partners.

A page of ratio analysis, a business plan detailing the

proposal for new stores and the five-year projection interested her most.

She liked the graph depicting growth. Averill's New York store tracked a phenomenal success. No wonder Climb wanted to extend the concept beyond the one store. High-tech clothing for high income and high status people, that's how she described the market. New York's profit said Averill had hit right on the target.

She skimmed the leases and debt agreements. The Bank of Boston rate matched the market. Not bad interest for a small company.

She set the financials aside without a glance because she had seen them before. The management letter finally issued by the auditors was an improvement over the draft George had showed her in Stowe. An attack of professional rivalry made her murmur, "silly Teal." Climb could never be a client while her relationship with Averill presented a conflict of interest. The alternative wasn't what she wanted under any circumstance, not even if Climb had been many times its size, had guaranteed her professional success. No.

She set the papers aside. The ringing telephone caught her at the door.

"Mr. Cunningham, please."

"I'm afraid he's not in. I can take your message," Teal said.

She pushed across the Climb documents on the cluttered desk. One page twisted on another's paper clip. She glanced down as she pulled it straight and saw a loan signature page with three names: Averill Morss Cunningham, George Henderson, Nicholas Jason White.

"You there?" the disembodied voice asked.

"Sorry, yes." Teal found a pad. "Go ahead."

"Ask him to call me. I'm manager in New York. I can't locate the Goretex wind shells listed on an invoice I found in his top desk drawer. No big deal, but I'm nervous with the Simon Brown visit. Also, the bank called. He should get back to them by next week—I said he was out until then, but they'd be happier with sooner. That's it."

Dinner was delicious.

"What do you think of Climb's prospects with the venture suits?" Teal asked after Averill recounted the progress of his day.

He flipped his palm up and back around.

"Hard to say. My friend is excited about Climb, and she'd like to bring us in; but her partners? She doesn't know yet. Climb's data should impress them, and I expect the store visits will clinch the deal."

"Store visits?" Teal's hopes sank. Was this the end of their California week?

"Boston and New York. Nick says he's ready. No change to our plans." Averill winked.

The tension drained from Teal's face. "It's smart to visit. I always learn more about a client at their facility. Reading stacks of documents doesn't quite do it. Should you be there?"

Teal wanted to hear another no, but she would make herself understand.

"No. Nick promises everything is under control."

Teal about hugged Averill at the table.

"Speaking of Nick," she said. "Is he a Nicholas Jason?"

215

"I'm not sure I know. Everyone uses Nick." Averill laughed. "Why ask?"

"Francesca says Mark Konstat played one of those complex computer games against an opponent named Jason. I saw Nick's full name today and think the middle name was Jason. It's just that if Nick knew Mark, then you both lost three friends this year. Konstat, Carroll and George—that's pretty awful."

The sounds of others diners filled their silence.

"Maybe Nick did," Averill said slowly. "No, he would have said something when . . . well, when Mark died. Nick is a fanatic about computers and computer games. I guess that was true of Mark, too."

"You're probably right. Nick said he'd never met Konstat at the Henderson's party, so forget my question. I want to banish thoughts of Konstat and all of them from my head. This is supposed to be a vacation!"

Teal was surprised at how much the answer about Nick had lightened her heart. Nick was Averill's surviving partner. She didn't want him to be Konstat's Jason; it could complicate things.

Averill lifted her left hand and stroked each finger. "Vacation, time with you—exactly what the doctor ordered."

He held her hand a moment longer. The conversation took up with their plans for Carmel.

"We can drive down tomorrow evening. Simon Brown will have a decision by then. I'll see if there's anything more I should do about their trip. Then, the rest of the week—" Averill looked into her eyes. "The rest of the week is as important to my life as the deal. More important."

Teal leaned across the white linen to kiss his cheek.

216

A few months ago she had been afraid to acknowledge her feelings. Now she was afraid to leave them unclear. Carmel came in good time.

"Actually, you do have at least one more thing to do. Your New York store manager called with questions about some shirts in your inventory he can't find. And you are supposed to call the bank."

Teal grinned at Averill's flash of irritation. "Do you think something as unimportant as inventory can ruin our trip?"

Chapter Twenty-four

They left for Carmel at two.

Climb On Up had been the first item on the Simon Brown agenda that morning, and Averill returned to the hotel euphoric. The group approved the equity Nick and he sought. There was an additional benefit in doing business with an old friend: Simon Brown would shorten their normal inspection of the company's operations as he had promised Nick.

Teal was happy to pack while Averill called New York to resolve the issue of the Goretex shells. A disputed invoice—that sounded familiar to Teal. Averill had refused the late shipment, something most of her clients would do. Then she stopped listening to wait, impatient, by the door.

Each mile shed their concerns, like a snake its skin, as Teal and Averill headed for Carmel.

First they wound through San Francisco's Presidio, the splendid acreage curving into the bay where public ownership gave access to the wild and rolling terrain.

Daly City, Pacifica and all the over building that represented the worst legacy of the California boom followed. Miles of tract houses, cheek by jowl, scarred the land where banks of parsley, fields of artichoke and dust brown hills once lay. San Gregorio came like a gift, the beach empty of all but sea gulls and wind, and cows along the interior road where they turned for gasoline. The hills nosed up dark and cool from the ocean. In Capitola, they stopped for ice cream.

The funky, tatty summer town barely had opened for the season. The tiny houses across the river waited, sealed closed, and half the main street stood empty. Dogs leapt for joy at frisbees tossed along the beach. A small boy burst into tears when his ice cream cone plunged to the sand. Teal moved a step back and into someone with a camera.

"Oh, please, excuse me," Teal said.

She pulled herself into balance. The man did nothing to acknowledge her apology. Doubt crawled up Teal's spine as her face, tiny and distorted, reflected back from black glasses. Something familiar in his stance caught her eye, and she had the chill impression she had seen him before. Wind tugged at his jacket, and Teal saw that what she had felt as a camera was the butt of a gun.

"Averill, we should go if we want to stop in Monterey," she prompted.

Averill turned from watching a teenaged boy converse with his mother.

"We'll talk to our children as they grow," he said.

"Of course we will. What made you say that?" Teal propelled them toward the car.

Averill stopped to point. "That boy. My father told me a story about his trip to San Francisco at thirteen.

He ate breakfast at a table all his own—the Victorian convention I suppose—and every morning my grandfather instructed the waiter to deliver the newspaper to the 'young gentleman over there.' Grandfather tipped well, no doubt. He took noblesse oblige to mean tip with abandon. The thing is, Father never acted any more at ease with me. I think he never knew how.'' Averill's voice caught. "You'll help me, won't you, Teal? I may not be much good at it.''

Teal heard a yearning that in all his tales of Choate and growing up, Averill had never expressed like this. His story touched her with its intimacy, and the cut of his profile, outlined against the sky, brought a surge of joy to her mind. Apprehension and love had colored their trip. Nothing was entirely casual about this California visit.

Finally they traversed the flat fields of greening vegetation tilled between the ocean and the road. At the turnoff for Salinas, they bent right to Monterey. The aquarium immersed them in an aquatic world of undulating kelp beds, surging tides, playing sea otters and innumerable species of Pacific fish. They ordered chicken at the restaurant and left satisfied.

Averill navigated the curves of the scenic Seventeen Mile Drive where he pulled them from the road to watch the sun lower over Pebble Beach in streaks of pink and gold. A sign marked the boundary with Carmel. Check-in at Lobos Lodge went quickly. Afterward, in their room, cheese and wine and crackers sufficed before they edged into bed. Everything that followed reaffirmed the vacation's purpose.

* * *

Teal hesitated at the dead end of Ocean Avenue and lifted each foot in place without a break. She considered the sweep of beach. The white sand shimmered in the early morning pallor, but the wind cut up the slope, damp and cold. She smiled at the sight of teenage surfers wading into the distant breakers. A few couples, heads tilted together, walked the soft sand. More serious runners than she beat across the hard pack where water overlapped land before it drew back. Teal zipped her sweatshirt closed and started a lope.

She enjoyed the thrust of her legs pounding the earth and the sweat beginning to bead and tickle her brow. Physical and emotional observation began to mix, Averill and California churning through her mind.

Each awed her. California, where nothing came in human scale, and Averill, the man who promised to liberate her most human emotions. She had allowed the patrician Bostonian to draw her closer as he trusted and loved her more, his own caution as seductive as a caress. She may have allowed Clayborne Whittier to consume her life, but no more. This week she welcomed commitment of a different sort.

Such a commitment never fit Hunt. "Why ruin a great relationship with marriage," they had joked if pressed by the intrusive and rude. Hunt suited best as a friend. Averill, different from the start, was a man to love, perhaps to marry. Their attraction had the purity of a natural force.

Like the tide—Teal jumped as a wave rolled across her careless feet. Even a tide could extract a price. Spindrift curved across her cheeks. She reversed her direction to head back, the crust of wet sand weighing each step.

She hadn't done nearly her normal four miles, but fighting the constant breeze made her cold and a little tired. Averill should be up and out of the shower by now, and she was hungry. She turned for a last look at the blinding sapphire water edging up the pearl-bright sand.

A flash of metal and movement beside a wind-tortured tree caught her attention. Teal blinked sun blindness from her eyes. Surely not the man from Capitola? He shifted from her stare. Perhaps she was crazy; but her heart clattered in terror, and she jerked her legs into motion. The steep grade brought her, sweating and breathless, to the lodge.

Teal panted, her fear quiet, then opened the door to step across the entry. Averill's voice sounded from the living room. A decorative arch hid the rest of him from her view.

". . . not meant to slight you, Steve," Averill said.

Teal suspected the Steve-person would be unaware of Averill's undertone of irritation. She wished Averill would finish the discussion. She felt the return of her fears and wanted his attention all the more. They were irrational, she reminded herself as the conversation continued. She hesitated, half in and half out, unwilling to interrupt.

"I can't say enough how much I appreciated you fellows; this just had to be an equity deal," Averill said.

Teal started toward the living room as he paused, wet sneakers dangling from her hand, but Averill resumed speaking.

"Your network's damned good. We thought we'd managed a quiet search. George came as such a terrible shock, and we needed to strike a deal with his widow before the vultures started to circle. Not that you're a vulture."

Chuckles interrupted the dialogue in a form of male bonding. Teal hated the sound of gender camaraderie that excluded her when it came up in business. But this had nothing to do with her, was nothing of the sort.

"No." Now Averill sounded adamant. "Borrowing to replace his equity wasn't right. That's why I didn't call."

Teal heard him pace the length of the cord.

"Yes. We got what we needed, but I am flattered by the bank's offer. The next time we want something, you know you'll be the first person I call." That same chuckle punctuated the last statement.

Teal found Averill's boys-will-be-boys laugh irksome.

"Steve, you've made doing business with the Bank of New York easy. I couldn't ask for . . ."

Teal's sense of propriety caught up with her. She looked like an eavesdropper. Her earlier panic had subsided, and she didn't need to hear another burst of male guffaws. She decided to slip outside until Averill was off.

The small garden, vivid with spring bloom, lay hidden from public view. Teal followed the path from their room. Morning sun settled on her back, clear and warm. Five minutes would give him time enough before her return.

She turned her thoughts to the unemotional issues of business. That world could be ordered and arranged. The memory of the strange man retreated as she considered Climb and the ramification of a partner's death.

Averill and Nick had been wise to seek equity to purchase the Henderson stock. Debt would have burdened their future. Teal was surprised any bank even considered assuming such risk. Climb's balance sheet already showed high leverage. Bank of Boston prided itself on supporting New England, but imposed tough limits on local businesses. Climb could hardly qualify for additional credit.

A fleeting observation poised on the edge of her conscious mind. Repayment requirements brought thoughts of Shag. But she was safe, she reminded herself. A door opened across the yard, and a woman came out.

Teal watched elephants dance across the woman's chest. "The Big Apple Circus" graced the bottom of the tee shirt. Teal smiled in recognition. She liked that circus and New York.

Now something new nibbled into her thoughts: Averill had said "Bank of New York" in the telephone conversation, not "Bank of Boston." Maybe she heard wrong.

But any bank's interest was odd. And so was a bank officer calling a company's vice president of marketing and not the officer responsible for financial transactions. Her contemplation circled around to Nick.

Nick had known William Carroll as a friend and a member of his company's board. Nick had started the business with George Henderson, a friend and a partner. There was even some evidence Nick had known Konstat despite his denial. A Jason had fought with Konstat's Beowulf in electronic bleeps fired over modems.

Nicholas Jason White?

Big deal, Teal decided. Konstat probably had any number of friends. Say, for example, Averill. But Averill, unlike Nick, was not in the company position where CPA's most worried about embezzlers.

Great, and now her imagination tagged Nick a thief and murderer! She had questioned this "obvious" quite enough. Nick White hadn't done a thing. *That I know of* crept into her brain.

"Forget it!" she about shouted.

She swung her sneakers over a bed of red flowers and knocked them hard together. Dry sand sparkled and drifted across the crimson petals like freckles of light.

This time, she entered with a noisy "Hi."

The word sank in the empty suite.

Teal walked from the table to the desk to the night-stand looking for a note. Nothing but the pad beside the telephone with a doodle: "50k" and "BNY" linked with entwined lines. Her habits ran to sketches of lanky dogs. She tore the page free and slipped it into her pocket automatically, as though she'd been caught.

She stripped and stepped into the shower. As the shampoo lathered up her head and snaked toward her closed eyes, the terror hit. Blind with soap and deaf with the water's thunder, Teal imagined Shag drawing back the curtain and raising the knife. Why had she ever seen *Psycho?* Fear puckered her skin. She jerked the water off, still slick with soap, and stood paralyzed.

Averill materialized out of the mist with a towel.

"Berries, tea and croissants await. And what a beautiful day! Glorious weather for whatever our hearts desire!" he said as he enfolded her within his arms.

"I'm achieving my objectives for this week one by one." Averill looked smug.

"And just what may they be?" Teal licked a crushed San Gregorio strawberry from her finger.

"Securing my company's future. And that's done for all intents and purposes. Climb is about to take off, Teal. The expansion will be a smashing success. Who knows what comes next—but we won't be viewed as a little regional specialty store anymore." Averill grinned. "The next objectives, you wonder? Since I've secured Climb's future, I want to secure ours. That's the real business of the week. Us."

Teal loved his confidence. Well, he should be confident. She certainly wanted to secure their future. The ghosts haunting her morning seemed silly. Averill had done an expert job with Simon Brown and with all his guidance to Nick on the buy out. Lingering curiosity prompted her next question.

"Did Nick think about borrowing to finance the acquisition of Nancy's shares?" Teal asked.

Averill's bemused expression made her grin. He raised his hands in mock horror.

"I talk of our future, and you worry about the company borrowing? All right, curiosity cat. No. Neither of us for a minute. Climb hasn't the capacity, and this Simon Brown relationship should work out well for all of us."

"Bank of Boston wasn't disappointed?" Teal asked.

It was a little pry, just to see if he'd tell. That's what she told herself. She couldn't admit she wondered about his partner, about Nick.

"Lord no. Nick assures me our sole institutional lender is very happy at the current level of debt. No more could come from them, and they won't permit us to borrow elsewhere. Simon Brown's equity is fine."

"No other bank has solicited Climb to become a client?"

"No other bank knows us, Teal. We need equity, not debt, remember. A capable lender would see that in a minute."

Teal opened her mouth to ask about the Bank of New York.

"What is all this—already bored with pursuing our personal interests?" Averill leaned his mouth to her lips.

Teal transformed words into kisses. Color fired her cheeks. Snooping was not an act of intimacy.

As Averill proposed activities for the week, Teal forgot about Nick. This was the relevant discussion. Breakfast ended with more kisses and a jolt back to reality.

"Nick comes out Friday to sign the deal. He's bringing Sara," Averill said.

"Great." Teal made the smallest of faces and left Averill to clear the table.

Before she balled her running shorts into the laundry bag, Teal retrieved the doodle. She considered it for a moment before she dropped it in the trash. Averill had his reasons to forget the Bank of New York, and perhaps so should she.

Chapter Twenty-Five

Dan Malley did not want to be riding the elevator to the Ivy Club. Surely Teal was wrong to believe someone had accompanied Konstat's final descent. Poor fool, fumbling his fancy injection pen. The fingerprint evidence showed he had neglected to draw off the top. No time, Dan supposed.

Teal's theory was not the true annoyance. Dan's greater fear was a renewal of his own hope. Senior detectives tagged him a cop who did not know when to let go, but they misunderstood. Dan considered every clue to present the possibility of finding the truth. Irony was, he had garnered his reputation for delays in record time, as well as for the wrong reason.

The Konstat case had sent him after every lead. He chased down each inconsistency and drove the lab crazy with the habits that distinguished his work and made it good. Good enough for senior detectives to lobby for him to be assigned their toughest cases. Good enough to support the rumor that when Dan Malley backed an arrest, the investigation might take forever, but the odds for conviction improved.

But Konstat had not turned out that way. Dan had failed his first important case. This goose chase only heightened the irritation because he could feel it start, his fool's hope.

Dan entered Ivy through the wrong door, as he had the time before. It sent him into a maze of service corridors. A lone staff swept breakfast crumbs from the tables in the dining room. She slowed her cloth to a stop.

"We're closed, sir. Service will open again for lunch at eleven," she said in a pleasing brogue.

"I'm looking for the maitre d'. Walter. Is he around?" Dan asked.

"I can check. You wait there." She pointed her dishrag to a comfortable room beyond the main hall. "Who should I say wants him?"

"Detective Malley, ma'am. Uh, Boston police."

Her clear, open Irish face slammed closed. She hurried backward to the kitchen. The poor woman probably suspected he was helping the Immigration Service, Dan realized. Boston harbored a raft of illegal Irish nationals. They worked construction and served in restaurants. They cleaned houses. They acquired licenses and social security numbers. All the papers you might want except what everyone wanted, a green card. Dan might claim the name Malley, but she wouldn't care. To her, he was the authorities.

Dan was almost surprised when Walter turned in the sitting room door.

"Detective Malley, may I ask you to come to my office? This is a club room," Walter said.

"Of course," Dan replied, chagrined with an Irish pride humiliated, the old Boston story. "I won't t-t-take

229

much of your time. This is a formality to follow up on our last talk. I was told Mr. Konstat met up with a friend, or friends, as he left the club the day he, uh, died. Would you remember that?''

"Met friends," Walter repeated. He settled at his desk. "Aside from Mr. Cunningham, you mean?''

"Yes.'' Dan inclined his head.

"No. Not in the dining room that I noticed. And I am sure I would have after all the attention to that day. Mr. Konstat and Mr. Cunningham left the dining room alone. Perhaps our coat check saw more.''

Walter tapped three buttons on his telephone and repeated Dan's question. After a few seconds, he wrote down three names.

"Here you are, sir.'' Walter handed the list to Dan. "Jose said they all ended up by his counter at the same time. You may speak with him on your way out. I would ask that you use discretion. We cannot upset either our staff or our members.''

"I understand. Thank you, sir,'' Dan said.

He hoped he sounded sensitive to Yankee sensibilities. *All in a day's job,* he'd heard the old-timer cops say often enough, *don't loose your shirt, Danny.*

He stopped at the coat check. Jose was full of information about Konstat's last day.

"I'm surprised you think you can recall who Mr. Konstat spoke to after all this time," Dan observed.

"Yes, sir, but after what happened to Mr. Konstat, I kind of couldn't forget anything about that day. It was strange from the start. Mr. Cunningham was in my line with the three members I told Walter about when a bicycle messenger pushed up to the counter. The guy was kind of older for the job, and he had a snake tattooed around his neck. Mr. Konstat was there.'' Jose pointed to the telephone cubicle across from his station.

Dan nodded encouragement.

"He was making a call to . . . to . . .'' Jose pulled a binder from his drawer and began to flip through the carbon pages. "Here. A Jason, no last name. I'd taken the call earlier. Mr. Konstat got the message when he stopped for his coat. He was dialing when the snake-man saw him. It was like the snake-man was surprised. The guy ripped open the booth and said something I couldn't hear, but Mr. Konstat became very upset.''

"What happened next?'' Dan asked.

The coat check shrugged. "Nothing. Mr. Konstat like tried to laugh it off, and the guy dropped his package with me and left. Remember I told you Mr. Konstat took a bunch of the chocolate covered nuts?''

Dan nodded.

"Well, that's when. It was like he was so mad he had to stuff his mouth with something. I don't think he tasted a thing. Would you like a chocolate mint, sir?''

"No thanks,'' Dan said. "Do you keep a package log?''

Jose checked his receiving records while Dan waited. He wondered if the messenger represented one more diversion from admitting that the case should be folded. Jose added a fourth entry to Dan's list—the name of the service behind the package delivery.

It took Dan two days to talk to every one of the three Ivy members, track down the name of the messenger and interview Mrs. Carroll again. He couldn't pursue the case full time, his schedule had filled with more recent and as senseless crimes, and for the brass, Konstat and Carroll had faded to yesterday's important case.

The three members gave stories that conformed to Dan's expectation. None was more than an acquaintance of either Konstat or Cunningham. None knew Carroll except by reputation. The information on the messenger turned out to be a different story.

He used his free time to pump iron—at the club where Shag worked. The messenger's rap sheet showed he regularly hired out to Shag's other employers. He enjoyed using his steroid-inflated muscles on flesh and bone. When his ex-wife filed an abuse suit, she exhibited the marks of his signature style. Nothing above the neck. Nothing below the knees.

Dan consulted a copy of Konstat's autopsy. Nothing above the neck. Nothing below the knees. The punk knew Konstat all right.

Mrs. Carroll tried to be helpful, but she was tired. She wanted the investigation to go away. She hated the memory of her husband's last, terrible week.

"He stood to lose his dream, Detective. Can you imagine how it feels to watch a man's emotional defeat? I never wanted him to run." She rubbed a weary hand to a haggard cheek. "You hope you can do good, and people respond by ripping every aspect of your life apart until you die from the exposure. Bill refused to drop out quietly. I guess someone didn't like that."

"Did your husband have things he wanted to hide?" Dan asked. He had asked Mrs. Carroll before. She had said no.

She dropped her eyes. "He was a careful man. Careful about the future and his past. I can't imagine he ever did anything to be ashamed of. Not even whatever it was about that loan.''

"What loan?" Dan leaned forward.

"I didn't tell you the last time? Surely—"

"Perhaps you'll tell me again," Dan prompted. This was the first he had heard of a loan from Mrs. Carroll.

"I don't know much. It was a business deal or something to do with that little company—you probably know it. Climb On Up? Bill sat on the board. Well, Nick White over there needed Bill's signature or used it or some such, and Bill got all upset. Ask Nick White," she suggested.

Dan tried. He made a string of calls, all unreturned by the next day. Finally, White's secretary gave him an answer for the delay.

"He has business in California. If it's urgent?" she said in a way that meant how urgent can it be.

"Yes," Dan replied. "No, not urgent."

"I will ask him to get back to you when he returns."

California. It brought Dan back to his search for the tattooed man and to Shag. Sure, Shag had agreed, everyone heard the rumor about a jerk-head journalist poking into private things.

"Does everyone include your friend with the tattoo?" Dan asked.

"Guy works out here? Probably." Shag shrugged.

Then Dan decided to squeeze a little harder. "Your friend around now?"

Shag shrugged.

"Parole board might have an interest in speaking with you. A few questions about—"

"He's outta the coast," Shag said.

"Business?" Dan asked, his eyes drilled to the punk.

"Maybe."

"Is he looking for Teal Stewart?" Dan didn't blink.

Shag shrugged less comfortably. "She's okay. She's not—he deals with me. Know what I mean?"

"Kathy, I want to talk to your boss," Dan said when she answered the telephone.

He wasn't alarmed, not yet. But his cop's instinct wondered if William Carroll had been on to something funny that Konstat's research first had turned up. Mark Konstat. William Carroll. University Savings. The old man. Dan realized he was sounding like Teal.

Kathy got back to him within the hour.

"They left the Mark Hopkins early, and she didn't give me an itinerary from there. She hates to let Clayborne Whittier come after her on a vacation. She only told me about the hotel because of her BiMedics offering. Should I try harder?" Kathy's voice betrayed concern.

Dan wasn't happy, himself. "I'm not sure."

"I know she's headed for Carmel and Big Sur, but no details. I could call the local tourist information lines and try the hotels—"

"No. I'll call the local police," Dan said.

"She's with someone," Kathy cautioned. "I'm not sure she'd be too happy to have the police—"

"She's not alone?" Dan asked. "This isn't business?"

"No." Kathy laughed. "She's with Mr. Right. But if you have to find her . . ."

Dan hugged the receiver between shoulder and chin.

234

He steepled his fingers. "With someone she should be fine. I guess."

He did not register his palms sliding together in a pose of silent prayer.

Chapter Twenty-six

The convertible had seemed a perfect choice—racy red, black top and only an additional thirty dollars on the week's confirmed rate. The "Sunshine Special" being promoted at the rental desk made no mention of the fog now chilling their legs, slipping behind their necks, obscuring the view. And what a view it was in the stretches where the air cleared, burned clean by the sun.

The Cabrillo Highway south from Carmel curved upward on a narrow shelf blasted from the side of the Santa Lucia mountains. Below the highway, the land dropped sharply to meet the Pacific. At the highest bends in the road, lingering fog curled around the blind turns and swirled in the dips and depressions ahead. Then every tail of mist lifted, and they realized the promise of the car.

Teal studied the narrow shoulder at her right, little more than a yard wide. The ocean slapped at the bottom of the precipice, restless and forceful. No more than a quarter of a mile ahead, the highway cut through a field of scrub and wild flowers where the land broadened into

236

a plain. There the air, still thick with damp, hazed a now more distant junction of continent and sea.

Averill drove with the happiness of a man challenged by the thrill of a curved road. Contentment relaxed his frame and burnished his thoughts to a comfortable glow. He enjoyed achieving his objectives, one by one. The blue box in his trouser pocket represented the next to be attained. Then only the living of it—the life squandered by his father—remained. Wealth and marriage would bring the true fulfillment of noblesse oblige, the responsibility of privilege, the mark of the godly.

He could envision them aging, as his parents had not, into a handsome, contented couple. Teal the doyenne of cultural charities, himself consulted on matters important to the state. The small box represented the future and all his anticipation. He was impatient to hear her say "yes."

Teal regarded the surroundings, eager to see Point Sur hung in gray, the brown of a dirt road cut into the hills, the cerulean sky. This week had transported her far from Boston and the questions that beset her there.

She turned to consider Averill's profile and his long, powerful frame.

He still sculled the Charles River each morning at five and retained the lean body of youth. Wind ruffled his blond hair, tousling the sober cut into anarchy. Something so appealed to her in the curve of his lips. Elegant, that was the word. She watched his fingers play, attentive against the wheel, as he responded to the nuances of the road. They could be so much to each other, she believed. Lovers with the intimacy of friends.

The disquiet nibbling at the edge of her consciousness

was no more than nerves. Love could seem a fearful thing, a threat to order and a life under control. But Averill? Averill represented unexpected joy. He entered her life and brought emancipation.

She leaned across the seat to lay a cheek against his shoulder. She heard his heartbeat resonate, deep, and slow. Settling back, her glance caught the rearview mirror. A Porsche was coming up hard.

"I don't think he can pass, Averill. Let's pull over when we have the chance," she said.

She turned back to look at the sports car, its tinted windows impenetrable as it hugged their tail. Averill accelerated to take the close, tight turns faster.

"Don't be silly," Teal said as she grinned. "This thing can't compete with a Porsche."

Teal's tease sounded sharp. She wanted the driver's seat. She would have jammed her foot to the gas pedal—just like him.

Now Averill flashed a smile. "Could your old Mercedes take him on?"

They crested the hill. A shallow turn-out lay two hundred yards beyond where the road began to drop.

"No," Teal admitted. "She's too much the dowager. Do let's stop."

The Porsche almost clipped their fender as they angled off the road. Relief calmed Teal's burst of nerves as the car surged past. They climbed out of the car, and she fished behind the seat for her camera.

"Stand there," she directed Averill.

He moved farther out the small point. No rail guarded the acute edge.

"Be careful," she cautioned.

"Indeed." Averill smiled.

Teal side-stepped right to frame the shot. Neither of them noticed the sudden stop of the Trans Am with a rental sticker, or the driver who climbed out.

Teal snapped the first picture. Automatic focus, f-stop and rewind whirred as the camera did the work. She raised her right leg and slid it back a foot. She raised her left—and collided with the man. The gravel rolled beneath her soles, and her balance faltered. Averill jerked forward to catch a forearm. The man grasped a hand. The men pulled her right as her own equilibrium failed.

"Lady—you better be careful."

Black sunglasses glared a humorless reflection of her face. The man let go. The movement flexed the tongue of the snake tattooed around his neck. Teal gasped. But surely his restraining hand had prevented a nasty, deadly fall. Averill stood by her, indifferent to the stranger.

"I'm terribly sorry," she offered, but the stocky man had turned his back.

He only paused a second in his return to his car. "You should be careful, lady. Get my meaning? Stay away from places you shouldn't go."

The Trans Am swerved onto the road. Like them, it headed south.

"He's a cheerful guy." Averill hugged Teal closer.

"I think he was in Capitola yesterday. Do you remember? On our ice cream stop?" Teal asked. "I don't think he likes me."

She considered the probability of bumping into him twice. Had he been on the beach in Carmel? That would make it three times. Too high for coincidence. This unpleasant thought rubbed against the day glorious with sun and love.

"I'll be happier when Francesca's article is in print. No point in the old man's threats then," Teal said.

"That Trans Am guy? Don't worry about him. The pebble dropped with Konstat's investigation. Your old man knows Konstat's questions started ripples nothing can stop. He has lawyers to keep him from getting caught. He doesn't need to endanger his reputation with a clown like that."

"Shows what you know about that world." Teal laughed, less than reassured.

"Your imagination is working overtime," Averill said before he kissed her furrowed brow.

Teal relaxed. Averill might be right, and anyway, how far could the old man reach? Not to California, surely. Coincidences happened.

Nepenthe's famous ambrosia burger came hot, and the separate order of french fries in a basket burned their fingers. Teal and Averill sat side by side at the rail, strangers to the right and left.

Yellow finches lifted from the trees which lined the hillside to steal food from their plates. One tried to plunder a french fry which left the bird too weighted to fly.

Nepenthe had opened in 1949 as the "home of the ambrosia burger." The years had added a history of gossip and California myth. The distinctive terraced stone-and-wood structure set on a hill and influenced by Frank Lloyd Wright gave amphitheater seating to nature's stage. Here, fantasy blurred reality.

Teal succumbed to a languor induced by heat and the

distant drone of traffic. Her mind drifted. it was coming together, she decided. She, too, was achieving her objectives, and Averill represented the most important one.

Her daydream faded as he shifted in his seat. A motion of hand to pocket caught her eye. He set a box no bigger than her palm between them. White satin ribbon obscured letters of black print. Teal could fill in the gaps. Tiffany & Co. She sat very still.

Averill embraced all of her with his eyes. "Will you marry me, Teal, my love?"

She lifted her mouth to meet his lips as some small anomaly tapped at her thoughts. The distraction was fleeting, no more than a nanosecond, a speck of inattention. Averill cupped her hands in his as he pulled back from the kiss. His gray eyes joined the gazes of everyone at the rail. Strangers repositioned their seats. Some stood to see.

The waitstaff hesitated as he thought the better of an interruption. Teal felt each second crystalize. Time became a distinct dimension, long and deep. Surely she wanted to say yes. Surely this was her objective realized.

Averill pressed the box against her palm. She smiled, old repression and new desire crossing in her heart.

"Nothing ever quite prepares one for this, does it?" she said.

She knew the only answer she could give then, and opened her mouth to speak, her wet blue eyes locked to his.

The couple beside her scraped back their stools. "Best wishes, dear, for a wonderful marriage." The older

241

woman patted Teal. "He looks a lovely husband. Good luck."

The man and woman moved past, arm in arm. Teal sat straighter and readied herself to begin again. She did not turn when someone claimed the empty spot to her left. Averill caressed her free hand as the other held to the box.

"I—"

A finger jabbed into her left shoulder. She turned on the defensive. Dead black sunglasses reflected the distant ocean.

"Can you pass the salt?" He smirked, and the neck tattoo stirred. "You just never know when we'll bump into each other."

He laughed and reached around her rigid body to the shaker, and, still laughing, he turned to his place.

"Let's get away from here, Averill." Tears glazed Teal's eyes.

"Of course, darling."

Averill gentled the box into his pocket and stood. The curious, with staring faces, averted their eyes. Others made a show of swiveling to the view. The man's sardonic chuckle followed Teal across the terrace as she escaped.

The turn for Pfeiffer Beach was little more than half a mile back.

A narrow dirt road plunged down Sycamore Canyon over the first mile, then flattened for the last. Few cars remained in the sandy lot. The trail to the beach skirted cypress, brush and grass. At the end, teenagers danced in front of a boombox.

Pfeiffer Creek pooled into a shallow, still lagoon before it met the tumult of surf. Spindrift drenched the air in sheets of fine mist. The wind could have ripped buttons out of buttonholes and swallowed their words in the din. Eroded rocks lifted from the waves offshore to form sea stacks marked by arches where the ocean surged through. Blowing sand stung Teal's bare legs.

They waded behind a line of boulders in the quiet of the lagoon. Teal tucked her filmy cotton skirt at her waist. Averill rolled his khakis to his knees. Still, rounding to the ocean's edge, water soaked cuff and hem.

Teal yelled to best the wind. "You asked a lovely question, Averill."

"And is that your prelude to an answer?" Averill drew her to him.

She understood his desire. "Prelude? Yes."

She held her eyes to his, bluer than either sky or sea. Averill steered her to the lee side of a tall rock. They settled on a shallow ledge.

Order versus disorder, Teal thought. Her legacy from the history of the Stewart family. She preferred to smooth the chaos of life. And death. She didn't want to dwell on the images of Konstat and Carroll and George, not now with Averill's question a celebration of order and life. But she had to know.

Nepenthe's funny little tap at her consciousness had matured to thought. Averill had given her the idea with his proposal. Marriage required an investment of loyalty in a partnership meant to last one's life. Life and death, loyalty and partnership—words as applicable to Climb. George and Nick and Averill, three partners committed to the company. And then the partnership reduced to two.

Averill, whom she loved. And Nick, whom she hardly knew.

"Averill, why didn't you tell me about the Bank of New York?" she asked.

Chapter Twenty-seven

Puzzlement widened Averill's eyes. "Whatever do you mean, Teal?"

"Just—why didn't you tell me you talked with the Bank of New York? They wanted to lend Climb money, didn't they? But you said Bank of Boston was the only bank to work with the company."

Averill drew his lips into a smile. "You overheard me on the phone this morning."

His statement was not a question, but she nodded.

"Steve's a classmate from Choate. We did some business a while ago; now he's after me to take Climb to the Bank of New York. The old school tie, you know. Maybe I'll convince Nick to agree some day. He hasn't yet, though." Averill shrugged.

Teal shifted off a spike of rock. Did she want to press Averill today of all days? But she wasn't comfortable letting the matter drop. No, it was something else. She couldn't.

"I saw the board resolution, Averill, in the papers I reviewed for Dan Malley. Carroll kept a copy of the resolution. It authorized your company to borrow from the Bank of New York. It was dated more than a year ago.''

The silence between them was not lost in the singing wind. Averill massaged his forehead before he lifted his eyes to hers.

''I'd forgotten. The board wanted to give us flexibility in financing the pilot. In the end, Nick stayed with the Bank of Boston. He wouldn't have used that resolution. Come on, Teal, what's really bothering you? Is my question so hard to answer?''

What was bothering her? she wondered. She studied Averill, ''Will you marry me?'' spinning in her brain to a tangle. She loved this man. Would she rather probe his conversation with a banker than respond to his marriage proposal? Was she that crazy? No!

If Climb's bank interested her this much, she could ask Nick when she got home.

Nicholas Jason White, vice president finance, keeper of the corporate books. That was her problem. Had Averill been fooled by his partner? Had Nick White fueled debt with debt to hide a crime of theft?

List all the banks, came the next anxious thought. List the players. University Savings. Mark Konstat. William Carroll. The old man. Bank of New York? George Henderson? Nick White?

Why not throw in Averill?

Teal laughed at herself until she howled. For a minute, uncomplicated yearning for Averill filled her heart. Averill offered the opportunity to choose love.

Her heart tore as her mind raced. Had Nick White deceived her lover and friend? Anger flushed her pink as her eyes glittered, wet and blue. She could not shed the discomfort.

"Humor me, Averill, please. Are you sure the resolution wasn't used to launch your New York store?" Teal asked.

Misappropriated funds could be hidden in manipulated accounts. And who would become suspicious when everyone's attention concentrated on New York's phenomenal results? Gross margins that exceeded the norm, sales per square foot double the competition's and positive cash flow from the beginning. But maybe someone had asked questions. Maybe Carroll. Maybe George.

"Teal, damn it—you're obsessed. Do you imagine I would hurt Climb to cover up for Nick? Is that what you think?" Averill's voice tensed. "Darling, the scare at Nepenthe has your imagination overstimulated."

He gathered Teal in his arms and laid his cheek against her head. She smelled salt air mix with sweat. She hadn't been—not thinking what he suggested, not about him. She slowed her breath and let the tension drain from her mind. Her meditation steadied to an even rhythm of inhalation and exhalation, her mantra merely "in" and "out."

An unexpected sort, in and out. In and out. Mark Konstat, William Carroll, George Henderson—in. The old man—out. Bank of New York—in. University Savings—out. Mark Konstat, William Carroll, George Henderson—each acquainted with Averill, lover and friend.

Was it his heartbeat drumming panic in her head? Her breath began to lose depth, the meditation failing.

Mark Konstat, William Carroll, George Henderson—each dead.

Averill's hand brushed over the back of her neck. His fingers circled to the hollow of her throat. Teal wrenched free from the embrace.

Confusion shadowed Averill's face. "Teal? What's wrong?"

He was up, holding her pinned against their stone bench. Outstretched arms held them awkwardly joined and as awkwardly apart. Wind-cut tears leaked from her eyes, or perhaps she was crying. She did not know. Averill drew her back to his shoulder.

Powerful emotions rattled her torso. Love. Fear. Hope. Yearning. Regret.

This man was her lover. This was Averill Morss Cunningham—Choate to Yale, Yale to Harvard Business School. No detours on his resume, no errors of omission. This was the Averill who had welcomed her into his life, introduced her to his ambitions, his dreams, his partners and his friends. This was not Averill the terrible.

The wind tears came faster now, her vision blurred with their sting. She shook from his embrace like someone waking from a summer's nap, logy with heat and sleep. He stood beside her, waiting out the storm.

"I've imagined unimaginable things." Teal ran her fingers through wind-snarled hair to lift the blowing strands from her face. "When you set your hands at my throat? I pulled away, afraid."

"Of what, Teal?" he asked.

"Of murder."

Teal burrowed against the soft texture of his sweater. The smell of Averill and the sea was perfume to her nose. She choked with a sigh.

"Hush. That creep upset you, that's all. Come, let's walk the beach." Averill linked her arm to his. "We can talk it out. Put your fears to rest."

"There's nothing to say except I'm sorry," Teal whispered.

"But something made you think I could hurt you. You imagined me a criminal, yes? I think I have a right to know."

Teal started, surprised at the baldness of his word—"criminal." Had she thought *that* of Averill? Nick, that's who she must have meant. The portrait of an embezzler could be fit to him, a stranger, but not to Averill. She knew Averill.

The Yankee Calvinism interdependent with the history of his family left him with the values of a world governed by strict rules and a faith in God's rewards for the chosen. Good works and upright deeds might not buy the kingdom of heaven, but they signalled God's blessing with riches and standing in the community. Averill, deny it as he might, was as much a Calvinist as his ancestors before him. The word criminal introduced a discordant note.

"It was craziness. That guy . . . you're right. He upset me," she said. "I didn't care about the bank. I thought you lied to protect Nick. And then, for a minute . . ." *For a minute I wondered if you lied to protect yourself,* Teal almost said. But she couldn't say it.

"And people complain that accountants are dull!" Averill grinned.

He laughed as Teal tried to smile.

"I kept thinking about Nick and how he knew both Konstat and Carroll," she said. Her palms opened in a gesture of apology.

"What else did you think?" Averill asked. His slight grin did not reach to his gray eyes.

"I'm sorry." Teal ducked her head. "If Nick had stolen from the company, he'd need to replace the funds before the audit. That resolution could get Climb a loan from the Bank of New York, and if he never accounted for the transaction on the books . . . ," she faltered.

"Yes?" Averill pushed. "You think he tried to make the cash records look good?"

"And then came the *Alt* investigation of Carroll and the risk of that resolution turning up," Teal concluded.

"You are good at the creative accounting stuff." Averill tapped her upturned chin.

"Maybe not." Teal dropped her eyes. "Because then I thought of you and the manager's questions in New York. Inventory seemed like another thread—George worried about it in Stowe and your missing wind shirts. Inventory provides embezzlers a good cover."

Teal stopped. Averill's strong profile showed a knot at his jaw. She recalled their chance meeting at the Ivy Club in September. He, stiff with grief at the death of his friend, and Teal trying to offer solace.

Her memory quickened with Mr. Hughes' caution. *Don't be afraid to challenge the obvious.*

Konstat had lunched with Averill that day, not as with a friend, but with a potential source for his investigation of William Carroll and University Savings. Then time ran out for Mark Konstat.

William Carroll.

The shattered face filled her mind as her intemperate thoughts raced. Carroll, member of Climb's board, signed as clerk the resolution authorizing *any one* of Climb's partners to borrow from Bank of New York. And now she saw Averill's scribbled "50k" and "BNY," reminder of the next payment.

In the spotlight of an investigation, William Carroll

250

worried about his political fate. He asked the wrong person to justify the resolution. Poor man.

George, the expert skier, troubled by New York's inventory discrepancies, shattered into body parts on a granite wall. Averill, himself an expert skier, never confused the purple jacket. Teal had not been the target.

"Are you as tough on all your dates?" Averill interrupted. "Or did I just get lucky, my silly Teal?"

She came out of the trance as the day sharpened to focus. Sun fired Averill's hair. Blond and smart and safe. Teal cleared the chaos with a laugh at herself.

His kiss threatened no more than pleasure. Teal knew Averill would never embezzle from Climb, his modern Calvinist's community. The success of the company, more than money, was his worth. Teal understood family myth—that legacy of expectation and religion casting shadows across one's life. Averill would never permit himself to be branded a thief. Never. Not with his identity vested in the approval of his community.

She knelt to scoop a fist of sand. Turned from hand to hand, the thin stream escaped in a string of glitter. Such turbulent emotions had erupted to confuse this day. The day she ate an ambrosia burger. The day Averill asked her to marry him. Sometimes realizing an objective did not work out as planned.

Nine months ago Konstat had fallen to her feet. The period of gestation.

She looked up at Averill. "Who did Mark Konstat run into at Ivy that day? You never said."

"Some friends, I didn't know them. Still, I never should have left him."

The fear returned, racing and hot. *Did you leave him?* Teal wanted to scream. She wanted to rip from her flesh the doubt tearing at her heart. She wanted to believe. Worse, she wanted to know.

She saw him as she had that day, elegant and sad, limping up to her in his beautiful suit. Forty-one flights was hell on the legs, like the construction worker said. Forty-one flights made a man crippled stiff. What a terrible price to insure approbation and success. That's what had confused her.

She gazed at Averill, lover and murderer. She fought the scream choking her tongue until her voice came, soft and calm. "Perhaps we should head back to Carmel."

Teal spread her fingers wide. The sparkling grains dropped to join the millions on the beach. She could never retrieve what she had held only a moment before. Not sand, not faith. Averill stroked her shoulder.

"Certainly, darling. But first, I want a picture of you here."

Teal prepared to stand.

"No, you wait. I'll get the camera. Please." Averill bent to tousle her hair, then left her sitting beside the sea.

He did not keep his word.

The sun lowered in the sky. Dusk shadowed a deserted beach. Teal understood. Averill would never return.

Bile pushed to her throat. The wind shifted and the waves receded. The tide had turned. Konstat, Carroll, and George, all dead. But not her.

"Love," she yelled.

She threw up ambrosia and passion's desire. Hope had betrayed her. This was the recompense of love?

252

Teal Stewart, certified public accountant, had thought to escape the human fray. Thought to press the anarchy of childhood, Mother's music cresting as milk boiled over and voices quarreled, to order. What had Averill thought to escape? The mark of failure.

Her bitter laugh became a howl.

Konstat's investigation of the underworld, a simple lunch between two old roommates, the confluence of chance and relationship—Carroll's with Climb, University Savings' with Carroll—and unexpectedly Averill was called to account for questionable behavior.

It was time to go home.

No red convertible waited in the lot. The uphill climb to Coast Highway 1 dragged on long and hot. There, a family from Illinois picked her up to drop her off at Lobos Lodge.

"I have to leave by tomorrow," she told the desk clerk.

The woman nodded. "Tab's been settled by your friend. We're sorry you folks couldn't stay longer. Visit us again. Checkout's by eleven and leave the key in your room."

The woman spoke in a pleasant, if impersonal, voice. People came and people went, she seemed to say. No need of involving her.

The red rental occupied the space in front of the door. The keys lay on the bed. A bed designed for two.

Carmel's romance perverted into mockery. She took no more than two minutes to decide. Starting now would bring her to San Francisco airport by nine. Time to spare to catch the last flight. The red-eye. She did not look back after she closed the door.

The blue box rested in the middle of the driver's seat,

Tiffany & Co. easy to read with the ribbon loose. Teal lifted the leather pouch and tilted the mouth to her palm.

A smooth, oval pebble bounced dark and hard to her hand. Her fingers closed to a fist. Too late, she thought. The ripples could not be stopped.

Chapter Twenty-eight

"Brahmin Scion Sought—
Dodges Detection in California"

Teal stilled her restless leg-to-leg sway and read the *Boston Herald* headline one more time. Averill looked as handsome as a movie star in the Bachrach photograph filling half of the page. She craned to see more, but the man in front of her snapped his newspaper closed as he ducked into his cab.

Teal paced around the sign marking the taxi stand. Logan Airport was quiet this morning, and few other passengers waited on the curb. Finally her taxi came. She sank onto broken springs and shouted her destination through the perforation in the scratched plexiglass. The driver cocked his head back, and she repeated herself with a louder yell.

"Police headquarters."

Now his head snapped around. She leaned against the frayed upholstery and closed her eyes. She couldn't get her last conversation with Dan Malley out of her mind.

She had pulled away from Lobos Lodge with nothing

more than escape on her mind, but within two blocks, Teal realized she needed to call the police. A gas station with a pay phone beside the building made her stop. She wanted Dan.

Kathy never asked why, but repeated the digits of his phone number twice. Teal missed the right buttons three times before she got the combination right. There was a long series of rings before Dan finally said, "Hello?"

Her suspicions sounded thin and false over the distance of the line, and her voice became defensive as it rose.

"It wasn't a lovers' quarrel, Dan. Honestly—he knew my questions were only the beginning."

The satellite returned Dan's calm voice. "I believe you. I made the mistake of thinking l-l-love would keep you safe. At least you are."

"In a way," Teal mumbled. "I'm coming home tonight."

She rolled the pebble across her palm, smooth and black; it burned with the fire of passing headlights. She squeezed harder and harder until a deliberate twist of her wrist let the pebble fall.

Boston had greeted her with a cold and drizzling morning. Late May could have brought better and could have brought worse. The plane landed before the rush hour, and her taxi sped through the tunnel connecting East Boston with downtown. Teal was at the station's front desk within minutes.

"Nick White will meet us in Cambridge," Dan said as he ushered her to his car.

"I saw the *Herald* headline. You worked fast."

Teal ignored the fatigue dragging at her brain. She wished she could believe Averill would greet them at Climb's door. She wished her suspicions were a mistake.

"Exposure may help us find him," Dan said. "The *San Francisco Chronicle* will have the same story this morning."

They turned onto the Massachusetts Avenue bridge to cross the Charles River into Cambridge. Before they arrived at the office, Dan pulled the car to the side of the road.

"I thought you should know—San Francisco picked up your tattooed friend last night. A rap sheet as long as his arm," Dan said.

"So, it wasn't paranoia," Teal said.

"No. And for the record, your buddy Shag wanted you back in one piece. I guess he likes you."

Teal tried to smile as Dan parked next to Climb. Nick waited in the lobby, and together they went up to his office. He spoke first.

"Detective Malley said you had wondered about my integrity."

He did not accuse, but acted confused.

"If Konstat started to question Carroll about his actions, Carroll must have wondered about what he'd done as a member of Climb's board. That board resolution would have led him to you."

Nick looked lost.

"And there was George," Teal continued. "Asking about the inventory. Inventory accounts can mask theft pretty easily, at least for a while. You were in the position to cook the books. Averill, with his position in marketing, never occurred to me."

"But you were wrong, right?" Nick asked.

"Not entirely." *But enough*, Teal grieved to herself. "Averill didn't embezzle—"

Nick's eyebrows shot up, *What do you mean?* about to explode from his mouth. Teal jumped in first.

"He committed fraud. He would have done anything to make the New York store succeed, anything to make Climb grow."

"He did do anything, including murder," Dan said.

Silence grew into gloom. Yes, Teal realized. Three men were dead. Two murdered. Mark Konstat's questions about William Carroll had had the unintended effect of spinning Averill's scheme out of control.

"But why?" Nick asked.

"Averill wanted to guarantee his vision could succeed. His credit line with the Bank of New York let him bleed cash *into* the New York store. He booked the money as sales and disguised the loan repayments as inventory purchases, but both were fiction. Like his claim of a dispute over the phony receipt of Goretex shirts."

Teal could have explained the accounting, the scheme's temporary boost to gross margin and the strain on Averill to maintain parity between the paper records and physical count of goods, but Nick was nodding.

"It wasn't for personal gain," he mused.

"No. Not directly. Before the store could produce it, he gave you the results everyone wanted—good margins, high volume and terrific cash flow. He planned to stop when New York turned profitable on its own. The fraud demanded daily control; it wouldn't last with added stores."

"I don't understand. Averill was my partner," Nick said.

"T-Teal has a theory your partner needed to demonstrate his worthiness, something to do with his family. He's just a criminal to me."

"I'll never get it." Nick grimaced. "Averill gave me more computer runs on that store, and I never once questioned the data. We wanted to expand, and his numbers proved to me we could. Why didn't he support a venture capital investment from the start? The cash would have bought us time without his resorting to—"

"Murder?" Teal said. "The first offer came too late. He had begun his activities and couldn't risk a review of his operation."

"I'm the one who hesitated about the venture capital this time." Nick snorted. "Averill made it sound so easy with his friend at Simon Brown. I agreed."

Teal nodded. "Averill prayed it would be easy. He had no choice. But if Simon Brown looked closely, he risked being found out."

"How did it start?" Nick asked.

"Your board resolution approving negotiations with the Bank of New York gave him the opportunity—"

Nick's hand flew up. "That's what's been bothering me—what loan are you talking about Averill using? The board never voted credit approval for any bank in New York. Bank of Boston is our lender."

Teal and Dan exchanged worried glances. The story had worked out so neatly. Too neatly? Dan pulled William Carroll's copy of the resolution from his pocket and handed it to Nick.

"Nope." He shook his head in disbelief. "I've never seen this. Did Cunningham and Carroll work together?"

"You mean collusion? I don't think Carroll saw the resolution until just before he died," Teal said. "Konstat's probing for information on the aspiring politician scared Averill because he had duped an unwitting Carroll."

"This week, Mrs. Carroll remembered her husband had been upset about the blank papers he signed when he joined the b-b-board."

"What?" Nick exploded.

"He stopped by the company the week before he died. After that visit, he complained to his wife about never signing a blank piece of paper because there's no telling what someone's secretary will do—"

"Let's pay a visit." Nick stood.

They caught Averill's secretary with his muffin and coffee beside a folded newspaper he hadn't opened yet. Nick asked most of the questions.

"Averill had me institute the procedure as a precaution," the flustered secretary explained. "I keep a set of signed blanks to speed things up when someone we need on a document isn't around." The man studied their faces. "You understand my boss is the board secretary?"

Nick slapped the desk. "Right. I remember. You had me sign one or two blank pages."

"Yes," the secretary agreed. "Everyone has."

"Did you ever have to use Bill Carroll's signature?" Nick asked.

"Sure. The Bank of New York resolution went out over Mr. Carroll's original signature. Averill had forgotten to ask me to prepare the document for the meeting when you all voted. It didn't cause a delay because his system works."

"Did Mr. Carroll speak to you about that resolution?" Dan asked.

"How did you know?" the man asked. "Mr. Carroll came by to see Mr. Cunningham a few months ago. I gave him a copy then."

"Was Mr. Carroll upset?"

"He didn't say anything to me."

"Might he have said something to Averill?" Teal asked.

"Not that day. Mr. Carroll stopped by without an appointment, and Averill asked him to wait. After Mr. Carroll read the resolution, he said he'd call back later and left. I forgot all about it. Then the poor man died."

Nick contacted the Bank of New York. Yes, Climb had $200,000 outstanding on a $500,000 line.

Teal spoke to Climb's auditors. After Averill had asked them to delete the inventory comment from the management letter, they had agreed. So much for independence.

Averill's bank account showed no evidence of unexplained deposits.

The last squash player on Konstat's list finally returned Dan's call. He remembered the article and Konstat. In fact, he had introduced Konstat into a great computer game, the same one Nick White played via modem. Beowulf and Jason.

The thing was, neither Nick White nor Mark Konstat knew his opponent's true identity—rules of the game. Dan and Teal decided not to say anything to Nick. It didn't matter today.

* * *

Teal stopped by her office to find Francesca's article in the center of the desk. Kathy brought tea and unspoken sympathy and closed the door for Teal to read. The old man's quote filled a sidebar.

> "The *Alt* performed a grave disservice to the citizens of Cambridge. University Savings' proud history of serving our community will continue under my stewardship as chairman. The libel against me by this author and paper are without merit, unfounded and unfair and unproven as my lawyers will prove."

The U. S. Attorney for Massachusetts dodged the issue with "no comment" when asked about the allegations.

Francesca called, pessimistic.

"I risk my hide. *We* risk our hides," she revised, "and the best the Feds can do is no comment. I'm tired of this investigative crap. Nothing will happen. I can tell by the profound silence this piece is evoking from the law and order establishment. *C'est la vie,* and all that shit. Of course, you and I can sleep more easily."

Teal felt as defeated. Nothing had turned out as she had hoped when she flew to California. Averill surely murdered William Carroll and George, and may have hastened Konstat's death. Averill, once lover, once friend. The pain cut to her soul.

"Some solace I am with whining. Sorry. What's to the rumors I'm already hearing about your Averill? Front

262

page coverage on the *Globe* isn't where I expected to see him next,'' Francesca said.

Teal had to smile. *C'est la vie* indeed. More like *c'est* Francesca. She pushed the words through stiff lips.

"Is this a last investigation before your retirement?"

"Hey, if you don't tell, I won't be mad," Francesca said.

Teal could hear the grin.

"What's to tell? I'm careful all my life, and when I decide to take the big risk it turns out like this. It's no secret Averill is the prime suspect in Carroll's death. And there I was, running off to California with him like a love-struck fool."

"Not what I hear, Teal. I hear you snapped the pieces into place."

"Damned inconvenient timing. I was going to say yes, Francesca. I was going to marry him."

"So. You didn't say yes, did you?"

Teal was silent.

"You still there?" Francesca asked.

"Um. I'm thinking about the tarot's prince of light, prince of darkness. I thought she meant two different men, when both were Averill. My subconscious saw it before I did. He asked me to marry him, and I wanted to say yes . . . well, I didn't."

Malley called next. "The Vermont police are reviewing George Henderson's death. Now, if we only had your Cunningham in custody."

But by noon, Teal knew they never would.

It ended like it had started, at the Ivy Club.

Walter fussed, curious about events and loathe to ask. He brightened when he remembered the envelope.

"It came for you, Ms. Stewart, express."

Teal stared at the San Francisco postmark, her name in Averill's bold hand. She held the white rectangle and focused out beyond the address, beyond the room. Like the day she had met him, tugboats filled the harbor. That day had been a beginning. Today was an end. She gentled the envelope open. Nothing but her eyes moved as she read.

"Teal—You know most of it by now. Please believe me when I write it started as a mistake.

"Mark went into shock the minute we stepped on that elevator. I hadn't taken a sweet, you see. I didn't realize they were coated peanuts. He found the hypodermic pen he carried so quickly that for a second I didn't understand what was happening.

"His hands were shaking by then, so I took the hypo. I wanted to help. But he'd been asking all those questions about Bill Carroll. I couldn't let him pursue the answers, Teal. I couldn't, not knowing what the truth could do. He slipped from consciousness still trusting me to use the needle. When I knew it was too late, I dropped the pen to look like his fumble.

"The key in the control panel let me lock out all the stops to forty-one. I couldn't believe my luck; no one saw me get off the car or go through the stairwell door. The walk down was long and solitary, but I didn't notice. My legs ached for days.

"Mark continued on in the elevator alone, poor bastard. We met because he fell at your feet. I wish fate had written a different beginning to our story.

"I never expected Bill Carroll to find out about that damned resolution. He kept hammering on and on about my using him. I agreed to meet that Saturday morning outside the *Alt*. He stood there and questioned my behavior, Teal. Accusation after accusation. He wasn't like you. He didn't understand. He wouldn't listen. He made a mistake with the gun. Mark had already died for me, you see.

"Bill had said, 'I thought of killing myself . . .' at the beginning of the conversation. He gave me the idea.

"Bill was stupid, Teal. He made the outcome a choice of him or me. I didn't realize he was meeting you. You should never have found him. I never meant to do that to you.

"George was the worst, but he badgered me about that damned inventory. Question after question as though I didn't want the very best for Climb. I knew he planned to ski that trail from his comments earlier in the afternoon. I took the access path to meet him and waited in shadow until he was heading straight for the wall. I yelled and waved at the moment he needed to turn. He met the granite at full speed. He never saw me.

"George loved to ski. It's not the worst end.

"Climb would have succeeded. All I needed was time. Mark and Bill and George should have given it to me.

"You are the best thing that ever happened to me, Teal. I am sorry."

Her hands rattled the lines into a blur while tears glazed her eyes blind, but it was too late to spare the truth. She had fallen in love with a man willing to kill to attain the veneer of what he could never be—an in-

265

dividual man who understood the compact between privilege and responsibility.

E. Teal Stewart, careful in her professional life, cautious in love—she almost could laugh. Almost. She folded the letter into a perfect rectangle and started at the corner. The words lay in the middle of her desk like a pile of confetti when she stood to leave.

Afterword

Nick White signed the decree of divorce and tossed out the pen. "Jason" and the special password retired the same day. His girls called him Dad-king and made a lived-in mess of his house when they stayed with him. Last week, they had agreed to try camping for his weeks of summer custody.

For the first time in years, he felt alive. He couldn't make up for George, or Carroll, or Konstat; but he could share his success with colleagues, family and charity, and he did.

Calvinist eyes might have judged him among those predestined to receive God's grace.

Dan Malley moved to another corpse, his second big case. The brass considered this an important investigation, but Mark Konstat would always be Dan's first. Dan planned to consult Teal Stewart again when money tangled in the motive for murder. And it gave him an excuse to visit Kathy at her work.

Dan never let himself dwell too long on Averill. Every

good cop could name the ones that got away. Maybe they made a guy do better next time.

Teal vowed she would never, ever tell anyone time healed all wounds. Time passed, was all time did, bringing her to fall, the snap of the sky a bright blue and the sun white on her back, antidote to a thin wind. Time had not eased the memory, but laid new events over the old. Averill filling her world. Averill lost and gone. Life at Clayborne Whittier continued on apace as each successive scrim of memory began to dull and curl at the edge.

Truth was, she realized, with all her dawdling through memory and the park, she was running out of time.

Hunt waited and worried. Teal had kept herself scarce since her return from California. She had surprised him when she agreed to breakfast today. He hoped the morning could begin to bridge their distance. The point wasn't to return to the relationship of another time, nothing so simple. No, he hoped to find something on which to go forward.

Argyle paced, as restless and anxious. Hunt knew the dog watched for her, too. The tea waited, fragrant and hot, and the scones snuggled in the oven. Finally the buzzer rang, hard and long.

It was almost old times. The conversation ebbed and surged. Sections of the Sunday *Globe* littered the floor. Now satiated with breakfast, both host and guest read.

Hunt took in a sudden breath. ''Teal—he's dead!''

Her hand shook as she took the offered paper.

And so he was. The obituary pictured a man in his prime. The prose gave testament to a life of high civic purpose and philanthropy. A wife, four children, eight grandchildren and one great-grandchild survived him. Who among them the rebel? Teal wondered.

She had to laugh. The old man had remained in command to the end. He had died in his own time, on his own terms, a successful fraud.

Teal skimmed the last of the national news as Argyle jumped up to whine at the elevator door, impatient for play. Hunt brushed crumbs to the floor from the table and cleared the plates.

"Ready for a walk?" he asked over the sound of Rodney Crowell on the CD player. Argyle added a bark.

"Soon," Teal murmured.

Her attention stayed with the short, unsatisfactory paragraph. A thirty-seven-foot Hinckley yacht had floundered off the coast of Fiji. The rescue vessel found no life aboard, no evidence of foul play. The weather in the area had been calm. Everyone refused to speculate about the boat that had been rigged for sailing solo.

An official of the government of Fiji stated little had been found to identify the boat's owner. He appeared to have been a citizen of the United States and the boat registered to a trust.

Argyle's nose rubbed dry and cool as he thrust his muzzle under her elbow. One snap of his head brought her arm up to bounce the paper on the floor.

"I guess it's time to go." Hunt laughed. "Argyle's patience is about worn thin."

"I guess so," Teal agreed.

Argyle danced to the door, and she knelt to straighten

269

the disordered paper before she stood. The last sentence of the story caught her eye.

"Aside from the boat, the most valuable asset discovered aboard was a 2.5 carat diamond ring crafted by the prestigious American jewelers Tiffany & Co."

Hunt reached out his hand to pull her up. Teal turned her face to his.

"Okay." She tried to smile. "Time to move on."

Please turn the page for an exciting sneak preview
of J. Dayne Lamb's next Teal Stewart mystery
A QUESTION OF PREFERENCE
to be published by Zebra Books in
July 1994

Chapter One

THE END OF JUNE

Nancy Vandenburg tightened her fist around her head. Thick blond hair, "blunt-cut and stylish," bent in disarray while "simple two carat diamond studs, her sole ornamentation," drove against an "impish" nose. Finally, "candid, jade green eyes" collided with "bisque pale skin."

Before her square, clean fingernails gouged through "high, broad cheekbones touched with the blush of modesty," she bounced her face to the floor.

As the mutilated page uncurled, paper eyes winked a mockery of her rage. Warm June sun illuminated the artist's studio and pink fluorescence highlighted the text. These marks showed a careful, even painstaking, application to selected letters.

laMode People in the News
—An Artist for a New Decade—
With Sotheby's going, going, gone at over 1.3 million for a canvas known as *FRIENDS* just last

month (April) and another presidential commission behind her, Nancy Vandenburg would not be impertinent to say, "Make room, Norman Rockwell, here I am." Of course, this charming artist follows the suggestion with a shake of her blunt-cut and stylish blond hair. America's foremost living painter of family and societal conventions herself lives a conventional life in a suburb of Boston, Massachusetts, with husband Michael Britton and young daughter Libby. While social problems—Adultery, AIDS, homelessness and death—are also depicted in Ms. Vandenburg's work, her genius lies in an insightful reaffirmation of American values, mixing humor, pathos, compassion and belief on canvases which speak directly to our hearts. The truth of basic values, not their perversion, infuse Vandenburg's paintings. Viewing her current exhibit at the Barrette Gallery on East 26th Street, I confess certain pictures move me inexplicably. Felicia Barrette, Ms. Vandenburg's career-long champion (Barrette Gallery has been the sole New York representative of her work) gives a simple explanation. "Nancy lets us feel it's okay to want to come home to a simpler ethic, despite how complex that ethic—discerning right from wrong, good from bad—can be." Later I asked Ms. Vandenburg if her paintings more accurately could be said to parody than reflect an idealized reality. Her candid, jade green eyes . . .

Wrinkles obscured the balance of the text, but the uneven strokes of pink remained all too visible. Nancy's transcription filled the margin.

"p u n i s h m e n t follows Adultery death f o l l o w s perversion confess n o w come home to th e right w a y" inadvertently captioned the image of a serene Nancy in her own, frenzied print. Ink smudged the spot where she had squeezed the paper like a neck.

Now her hand beat lightly against the windowpane. The fields beyond lay furred with early summer's tender grass. Two horses frolicked past the barn. Red barn, green grass, white farmhouse, blue sky and Libby with the collie by the leafing maple tree—a scene Nancy could have painted.

Her hand drew back in a jerk, then sailed forward, barn shattering, sky falling, blood running. The shock of pain snapped her to attention as her inked "Adultery" bled black beneath drips of red. She stamped her foot to the upturned face as if to conquer fear with anger.

Fear won. Nancy Vandenburg needed help. Teal Stewart's kind of help.

Chapter Two

THE END OF JUNE

Teal stared at the stack of bulging files in the middle of her desk. She scanned the pile to the right, then swivelled to assess the heap on the credenza behind her. Her blue eyes grew dim. *Audit papers*, the physical record of the analysis and testing performed on the financial records of a client company by a certified public account, a CPA, like Teal.

For a fleeting moment she wanted to scream. But senior managers at Clayborne Whittier, the prestigious international accounting firm, did not scream. They did not crack under pressure. They did not let the *great* firm down.

Especially not in this case. Not when Teal herself had raised the charge of embezzlement against this particular client's chief financial officer. Now that client expected Teal to provide technical evidence of financial malfeasance adequate to convict against the defense mounted by Boston's hottest white collar crime lawyer, Renee Maxwell.

Teal stroked the top page of the top file. The audit papers held irrefutable proof. The trick lay in assembling the complex data. But she would. No embezzling jackass of a CFO was going to end her career. She'd pit her skill as a certified public accountant—hadn't the *Boston Globe* once described her as a "financial Sherlock Holmes"—against anyone, any day. But did it have to be Renee Maxwell? Did it have to be this year. The year Teal was up for admission to the Clayborne Whittier partnership?

Teal knew the unspoken price of failure. Goodbye Clayborne Whittier, goodbye big corner office, goodbye to her name spelled out under "PARTNERS" on the lobby directory. "E. Teal Stewart"—it could look nice. Whether or not she wanted it there was an entirely separate matter. An undecided matter. Still, she wanted the choice to be hers.

E. Teal Stewart shook her head and opened the file. This CFO had been greedy, not clever. Greedy enough to get very sloppy in his schemes of fraudulent invoices and payments. The proof was in the pages in front of her, in the company's bank statements, in his. Let the company's attorney worry about R. Maxwell, Esquire. The company's attorney would be the one to face Ms. Maxwell in court.

Teal set to provide the evidence adequate to convict. She liked puzzles she could solve, questions she could answer.

Suddenly she wished she hadn't agreed to meet Nancy for lunch today, not with so little time until the trial. But Nancy had insisted. Teal closed the top file and rose reluctantly.

"Carole will know what to do, Nancy, or Michael, maybe." Teal tried to filter the impatience from her tone.

"Don't put me off. This isn't some little problem with a show, Teal. This isn't something for my sister or, God knows, my husband. Please, I mean it. I need you." Nancy jabbed Teal's peppermint tea aside, sloshing pale green across the white cloth. She slapped the abused magazine page down on the table. Her ruined face stared up at Teal.

"Punishment follows adultery, death follows perversion. Confess now. Come home to the right way." Teal read aloud slowly.

She took in the photograph. Richard Avedon wouldn't be happy with the dried blood effect. She registered the laudatory profile. Nancy didn't have career worries. Teal's thought was sharp and small and unattractive.

"It isn't true?" Teal straightened, alert to the sudden tension between them.

"I hope not—I'd be in big trouble."

Their eyes locked, the golden-flecked green to Teal's smoky blue. The hum and murmur of other conversations in the restaurant continued unabated around them.

"The threatened outcome aside, Nan, is this about adultery?"

"Yes, I suppose." Nancy dropped her gaze to the article. "They don't understand. I'm finally home."

"What about Michael, Nan? Does he know?" Teal asked carefully, like Nancy, easing away from the friction.

Teal had never like Michael, never understood the attraction he held for Nancy. Teal never asked, fearing knowledge too intimate for even the best of friends. She knew one view of Michael had changed with the years. It was not hers.

Nancy gave a mirthless laugh. "No. Look, I'm going to sort this out, but not this way. Not because of some creepy emotional terrorist. Help me."

The complexities of self-interest stalled Teal's assent. She knew the chief financial officer held a monopoly on her time. How dare he jeopardize her future with his inept greed. She could kill him!

How casually considered and ardently felt, Teal realized. *She could kill* ceased to be a mere turn of phrase. Could someone mean the threat of death to Nancy literally? No. No way.

Teal fingered the garish message. A joke. "Death follows perversion," Teal read. Could she gamble with her best friend? Her eyes moved from the blood-flecked picture to Nancy's scabbed hand.

"Should you tell me about that?"

Nancy shifted in her chair uncomfortably before she fanned her fingers. "It heightens the dramatic presentation of my personalized junk mail, doesn't it? Please, say you'll help."

"I'll do what I can." Teal suppressed an internal sigh.

"You're so wonderful! I knew you would!" Nancy arched her long, lanky frame over the table and hugged Teal.

The room rippled to silence. Convert glances flicked over Nancy's body, vivid in a yellow angora sweater and black leggings. Nancy lowered her imposing stature back into the seat, and the staring eyes dropped away.

Teal recomposed the strands of hair escaping from her chignon and squared the shoulders of her dove gray Italian dress. Nancy must be upset. She never displayed overt affection in public. Teal signalled for their check and placed the ragged paper into its envelope.

"I'll need to know everything. You can start on the walk back."

There was half a minute, getting their coats, when Nancy's radiance disturbed Teal. She felt the gosling beside a swan.

Obvious stares had followed Nancy from the dining room to the foyer. All minds concentrated to search memory. Who was this woman? An actress? A model profiled in last week's *People?* In seconds, someone would ask Nancy if she'd been on TV. It took all of Teal's concentration to remember that long ago she had accepted that Nancy's presence could eclipse the rising sun.

But Teal had her own moments, like the afternoon a man had stopped her in the street.

"I saw you on *Boston Magazine!*" he'd said, satisfied with his recognition.

"Yes," Teal replied. " 'Biased in Boston? Professional Women May Just Agree.' The cover story."

The man turned to his companion. "Wish my CPA looked like that."

Teal grinned at the memory. That she wore a chic linen dress and stylishly restrained hair for the work day did not make her a little gosling. It didn't make Nancy any less gorgeous, either. Teal laughed.

"What are you finding funny in my predicament?" Nancy asked as she tossed a fire red baseball jacket over her shoulder and pushed through the revolving door.

"Nothing. I amused myself. The worm of envy, Nancy. It isn't always easy being your friend."

Nancy turned a blank face to look at Teal.

Teal waved a hand. "Surely you haven't forgotten my zeal to put you in your place freshman year?" Even now, Teal remembered the messy, adolescent fight with chagrin.

"Oh, that. Over fifteen years ago! I hate thinking about that. I didn't do anything to be blond or tall—"

"Or beautiful and talented. That's what you said, Nan, but you were then and are now and there can be moments . . ." Teal stopped. If she could be envious, what could a sibling be? Seethingly jealous? Sending threats? A sibling could be Carole, of course. Nancy and Carole formed a mutual adoration society. Teal's insight deflated.

"Yeah?" Nancy said. "And you forget there can be moments when your best friend, her hair glowing chestnut and her height a graceful, reasonable five-seven, is not only attractive, but the most outspoken individual on campus while I could hardly say my name without blushing." Nancy stared at Teal. "How did we start?"

The hardest thing to forgive, Teal felt, was Nancy's utter innocence of her effect. Merely entering a room, she stopped conversation. Yet her grace and graciousness were unfeigned. Teal spent freshman year looking for Nancy's clay feet and little, prehensile claws. Teal found her own smallness and that was all. They roomed together the four years, inseparable.

"Glowing chestnut, indeed. Is that off your latest tube of brown paint?" Teal laughed and raised her eyebrows. "Now, tell me more about this magazine graffiti."

It seemed to Teal that Nancy did a little stutter step, a mere second's hesitation.

"I found it in the Lincoln post box yesterday. Most

281

business mail, about shows or buying or interviews, comes to Carole here in Boston. Personal mail goes directly to my house, so I don't make much effort to clear the box more than once a week." Nancy shrugged. "That piece of trash could have been there for days."

Teal read New York from the envelope's postmark, but the date was illegible. Nancy explained that Avedon shot the photo in March, *laMode* interviewed her in April. Teal remembered buying the May issue. She expected all of Nancy's friends to have done the same.

Entering the lobby of the First New England Bank building brought Teal's primary concern back in a surge of anxiety. She'd lost over two hours on Fruiers to this lunch. Worse, Nancy's narrative lacked detail, but Nancy expected Teal's help.

"Look, Nan, I need more. What's happening with Michael? What's up professionally, aside from the promo here?" Teal shook the envelope impatiently, then paused. Nancy's partner in the affair was unlikely to be just anyone. "Could this be meant to hurt the man you're seeing?"

"No." Nancy's eyes shifted to evade Teal's.

People pushed past in a commotion of coming and going.

"Michael is busy with the retrospective. He's a good publicist for all his clients, including me."

"Well, you're his biggest, aren't you? The most important?" Teal asked.

"Yes." Nancy shrugged. "If you're asking if Michael could have sent this—maybe, but it's not his style. Anyway, he doesn't know anything, Teal. No one knows."

Teal watched Nancy absorbing the visual of the lobby. Light, distorted through a wall of glass cubes, fell on floor tiles arranged geometrically to tease the eye. Nancy did not ask Teal about Hunt, the architect who had designed the FNEB building and stopped living with Teal in the same year. Teal couldn't afford to show Nancy equal tact.

Impatience sharpened Teal's words. "How is Carole?"

"Consumed by the retrospective's opening this fall. San Diego, Chicago, Washington, Boston and then Europe. Carole actually enjoys this chaos. Not me! And no, I haven't told her anything about this . . . new aspect of my life. Not yet."

"Afraid she'll be worried about you?" Teal asked. Nancy grinned back, nodding her head. Teal resumed. "Okay. Your husband, Michael, doesn't know anything. Your sister, Carole, doesn't know anything. You didn't confide in me until today—and from my point of view, not much. That leaves who? Felicia?"

"No."

The silence crawled. Teal changed tack. "I always liked *FRIENDS.*"

The painting of two men on the beach had been Nancy's first critical triumph. One figure leaned into the side of the other as they sat by the water. The rectangles of their backs filled the canvas. Water and sand were depicted in splashes of color over shoulders and beside buttocks. The simple tenderness of posture spoke legions about the depth of relationship, man with man. Nancy's genius was evident and startling, her tacit understanding of friendship's dimension and vulnerability clear. She had been twenty-two.

"One point three million." Nancy shook her head. "I think I received two hundred when Felicia first sold it."

"The benefits certainly come now, for you and Barrette Gallery. *FRIENDS* should push your current works into the stratosphere. And what's this I've read about the buyer. A 'prominent, adulterous, bisexual capitalist'? Not the profile of your usual collector. Maybe that inspired the nut to color in *laMode*. The profile starts with *FRIENDS*.*"

"The message is—don't let bisexuals own my work?" Nancy started to laugh. "As though I control my buyers or sellers."

"I don't know." Teal floundered. The real question remained. Who stood to gain by scaring Nancy?

"Teal, I've been successful for years and never been held accountable for the peculiarities of my collectors. You remember the president who believed in the imminent coming of Armageddon. He based travel plans, and art purchases, on the stars." Nancy's voice rose.

"Leaving your friend. Who did he tell?" Teal asked.

"Don't you get it, Teal? *No one knows about us.*"

For a second Teal wanted to say, *Don't you get it, Nancy, somebody does,* but someone yanked at her wrist.

"I've been looking all over for you." Teal's secretary, Kathy Jones, nodded to Nancy. "Hi, Ms. Vandenburg, sorry to interrupt. Teal, the PIC wants to see you ASAP. He's been calling every five minutes."

Don Clarke, Clayborne Whittier's partner in charge in Boston, could want her for only one thing, that damned CFO. Teal took a deep breath. "Tell him I'll be right up."

"I should let you go, Teal."

Teal sensed the faint relief humming in Nancy's voice. Guilt at her own inclination to dismiss Nancy prompted Teal to wave the envelope. "I'd like to keep this, Nan."

Revulsion tightened Nancy's jaw as she nodded assent.

"And I'll need to talk to Michael, Carole, Felicia, even your friend. Discretely, of course." Teal couldn't imagine how else to start.

Now Nancy shook Teal's arm. "No! I mean not yet. They don't know anything—what could you learn? There's got to be a better way."

Teal looked at Nancy, vivid in black, yellow and red, jittery with apprehension. Standing with her back to the street, daylight illuminated a faint glow around her shadowed face. The years of friendship had survived their share of ups and downs. Nancy was as close to a sister as it came.

"The better way, Nan, is for you to tell me the truth."

**LOOK FOR *A QUESTION OF PREFERENCE* ON
SALE AT BOOKSTORES EVERYWHERE
IN JULY 1994**